I0664853

Highway to the Stars: The Beginning

By: B. E. Wilson

Copyright © 2014 B. E. Wilson

ISBN: 978-0-9904733-1-2

Edited by: Scribendi Inc.
405 Riverview Drive, Suite 304
Chatham, ON N7M 0N3
Canada

www.bewilson.com

God made the two great lights, the greater light to govern the day, and the lesser light to govern the night; He made the stars also – Genesis 1:16

Dedicated to my mother, Mary: She had the courage to take two young boys out of a bad situation and give them a life. She would sacrifice her own needs, her own wants, to make sure we had a wonderful life.

She was unselfish in her generosity and fair with her discipline. (Even though I probably deserved every bit of discipline I ever got. And if she ever finds out about the other stuff I've done that she doesn't know about, I'm really in trouble! Just saying.) Love you Mom!

Highway to the Stars: The Beginning

1

It was a typical morning for John Kemp. He was late, again. He hustled to find the paperwork he brought home from work the night before. He could hear his wife, Gloria, yelling at the kids to get ready for school and to get downstairs for breakfast. The smell of bacon was in the air, oh how he loved that smell, but he knew he would be lucky just to get his morning cup of coffee before he rushed out the door.

"I'm late, I love you all, but I got to go," John said, as he placed a kiss upon both children's heads, and a kiss on his wife's cheek as he reached for his morning coffee, which she was holding ransom so that he would listen to her.

"John, I really need you to fix this garbage disposal tonight, do you think you can do it or do I need to call a repairman?"

"Sure honey, I'll take care of it," he muttered. He would tell her anything she wanted to hear, as long as she would just hand him that cup of coffee.

With coffee in hand, he was out the door, racing for his car, fumbling for his keys, papers shoved up under each arm, a page fell here and a page fell there; it was John's typical morning. No matter how hard he tried, he just couldn't find a way to be on time. He was always rushing to do anything. If his wife wasn't barking orders at him, his boss piling more work on him or his kids wanting anything and everything that didn't even seem reasonable at the time, he always felt late and he always felt behind.

John was your everyday typical man; in debt up to his eyeballs, worked for twenty plus years to barely get ahead, but he was happy with his life. He had a wife and two great boys, Thomas (thirteen) and John Junior (six), who were active in school and in sports. They had good neighbors (so he thought) and lived in a quiet little town in Ohio. He had been an engineer in the automotive industry for those twenty plus years. At times his job was demanding, with long hours for mediocre pay, but he loved what he did and it provided for him and his family, and he was okay with that.

Now finally on his way, John knew that if he didn't make it to the highway on time, he could run into that morning traffic jam and be even later for work than he normally was, and that's exactly what happened.

"Son of a bitch!" he yelled as he saw the cars packed on the highway on-ramp. "Tom is going to kill me."

Tom Hawkins was John's boss at the factory where he worked, a short burly guy who didn't have the best demeanor for dealing with people to start with. He was a former Marine drill instructor who still thought every employee was a new recruit.

As John pulled up to the factory, he could see Tom standing outside the front entrance, arms folded, cigar pursed in his lips. Tom was waiting on him. John hurried as fast as he could to find a parking space. He threw the car in park, gathered almost all of his stuff, or at least what he could fit under each arm, and rushed to meet Tom.

"You're late again Kemp!"

"Sorry Tom, traffic was horrible this morning."

"Drop that crap off on your desk. We need to see you upstairs this morning," Tom gruffly said as he pitched his cigar butt into the grass.

"Yes, sir," John replied, scrambling to open the door for his boss.

John did what was requested of him; he dumped everything off on his desk and noticed his coworkers didn't even look up at him as he made his way through the office. *Not even a single good morning today. I must have pissed off everybody by being late,* he thought.

Once upstairs, John knocked on Tom's office door. He heard some mumbling he could not completely make out, but the voice sounded familiar. The door opened and John immediately got that sick feeling in the pit of his stomach, that feeling like something bad was about to happen. John immediately noticed the head of Human Resources, Amy Howell, was not only in Tom's office, she was seated behind his desk.

"Good morning Amy," he said nervously.

"Good morning John, please take a seat," she replied, pointing at the one lone chair across from the desk.

John fumbled his way to the chair, twisting and turning once he was seated as if he was truly on the proverbial hot seat.

"Amy, would you like me to start?" Tom asked.

"No, I'll take care of this," she said, pulling a red folder out from underneath Tom's desk calendar. "John, this isn't always the easiest thing to do, but in business, we as managers have to make hard decisions."

John could feel his pulse starting to beat faster, a warm sensation washing down over his body, while a single bead of sweat was starting to drip down his brow. He knew this conversation did not start out with words anyone would want to hear, even those who might have been sitting in the very seat he felt glued to at this moment.

"John, at this time we have to let you go. The automotive industry is in a recession, and cuts have to be made," Amy said firmly as she leaned forward, resting her forearms on the edge of the desk. "Your research program doesn't have a budget after today, which means your department will be the first to be cut."

"I'm sorry John," Tom said. "But without a budget, I won't need you, or your team."

"But what about all the work, what about all the countless hours, what about all the advancements we've made?" John asked, his voice shaky, his tone uneasy. He wiped the sweat off his brow, leaning forward in his seat to match Amy's authoritarian posture.

"That's not yours to worry about John. We've put together a very nice severance package for you," Amy tried to explain, but John stood up, his temper was starting to get the best of him.

"I don't want to hear any more of this. I'll just go clean my desk out!"

"Sorry John, we can't let you do that. If you have items in your desk, we will collect them and mail them to you," Tom said firmly as he placed his hand on the door so that John couldn't leave. "Security is outside; they'll escort you out of the building."

The two men exchanged disagreeable and uncomfortable stares for a few harsh moments.

John replied gruffly, "Twenty-five years of service, and I get thrown out like the common trash?"

"Don't look at it that way John. It's company policy. Again, we are sorry," Amy tried to explain, but John wasn't having any of it. He grabbed his severance folder and whipped open the office door, only to be greeted by two security guards.

2

John sat in his car for what seemed like hours, in disbelief and fear, trying to comprehend the simple fact that he didn't know what tomorrow would bring. Would he be able to find a job quickly, would his wife understand what had just happened to their family and not judge him, and would he be able to continue providing for them?

He started the car and took that long drive home; he wasn't looking forward to telling his wife when he got there. He knew she wasn't always the understanding kind; for the most part, she wasn't tolerant of very much, it seemed. It seemed she was always riding him over everything, do this, do that, don't put that there and move this. At times he prayed for the sweet relief of death (freedom) to avoid her nagging, but it never came, so he become tolerant of it.

They had been married twenty years after starting as college sweethearts. Once John was successful in his career, they took the plunge and got married. John had insisted that she didn't work; he felt she would be able to raise the kids better if she stayed home. She was all right with the idea and took to being a housewife at first, for a little while or about one year's time. To tell the truth, she loved not working, but the idea of being a stay-at-home mom wasn't her cup of tea. She always had this adventure, this or that women's club; most of her time was tied up in something that had no value to the family and also took funds away from them to afford her lifestyle.

John was all right with this. He was the first to keep the peace and not make waves when it came to Gloria, due to the fact that Gloria could make his and everyone's lives around them a living hell. So in order to keep the peace, he allowed her to keep up with the Jones per se; it meant less turmoil for him and the kids.

John pulled into the drive a little after noon, took a deep breath and decided he'd better go get this over with. As he placed his key in the lock, he could hear noises, muffled noises. He wasn't sure what they were. He stepped in the door, and the noises became quite clear. Either his wife was having an affair or she had developed a porn addiction.

He snuck his way up the stairs as his wife's sounds grew louder; he crept down the hallway towards their bedroom. Noticing the door was slightly open a few inches, he peeked inside. His fears again came true today, not once, but twice.

John saw his wife in the arms of another man, not just any man, but his neighbor. The neighbor who borrowed his tools, came to his cookouts and even carpooled to sporting events for the kids.

He kicked the door open the rest of the way.

"What the hell are you doing?" he screamed, startling the cheating pair.

Gloria jumped from the bed in shock; Fred, his neighbor, jumped to the other side closest the bedroom window, possibly to make a break for it, if needed.

"John…John, I can explain," Fred stuttered as he reached for his clothes.

"Explain what, that you're fucking my wife?"

Before the Fred could get his next word out, John was on top of him, swinging like a mad man, tears welling up in his eyes as he delivered punch after punch to the top of the man's head. Fred tried to cover up, but it was to no avail; John's fists were true in finding their mark. Gloria had locked herself in the bathroom by this time, in fear she would be next.

As Fred lay there in a pool of blood, John slumped onto the bed, staring at the broken man gasping for air. His own chest heaved as he tried to catch his breath.

"Fred, you have ten seconds to get out of here, or I'm going to beat you again…badly…until you're dead."

Fred nodded and crawled to the bedroom door. He wanted no more.

John sat there staring out the bedroom window. *What else could go wrong? God, why did this happen to me today?*

"Gloria, you can come out now, I'm not going to hurt you," he said, his voice still shaky.

Her heart was racing. The man she knew to be a gentle pushover just exploded at her lover with aggression she did not know he possessed. John's calls startled her each time, she was afraid, terrified she'd be next.

"Gloria!"

John paused a few seconds, waiting to hear a reply.

"Gloria!"

"Come out here, we need to talk."

Still sitting slumped on the bed, he heard the door behind him open. Gloria carefully walked towards the bed. Her hesitation was pure fear for her infidelities. John didn't even turn to face her.

"I lost my job today."

"John?"

"It's over, my project is cancelled, my team is gone, and you're gone. I want you out of this house tonight by the time I return," John said as he raised his body up from the bed.

He didn't even look at Gloria; he just left the room a broken man.

He could hear her scream his name as he walked down the stairs, grabbed his keys out of the lock where he had left them hanging, and shut the door behind him.

Now John is a lot of things, but a good husband, good father and a good provider he was. He may not have been the most organized guy in the world, and yes, he wasn't the most punctual, but he didn't deserve a day like this. As one weight was put on his shoulders, another lifted and another was placed back on. He wondered how he would provide for his children. They were innocent in all this, and he felt like they were the victims.

John left his house not knowing where to go, what to do; this wasn't his daily routine. At this time of the day he'd be watching the clock and thinking about his drive home, which kid had football practice or what his wife might pick up for dinner. She wasn't much of a cook, but he enjoyed those evening meals when it was just them around the dinner table.

He found himself at the local liquor store. Scotch wasn't the answer, but it would provide answers to questions that didn't matter. With a bottle of forget-me-not, he nestled in at the local park. He found a bench to his liking and settled in. He could feel the warm sun shining down on his face, and heard the birds chirping in the distance. Kids in the background played and mothers yelled, "Don't put that in your mouth!"

It reminded him of the times when his kids were small, and Gloria and he took them to the park to play. Times that were long gone now. Things were going to change. How would he build memories now? And if he could, would those memories be worth remembering?

With his knuckles sore, his head distorted and his pride pretty much gone, he sat on that bench and wept. This was not the life he imagined for himself, but then again, what man does?

After polishing off half that bottle, John decided it was time to go home, while he still could make it. Placing that bottle back in its brown paper hiding place made him giggle. The sack wasn't going to fool anyone and he knew it, and if they saw it, who cared? He had no dignity left.

John safely made it home, which at that point was a surprise on its own. He hadn't drank like that since college, nor tried to drive anywhere while doing so. The first thing his hazy mind noticed was that he never pulled into the driveway when there weren't any lights on. The house seemed deserted.

No take out meal to enjoy with his now-broken family, he found a bag of cookies to go with the remaining scotch. Sitting in the dark, in his drunken stupor, staring at a blank wall, he drifted off into self-induced unconsciousness.

3

Ring!! Ring!! Ring!!

"What the hell is that?" John barked, as he raised his heavy, throbbing head off the arm of the couch.

He wasn't sure of his whereabouts or what truck had hit him; all he knew was the room was spinning, and a ringing noise was making his headache worse. He wrestled through his pockets to retrieve that annoying phone he suspected was the source of his current pain.

"What?" he said gruffly.

"John, you okay?" asked the voice on the other end of the line.

"Who is this?"

"John, it's Rob. They killed the program, and they axed us all this morning. We heard they got you yesterday. We tried to get a hold of you numerous times. You doing okay bud?"

Rob Yarborough was another engineer, and friend, who also worked on John's project. He wasn't really an engineer by degree standards, but had worked his way up the ladder due to the fact he could build just about anything. He was one of those closet geniuses who couldn't survive in the scholastic world because he had the attention span of a gnat when it came to sitting in a classroom. If it wasn't hands on, he wasn't interested. Now he could sit down and read anything off the Internet for research, but if it came from a book or a stuffy old professor, he was out of there. He had an average build, sort of humdrum, balding with pop bottle glasses, a scruffy salt and pepper beard with attitude to match. He had a dirty mind and told raunchy jokes but was as loyal as Labrador retriever.

"Yeah Rob, I'm okay. It is what it is, and sorry about the phone. I really wasn't in the mood to take calls yesterday."

"They got all of us John, all of us but Jasper. They sent that little kiss-ass to Detroit."

"You got to be kidding me!"

"No John, I ain't kidding, we heard he's continuing the project. They sent him and dismantled the lab to take with him. All the files, all the test samples, everything!"

"Jesus H. Christ, he wasn't good for much more than making coffee. They told me the project was scrapped, what the hell?" John said as he stood up and started pacing, his temper flaring back up. "They told me they had no budget for our project, and they packed this little shit up and let him run to Detroit with it?"

"I know John, we can't believe it either. I'm here with Bobby and Frank right now. We are all over at Bobby's house trying to sort out what just happened."

"How they taking it, they okay?" John asked.

"They're just as shocked as we are. We all got the same speech and the same long walk to the door. The worst part though, is we were all in the lab when they came to dismantle it, before they called us upstairs."

"Holy shit, I'm so sorry guys."

"It's not your fault John, we know this," Rob acknowledged. "You think you can come over to Bobby's so we can all talk?"

"Yeah, I guess so, ain't much left for me here. Job is gone, and the wife is gone."

"The wife is gone?"

"Yeah, long story, don't worry about it. Give me a few to get myself together, and I'll be over."

"Okay bud, see you soon."

By the end of his call, John found himself standing in front of a framed picture from his wedding day. He stared at the picture, his face turning a bright crimson red, his anger boiling hotter, thinking about the previous day's vision of his wife with another man. He picked up the frame, gave it one last glance, and smashed it on the hardwood floor at his feet. The glass shattered in a thousand hateful pieces, the frame mangled from the impact. He stepped over the debris and ran up the stairs.

That rotten bitch!

John found himself in the shower, washing dried blood off his sore knuckles, watching the dark red swirl disappear down the shower drain. His wedding ring was encrusted with what he presumed to be residue of the man's skin. His mind was going in different directions about what had occurred the day before. How could she do this to him?

Did she ever really love me?
Didn't I give her everything she wanted?
Wasn't our family enough for her?
What is she telling our children?

He had no answers for the questions swirling in his head, but what man does in this situation? Life threw John Kemp a curveball he was not prepared for. All he had left was the air he was breathing.

John finished his shower, quickly got dressed and stumbled out the door. He noticed up the road that Fred's wife Kathy was outside watering plants she had planted that spring.

He slowed his car down to see if she noticed him coming. He didn't know if the cops were after him for beating Fred, or even if Kathy knew what had happened at all.

She looked up from her chore, smiled and waved at John. She didn't know. John pulled the car up to the curb and rolled the window down.

"Kathy, tell Fred if I catch him near my wife again, I'll kill him."

"Fred what, your wife…what are you talking about, John?" she said in astonishment, the tone in her voice rising. "Fred called and said he had to go out of town for business."

"Well, you just tell him what I said."

John pulled away before Kathy could respond again. He felt bad for saying anything to Kathy, but if it screwed Fred's life up like it did his, so be it. He didn't want to leave her hanging, but he didn't have the heart to tell her everything that had happened. He felt it best that Fred now answer all her questions. Part of him wanted revenge, to beat Fred one more time. Perhaps being stuck with Gloria for the rest of his life might be all the revenge he needed. John was torn.

He tried to call Gloria as he was driving. He wanted answers, and he wanted to brag about letting the cat somewhat out of the bag with Kathy.

The phone rang until a message picked up saying that this number has been disconnected and is no longer in service.

She's already turned her phone off?

John tried one more time; maybe it was a mistake, but again he got the same message. He tossed his cell phone in the passenger's seat, turned on the radio and stomped the accelerator.

Fuck her! Fred can have her!

4

John arrived at Bobby's house; the guys were sitting in his garage washing down their sorrows with cheap beer and what looked to be a mason jar of moonshine. As John pulled into the driveway and was immediately welcomed, John could see the disappointment in their eyes. As soon as he could exit the car, Rob grabbed him in an attempted bear hug. John didn't accept the hug and half-heartedly returned the gesture.

"John, we're so sorry."

"Don't worry about it Rob, shit happens," John replied.

One by one the men tried to hug John; each wanted to give the other their condolences over the devastating news. It was the first time since John took his long walk with two security guards that he felt the slightest sense of compassion, although it made him uncomfortable. He didn't want to be thoughtless. "I appreciate it guys, words can't say what I'm feeling, but it's good to see all your faces."

John spent the next few minutes explaining to the guys what happened after he was released, his troubles at home, his day at the park, his cookie and scotch diet.

"Somebody else got their number disconnected as well," Frank said. "Been trying to get a hold of Jasper, he must have turned his cell phone off too this morning."

"That little troll," Bobby responded.

"I'm curious, how did you guys find out about Jasper continuing the project?" John asked.

Bobby answered with disgust. "I overheard Tom and Amy discussing it before they canned my ass!"

"Tom said if we found out about it, that we would go ballistic. Amy told him there is nothing we can do; the company owns the rights to the project, and we all are just collateral damage," Frank said.

"Anybody got any good job leads?" Rob asked with a little laugh. He wanted to break the tension. It was starting to turn ugly, and they really needed to get off the subject. "I'm thinking about becoming one of those underwear models now that this engineering thing is over."

Rob stood up and with a little jiggle of his hips he jested, "I might also become one of those male strippers, probably get some work down at the old folks' home, they only pay once a month…unless you accept denture cream!"

Rob had gotten the response he was looking for. He didn't want to see the guys beating themselves up anymore, and he himself didn't want to think about what had just happened. He wanted some camaraderie from his friends, to drink a few drinks and tell some lies. He knew that the coming months were going to be hard on them all, and he wanted to enjoy the moment and worry later.

The guys settled into the garage, talking, laughing, and telling those lies and tall tales that all men do when liquid courage is involved. Bobby broke out the grill, burnt some steaks, which the guys jokingly referred to as *The Last Supper*.

To the torment of Bobby's wife, Lora, the men stayed up into the wee hours of the morning. It was like four grown kids reliving their adolescence.

Bobby White was a mechanical engineer, which surprised most, due to the fact he looked like a NFL lineman. He was a monster of a man who stood somewhere in the vicinity of six feet eight inches tall. His wife, on the other hand, Lora, who barely made it up to Bobby's waist, was one to be reckoned with. She might have been a tiny woman, but her attitude was ten feet tall and bulletproof. Bobby knew it, and for the most part walked a fine line when it came to dealing with his little lady. Bobby had been on John's team at the plant for about six years. At one point John had begged to have him added to the team due to his work ethic and his knowledge of mechanical engineering. He would draw it up and Rob would build it, make it come to life.

Frank Henry, on the other hand, was the opposite of Bobby; he was often kidded about having to look up to Bobby's wife. Although he was taller than Lora, it wasn't by much, which made kidding him even more fun. He was also a self-professed ladies' man, a legend in his own mind; this also didn't help his cause in winning any respect from his team. If he told one story, they pretty much knew, when he started it was bullshit. His weekly sexual trysts became office legend, not the legends you'd want to be famous for. But they let him have his moments, to say the least. If anything those stories were somewhat entertaining and broke up the monotony of everyday life. But to Frank's credit, he was as smart as they come; he was a problem solver, a thinker, a process engineer like no other. And if anything had to do with computers, he was the guy to ask; he could work magic with one of those things. He was with John when they inherited the project.

Now the project, that was a different story. It was kind of a fluke; it just happened one day that some guy (the company never disclosed his name) found a way to chemically change diesel fuel, for a few seconds, but never could sustain his results. In theory if they could sustain the fuel, it would burn much longer, decrease usage, increase fuel mileage and lead to the next big thing, allowing the company to sell more vehicles. The longest time that they had achieved any sustainability with the fuel was about an hour, then the chemical change would revert back, and so would the fuel mileage, hence losing the results. John's team worked on this project for the next ten years. What started out as a *See what you can do project* turned into a *We need results project*, almost overnight. The uppers started about a year ago before the current layoffs, demanding we need results now. Although it was never an easy task, and the company knew this, they had to win this race, be the first to develop the technology.

A year ago is when the company introduced Jasper to John's team. He never really fit in, and for the most part he was a contradictive little prick. If he wasn't messing something up, he was somehow stirring up trouble within the team. Numerous times John tried to get him removed from the team, but as the company put it, "If he goes, so do you." John was unfortunately stuck with him.

Jasper Van Winkle was a snot-nosed little college boy, kind of wiry, with a thin frame and slicked back hair. He wore these fancy little glasses that he sometimes pushed on top of his pointy head to keep that greasy mess of a hairdo in place. Rumor had it he was the nephew of one the bigwigs up north; they needed some place to stick him, so they put him with John's team. Since Jasper had his college degree, he thought he knew more than the engineers he worked with, some of whom had twenty plus years in the industry. He was an arrogant little brat, and he didn't care whom he snubbed when he thought he was right, which happened to be all the time. It was hard for the team to deal with him on a daily basis due to his high connections, but they managed, often using Jasper as the target of some of their juvenile pranks.

One time Jasper was in full swing and full of himself, tattling on his peers to see whom he could get in trouble. He didn't like the test results of a trial run of fuel samples, mainly because he didn't get his way, and the team wouldn't run the test samples as he wanted. He told upper management that there may or may have not been a little fire in the fuel lab. Well, with *safety first* always being the main policy in a manufacturing plant, upper management investigated, and sure enough, John and his team were disciplined for the fire. It didn't sit well with the guys that there was dissention in the ranks, so they set out to get even with Jasper. The rest of the guys drove typical vehicles, nothing fancy, but Jasper's prize possession was a cute little foreign convertible Daddy had bought him for graduating college. So the guys took it upon themselves to welcome Jasper into their club by loading his little car with cheesy popcorn and blow up dolls. Not only was Jasper fit to be tied, their behavior did not sit well with upper management, and yet again the guys got written up and disciplined.

As the beer supply dwindled and the cold from the morning air set in, it was evident that the party was ending. Rob was the first to depart; his wife Heather picked him up, disapproving of his current condition. Frank's taxi was next to arrive, which left John wondering how in the hell he was going to get home. Lora suggested that he stay, sleep on their couch and have breakfast in the morning. John graciously declined and said he would walk; the fresh air would do him good. Part of him was wondering if Gloria had returned home, although he probably wouldn't have admitted it if asked.

The walk, however, was a bad idea for John; it moved his hangover along quicker than it should. The sun was rising in his direction and it didn't help his bloodshot eyes; he was struggling to focus. Each step he took felt like someone hammering a nail into the side of his head.

When he finally arrived home and made it through the door, he realized something else was terribly wrong. He had no furniture.

You got to be kidding me! he thought.

"WOW! Why did I marry such a bitch?" he yelled.

Searching through the house to see if she left him anything at all, he was mesmerized at how quiet it was, how eerie this once-lively home had become now that it was deserted. She had emptied the entire house except for one room…theirs. She left his clothes and one single piece of furniture…the bed. The very bed in which she had cheated, the bed where John had found Fred and her only the day before. The bed was still in its previous condition, unmade and still soiled, except for the lone note she left on the pillow.

This isn't working anymore John. You will be hearing from my lawyers.

5

John woke that morning with his back aching and his head throbbing, as if someone was standing next to him, tapping him on the temple. He swore he could hear his pulse beating like a drum. He hadn't slept in the adulterous tainted bed his wife had left him; he opted for the bathroom floor, just in case he needed to make a donation to the great white wishing well. And the very thought of touching and changing the sullied sheets turned his stomach even more.

I'm not as young as I used to be, he thought as he tried to lift his weary carcass off the floor.

John crawled over and slumped into the tub. He didn't even take time to remove his clothes. He just turned the water on and lay beneath the showerhead. He found comfort in the warmth.

Thinking to himself: *Is this all I've worked for? Is this the reward for hard work and dedication? I try to be a good husband and a good father, do the best I can to provide. Is this my life's reward? Then this sucks!*

John hoped that this was all just a dream, but the reality is that this is life. It's a gamble. And right now he was losing.

John eventually picked himself up, took a proper shower and got dressed. He needed to get back to Bobby's to reclaim his car and figure out what his next move would be. The walk back was no better than the walk home. He couldn't call Bobby to come pick him up as he had left his phone in the car.

When he finally arrived at Bobby's house, he noticed his car was missing. He knocked on the door and Lora answered.

"Hey John, come on in."

She gave him a hug as he entered.

"Where's my car?"

"Gloria had it towed this morning John. We tried to call you, but you wouldn't pick up," she replied frantically.

"Yeah, the phone was in the car. This is just perfect."

"We're sorry John, we tried to stop them, but they had papers, and we didn't know what else to do."

"It's been one day and she has my car towed. How in the hell did she know it was here?" John said as he hung his head, rubbing each of his temples with his fingers in a slow circular fashion. The news wasn't helping his self-induced headache. He looked up at Lora and saw the pity in her eyes. John could tell she didn't have the words. Not wanting to make Lora feel any worse that she already did, he tried to hurry and move on from the conversation.

"It's all right, don't worry about it. Where's Bobby at?"

"He's in the garage cleaning up from last night."

"Thanks," John said as he gave her a hug and headed towards the garage.

As he stepped into the garage, Bobby was unaware that John had joined him. John tripped over an empty beer can, which alerted Bobby to his presence.

"Holy shit, you look like hell!" Bobby pointed out.

"Thanks. Guess you're not taking me to prom then?"

"Hell no, not until you shave them legs."

"Well, that ain't going to happen. As big as you are, I'm pretty sure I'd be the bitch in that relationship." John grinned over at Bobby, who wasn't cleaning the garage like his wife said. He was looking through a file box.

"What are you looking at, Bobby?"

"You know how Rob is, he had been taking stuff home from time to time. These are copies of our recent sample tests."

"No shit, really?"

"Yeah, he dropped them off this morning, even said when you stop by to give you these," Bobby said as he placed three vials in John's hand.

"Are these what I think they are?"

"God love old Rob and his dirty little sticky fingers." Bobby laughed as he leaned back in his chair and lit a cigarette. "You want a smoke?"

"Sure, why not? Everything else is trying to kill me."

John lit a cigarette, took a slight drag, and immediately coughed. "Haven't had one of these since college," he gurgled. "Now I see why."

"Here, take a draw off this. It will help what ails you," Bobby offered as he raised a jar of shine from the night before. John waved the jar off with his hand while turning his head away from it. Catching a smell of the pure grain alcohol turned his stomach once more.

"Those three vials are the closest we have gotten to sustainability with the fuel samples. Are they pure or have they been mixed with diesel?" John asked, as he tried one more quick drag and quickly extinguished his cigarette.

"Nope, Rob said those are pure samples, S901, S902 and S903."

"When did he get these?"

"Said he took them that morning, before they called us upstairs. Said he could see the writing on the wall and he wasn't letting them take all of our work. When they came to dismantle the lab, he snuck in the back to the chemical containers and got three samples before they even knew he was back there."

John walked over to the box containing the test result papers. "How'd he get these out?"

"Those he had all along. He had been taking pictures with his phone, the little sneak."

"Well, it's certainly nice to see all this, but what can we do with it? We have no lab, we have no funding. For fuck's sake, we have no jobs," John snarled as he tossed the paperwork back in the box. "I personally don't have shit, not even a car now!"

"Well John, I hate to tell you this. It kills me, it really does," Bobby said as he stood up, placing his hand on John's shoulder. "Gloria said this morning she was going to file a restraining order. She's afraid what you did to that other guy, you're going to do to her."

"Trust me, I wanted to!"

"John, I don't think you understand. She's going to take your house too. If she gets the restraining order, and they tell you to stay away, you don't have a home either."

"But she removed every piece of furniture, she took everything, she's the one that left."

"Judge tells her it's hers, it's hers. Nothing you can do about it, it's the law."

"*Son of a bitch!*" John kept mumbling over and over, pacing around Bobby's garage.

"John, I don't know if this helps, but I do have some good news."

"Really Bobby, is there such a thing as good news?"

"Well, as of nine-oh-one this morning, I got another job."

"That's fucking great Bobby, good for you. I've lost everything in my life, and you got a job. Awesome, just freaking awesome!" Disgust billowed from John's voice. "I got to get out of here. Sorry Bobby, ignore me. Good for you, I'm really happy for you, I'll catch you later."

"John…John." Bobby gave chase as John was storming out. "John…you have a job too!"

The news stopped John dead in his tracks. He turned to face Bobby. "What the hell are you talking about?"

"Rob's wife, Heather, you've met her right?"

"Yeah, and?"

"Rob never told any of us this, but she's loaded!"

"I'm lost. I don't understand. What the hell are you talking about?"

"Come back inside, and let me explain, please?"

Johns stood there biting his lip, hands on his hips as his foot tapped the pavement, looking up at Bobby, back at the ground, back at Bobby. "What the fuck have I got to lose? Sure, why not, this day can't get any crazier than it already has."

Rob Yarborough had met his wife Heather a few years back. The guys didn't really know much about her. She seemed very nice, and she wasn't bad on the eyes either. The guys wondered what she saw in Rob; he had definitely married up. What they didn't know, and Rob surely didn't share with them, was that Heather came from money. Her family, her father in particular, had done very well for himself in the oil business. Supposedly when he passed he had left Heather a good portion of his estate. She didn't know anything about the oil business; however, she did very well for herself investing and buying a few small businesses that afforded her a comfortable lifestyle. She was a tad frugal, which was why she shocked Rob when she said that she would volunteer to invest in a project that hadn't proven successful yet.

As Bobby laid it all out for John, there still seemed to be some missing pieces. How do they lose their job one day, and the next, they have one funded by Rob's wife? How was this to be?

"Heather didn't even know Rob lost his job until she picked him up last night," Bobby said. "He explained it to her on the way home, and as they talked about it, she offered to back him if he wanted to continue the project."

"Didn't he explain the legal ramifications?" John asked. "I mean for one, we all had to sign a conflict of interest and a privacy clause when they hired us."

"John, you have been working on this project for about ten years. The clause is only good for three more once you leave the company. Look at it this way, if we discover how to sustain the fuel, we'll sit on it for those three years, still draw a paycheck, and then release the results, become rich and retire," Bobby said as he leaned back, crossed his arms and grunted, like he had just presented the new Ten Commandments.

"What if they sustain it first?"

"Do you really think Jasper can figure it out?" Bobby said with a smirk, throwing both hands in the air to emphasize his point. "He can barely tie his own shoes!"

John paused while searching for possible answers to the questions his mind was asking. He could find no answers. He scratched his head and replied, "Good point."

"But I'm going to tell you this, there is one little catch. Okay, maybe two. Don't get mad."

"Okay, what's the catch?" You could hear the skepticism in John's voice.

"The pay is under the table, and the project won't start for six months. Do you think you can hang on that long?" Bobby said as he tilted his head and looked over the top of his glasses at John.

"Doesn't sound like I have much of a choice. Why the delay, why six months, what exactly are we waiting for?" John asked.

"Rob said she had to sort out a few money issues, move this here, move that there, and secure a facility. Red tape shit, you know how it goes."

"Guess that leaves me with no choice. I'll need to find a place to stay, sort out this shit with Gloria. I can wait six months, I hope. You got a car I can borrow?"

"I got that old Ford LTD out there. She's rough, but she runs. She's a 1979, and she ain't going to turn heads, but she'll get you to the prom."

"You know how the old saying goes, beggars can't be choosers. I appreciate it Bobby," John said as he stood up to shake Bobby's hand.

"She's yours if you want her, my friend, she's yours."

"Question. What happens if we all find jobs before the six months is up?"

Bobby shrugged his shoulders. With uncertainty in his voice, he replied, "I don't know John, I guess we will have to work both jobs."

6

Six months had come and gone. John found himself at his lowest point, with no job and still collecting unemployment, although Bobby and Frank had both found other work.

Gloria had continued the restraining order against him. He only was able to see his kids through a court-appointed guardian, and of course at his own expense.

He had to move into Bobby's garage. His home, still occupied by Gloria, was headed for foreclosure. She had one vehicle in her possession, the other repossessed for failure of payment. Bills were piling up around him; he saw no end in sight. What money he did receive went to Gloria and lawyers. With divorce proceedings around the corner, she agreed to stop the restraining order and allow joint parenting for the kids. Surprisingly, she wanted no alimony; rumor had it she was moving in with Fred since his wife had kicked him out after finding out about the affair. John had been quoted that he prayed for the *sweet relief of freedom*, although no one could tell, because John still wore his wedding ring.

John was looking forward to getting back to work on his project. He had invested so much time into it, and he wanted to find all the answers to sustainability. That and seeing his kids was all he had to look forward to in life. It wasn't just the project he missed; it was working alongside his team. He enjoyed how they operated together. Sure, they had hung out together in the last six months, but it wasn't the same. He didn't know if Bobby and Frank would make the same contributions to the project now that they had found other work. He didn't know how Rob's wife being involved would change the chemistry they were so accustomed to. All he knew was there were changes.

John was lying on the couch in the garage. He raised his head and looked up when he heard a gentle knock at the door; Bobby leaned his head inside the dark refuge where John lay in his self-pity.

"You awake?" Bobby whispered.

John whispered back, "Yeah, but why are we whispering?"

"I don't know, thought maybe you might be asleep."

"I don't sleep at night, what makes you think I sleep during the day?"

"Well, it beats the hell out of me!" Bobby shouted as he flung open the door and smacked at the light switch. Lights popped on one by one, causing John to squint his eyes as he tried to focus on the larger man-child, who was giggling like a little schoolgirl.

"What the hell are you so happy about?" John asked as he sat up, his hair a mess, his clothes unkempt. He looked like he hadn't shaved in days, and the stubble on his chin was starting to show a little grey.

"We all should be happy. Rob did it."

"Rob did what?" John asked, as Bobby romped across the garage floor, plopping his big frame down next to John.

"He got us a place, a place to start the project back up, it's on!" Bobby said excitedly as he reached over John's shoulders and pulled him in, giving him a one-handed bear hug. "We got a place! Aren't you excited?"

"I'd be more excited if you'd quit hugging me." John said as he pulled away from Bobby's grasp.

"And I'd be more excited if you went and took a shower. I got to tell you, you smell foul. It's like whiskey-tainted gym socks on a dead hooker; even the flies in here are wearing gas masks."

"Thanks Bobby, you really know how to make a guy feel good."

"Anytime, my friend, anytime. Now why don't you go jump in the shower? Because when Rob gets here, we are going over to take a look at the new facility."

John, shaking his head in astonishment, sighed as he lifted his stiff body up off the couch. "All right, I'll go take a shower, don't get pushy."

John headed off to the bathroom to do what was requested of him. He thought he'd be more excited about the news, but he couldn't stop himself from thinking about his life. Part of him wondered if this was all just another illusion, a fantasy. Would he actually get excited and then watch his dreams get pulled out from underneath him once more?

John leaned against the shower wall, his forearm resting on the cold tile. His eyes fixated on the water as it flowed down the drain. The warm water drizzled down the back of his neck as droplets plummeted from his arms to the awaiting swirl below. He was mesmerized. At this moment he related his life to the drain. John was so fixated on the swirls that he didn't even hear the bathroom door open.

Before John could snap out of his hypnotic trance, the shower curtain was ripped open and there was a single flash. It was the flash of the camera phone that awoke John from his state of unconsciousness.

"What the hell are you doing?" John screamed as he scrambled to cover up his private parts, startled by Rob's juvenile antics.

"I'm making a photo journal for our restart. Day one, John naked!" Rob said as he ran from the bathroom, running and bumping into the walls as he made his escape down the hallway.

These idiots are going to be the death of me, John thought.

Once John was dressed he found both Bobby and Rob outside tossing a football around, impatiently awaiting his arrival. Somehow both middle-aged men had found their second childhoods. John wished he could have the same enthusiasm, but longed for the slightest touch of normality.

"Where's Frank? Isn't he going too?" John asked.

"He had to work, so I texted him the address. He'll meet us when he gets off."

"Working on the weekend, that brings back some memories. Remember those days?" Bobby asked as he threw the football to John, who just smacked it away.

"I don't remember. It's been too long."

"Somebody woke up on the wrong side of the couch this morning," Rob joked.

"Let's go. Let's see if the new place can bring some life back into the old dog," Bobby said as he opened the passenger side door of the car for John. "Your chariot awaits, my lady."

"Quit bowing, it's not becoming of you," John said as he entered the vehicle.

"Robert, her royal highness is ready to depart, shall we?"

"By you my liege, let us embark on a wonderful journey."

"It is our journey, isn't it?" Bobby asked. Both men nodded, bowed and then curtseyed. With a quick laugh they joined John in the car.

"You two are real cute. Funny, very funny," John said sarcastically with a scowl. "So where are we headed?"

Rob, still snickering, replied, "It's about twenty minutes outside of town."

"Twenty minutes? You couldn't find anything closer?" John asked.

"It's what we can afford. Plus, nobody will care or find out what we're doing out there. Nobody will give us a second look."

"Like you always say John, beggars can't be choosers," Bobby said as he reached up and patted John on the shoulder. "It's our journey."

7

John stared out the window of the car the entire trip. Both Rob and Bobby were going back and forth insulting each other, laughing and carrying on like little schoolchildren on a bus trip. John zoned out. Once again he let the daydreams about his past control his memories. He was starting to imagine that it was his kids in the back seat arguing while they were driving on a family vacation.

"Here it is boys!" Rob informed his two passengers excitedly.

John snapped out of his daydream. He noticed they were turning down a long drive, unpaved and untended. It was hard in places to distinguish if the drive continued or stopped. It had definitely been some time since this beaten path had been traveled. Overgrown tree limbs scraped the roof of the car. John could feel the car jostle over fallen branches and hear the cracking noise of the dried wood underneath the weight of the tires.

"What kind of facility is out here?" John asked Rob.

"Not so much a facility as an actual house with a garage," he replied.

As the car came to a stop, the men exited the vehicle, both Bobby and John in awe.

"What…is…this?" Bobby asked.

"It's our new lab, see. You have a house with an attached garage. With a bit of work we can make her good as new," Rob said as he placed his hand on his hips. He was proud of his new investment, although the others didn't share the same enthusiasm.

"It's a trailer with a shack next to it!" John proclaimed loudly.

"It's not a shack. It's got a garage door," Rob said, defending his purchase.

"Okay, it's a fucking shack with a fucking garage door!" John shouted.

"All right, it is a shack, but it's a shack within our budget."

Rob's last statement got the other two men's attention as they shot a quick glance at each other.

"We don't have much of a budget, do we?" Bobby asked. "Is there something else you might want to tell us Rob?"

"With buying all the equipment we need, which I'll tell you now, it's not the top shelf equipment we had, but it's equipment that will do the job, I had to cut a few things out here and there," Rob answered, his voice a bit unassertive. "I did the best I could guys."

"Rob, I do appreciate everything you and Heather are doing for us, I really do. But what do we have to work with here? Really, what kind of budget are we looking at?" John asked.

"There's a recession going on, the whole country is hurting. Heather sold a couple of businesses to make this happen, and to tell the truth, she didn't get the selling price she was asking for."

John nodded at Rob, smiling with gratitude, and crossed his arms. He took a few steps toward the decrepit old homestead, his back turned to the other two. He just stared at the neglected property, studying every possibility of its structure. The shack was a shambles. The trailer was intact but looked as if it had been battered by Father Time for being older than he was. He didn't want to disrespect Heather or Rob. He was looking for some angle to make it work. He couldn't find one, but he was going to let on as if he did. This old dilapidated shanty was to be his new lab. It had to work.

"How long do we have before the money runs out?" John asked.

"A year, year and a half maybe," Rob answered. "But there's one more catch, a minute one, but there is a catch, if you guys can accept it, I hope."

"A catch, yes, there is always a catch," John said, grinning as he turned to face Rob.

"And what would that be? It's haunted? The Clampetts are due to return? The three bears might come back looking for their porridge? What's the catch?

"We can only pay you guys about four hundred dollars a month. I'm not even taking a salary," Rob confessed. He was starting to get nervous about this newfound revelation, as if him not taking a salary added to the acceptance of the equation. "I know it's not much, but if we do this, we discover sustainability, we won't ever need to worry about money ever again."

"You know, I used to make about fifteen hundred dollars a week, now I'm down to four hundred a month for the same work," John said, shaking his head in pity at the new price of his life's work. "But its four hundred dollars I don't have. It is what it is. Guess I'll have to find a way to make it work."

"I already got another job, screw it. I'm in!" Bobby said as he grabbed Rob to hug him, reaching over to pull John into his group hug. It was the first time John wasn't totally uncomfortable receiving a hug.

At that exact moment, Frank pulled up the drive to find the other men in an embrace. Not realizing that Frank had arrived, the men were oblivious to his presence.

"What the hell's going on here? You all getting ready to go brown trout fishing on Broke Back Mountain?"

"Not without you to paddle the canoe, get in here," Bobby demanded, waving Frank over to join them.

Bobby explained the situation to Frank as the other two explored their new so-called research facility. Rob took John into the trailer to look around at the possibilities.

"John, I'm sorry about you and Gloria. No one saw that coming."

"Don't worry about it Rob. I'll be all right."

"I know it's not much, but we can fix this place up. If you want you can stay here, and it won't cost you a dime."

"I don't know Rob, Bobby's garage is pretty nice," John said, smiling at Rob.

"I'll help you. We'll make it livable, and for the most part, you can have some privacy."

"I appreciate it Rob, I really do. Thanks."

The men spent the next few hours planning their angle of attack, how to transform the pigsty into a home and a research facility. It wasn't going to be easy on the limited funds they had. And they hadn't seen what Rob had bought for test equipment yet. Although he promised them all over and over again that he did the best he could, there was still doubt.

"Guys, we have one problem that I see that we cannot budge on. We need a current model engine for the tests. We can't just test on any engine," Frank stated.

"One step ahead of you Frank," Rob answered. "I may or may not have our old test engine soon in my possession. Well, not the old one, but the same model, I should say."

"How do you plan on pulling that off?" Bobby asked.

"If you know the right maintenance guys at the plant, and I do, we can have that very engine by the end of the week."

John started laughing. He knew if Rob could sneak the current samples out of the plant, why not an engine? "And this is going to cost what?"

"Nothing. We made a deal."

"What kind of deal?" Frank asked.

"I need to hack Tom Hawkins' personal computer, download some images he has on there, hack into the plant's mainframe and upload them there."

"What kind of images?" John said, still laughing.

"Let's just say that his secretary is kind of flexible." Rob chuckled.

The guys were unsure about Rob's plan of attack. It wasn't going to be an easy task to pull off with Rob's limited computer skills, and it left them all with just a slight grin instead of the hardy laugh they had been sharing, until it registered with Frank what was happening.

"You can't hack into a computer, can you?" Frank asked.

"No, but you can," Rob said, smiling as he gave Frank a slap on the back.

"You guys are going to get me thrown in jail," Frank replied. "But I'll do it, I've always had a thing for Tom's secretary."

8

Wasn't long and Tom Hawkins found himself begging for a job. The guys had somehow pulled off the impossible and set Tom up to get their new engine. Jasper Van Winkle wasn't having any luck either, as he tried to head a project he knew hardly anything about. He too was often begging for his job.

"Jasper!" the tall man at the end of the hallway yelled. "Come down here I need to have a word with you."

He stood at the end of the long hallway, his arms firmly crossed atop of his Armani suit. He stood there like a statue, tall and proud, and stone-like. It was Alex Wright, the CEO of the company, and probably one of the richest men in the world. Even at 62 years old, he was still an intimidating figure. Broad shoulders, slim waist, with a tan that most supermodels would die for, his lustrous silver hair neatly trimmed, not a one was out of place. He was not known for his patience; when he wanted something he got it. And if you could not provide it for him, he was sure to find someone who could.

Jasper wasn't very comfortable taking that long walk down the hallway to meet Mr. Wright. It wasn't his vision to restart the project on bad terms with the big guy. The hallway seemed a mile long. On each side of the corridor hung pictures of former vehicles from every year the company had been in business. They were a symbol of the success and heritage. Jasper looked at everyone as he nervously made his way to meet his new boss.

"Good…morning…Mr. Wright," Jasper said, his voice squeaky and hesitant. He stuck out his hand to shake.

"Um…yes, good morning," Alex Wright replied as he waved off Jasper's handshake attempt. "Sorry, I don't touch other people."

"Oh sorry Mr. Wright, yes…yes I read that in your biography, great book one of my favorites sir, let me tell you when I read your book it changed my life, I can remember…"

The older gentleman cut him off. "That's wonderful, thank you. Now walk with me."

Jasper jumped in line behind the elder statesman's heels, like a pup chasing its master. If the sun hit them, Jasper would have disappeared in his shadow.

"The reason we brought you up here," he said, turning to his right, back to his left, Jasper moving with him each time. "Where the hell did you go?"

"I'm here sir!"

"Well, walk beside me so that I can see who in the hell I'm talking to!"

Jasper, responding to the order, jumped out from behind Alex Wright, his hands clasped behind his back, his pathetic fake attempt at a smile on display for the whole world to see.

"My apologies sir," Jasper said, bowing his head as if he were talking to the king.

"Yes, okay, whatever," Alex said as he started to walk again, Jasper increasing his gait to keep up, skipping to stay alongside at the brisk pace Alex had set.

"The reason you're here is we are losing market share to other engine manufactures."

"Oh, that's a shame," Jasper interrupted.

"Yes we know. The reason you are here is to find the answer to this fuel problem. I need these results immediately."

"Well sir, I will do my very best."

"No, you will do it yesterday, as if today was yesterday!" Alex barked.

"Sir, I'm going to do everything in my power. I love this company and I love my job and results are what I shall give you."

"Good, but let me put it this way. If I don't get my results, you don't have a job!"

Jasper felt a lump in his throat. He found it hard to swallow. He stammered, "But sir, sir…"

"No buts, no excuses, just bring me my results. Do I make myself clear?"

"Absolutely, without a doubt, I will do whatever it takes Mr. Wright."

Alex Wright leaned over the smaller man, establishing his authority. Jasper, alarmed and terrified at how puny he really was standing underneath this behemoth, could feel the man's breath on his face. He felt like David facing Goliath, and all he had to throw at this hulking man was a single grain of sand.

"There is only one answer when Alex Wright tells you to do something, do you know what that is?"

"Yes…sir," Jasper said hesitantly.

"That's right," Alex said as he stepped away from Jasper, a smug little grin across his lips, folding his large arms back across his chest. "People around here often find themselves at the bottom of Lake Erie. Do you know how that happens?"

"Yes…sir."

"Good, we are on the same page then. Next time I see you, I better see results. You are dismissed."

"Yes…sir."

Jasper quickly scurried away. He could think of a thousand places better to be than at the bottom of Lake Erie. For one thing, he couldn't swim. He hurried back to his lab, as if somehow it would shield him from the big bad wolf. He realized everything was still in crates. The fuel test samples were still in transit and would not arrive until tomorrow. How was he going to pull this off?

Oh god, what did I do? I should have kept those guys, he thought.

Standing safely behind locked doors, he kept thinking about how badly he had screwed up. See, now the automotive recession was indeed a real thing, and he used that excuse to get rid of his teammates. The whole time he had been behind the scenes, making phone calls, cutting deals, and making promises to people to whom no one should make promises. He promised that he could deliver results. He was indeed writing checks his ass couldn't cash. Being straight out of college, he was in very deep over his head. He didn't have the knowledge or the skills to deliver, but the team he had gotten fired did. His desire to be the boss and the next big dog might now cost him his life.

The test results the company wanted to see was to take diesel fuel and sustain it chemically while taking the fuel mileage to one hundred miles per gallon. Not only would it make someone a billionaire, it would be a monopoly on the market for the company who developed it.

That guy who no one mentioned, who made this little discovery, had disappeared. The project actually started in the early 1970s and only three teams had worked on it. One that nobody knew anything about but possibly could get answers if they swam to the bottom of Lake Erie to ask. The second was trying to continue the work in a dirty little hooch in the middle of nowhere, and the third, which wasn't even fully assembled yet, well, their soon-to-be leader was currently trying to figure out how to open a crate with a stapler.

9

"Hey, the place is looking good," Bobby said as he interrupted John's cleaning.

"Yeah, the carpet still smells bad. The plumbing half ass works. But these rat droppings are history."

"Oh darn, I thought those were M&M's. I shouldn't have ate one the other day then."

"No, probably not," John agreed.

"So where are the other guys at?" Bobby asked.

"Frank's not off work yet, and Rob is picking up the carpet cleaner for in here. Then Frank said something about picking something up at the airport after he got off work."

"What the hell would he pick up at the airport?"

"I don't know, he was a little giddy on the phone this morning and it was hard to understand him out here. Service isn't that great you know. Some sort of programmer thing, hardware-software. I don't understand half the stuff he talks about when it comes to computers."

"I feel you there. I've been working on computers my whole life, and most of the stuff he talks about is over my head," Bobby replied.

"I know what's not over your head. There are some surprises out in the shack for you, sorry, I mean garage." John said.

"No shit. Don't let Rob here you say shack, you might hurt his feelings again," Bobby kidded.

"Let's go take a look, I think you'll be pleasantly surprised," John said.

Once outside, John encouraged Bobby to open the door, "Go ahead big man, do the honors. It will feel like Christmas."

Bobby reached over and gave the door a tug upwards. Settled dust started sailing outward as the evening sunlight exposed the spoils inside.

"Is that what I think it is?" Bobby asked giddily.

"Sure is. That's a laser cutter. We also have, if you look over here, two more laser setups on a steel jig table."

"Twenty watts, one hundred watts and the cutter is three thousand watts," Bobby said as he read the tags off of the equipment. He rubbed his hands across the newfound treasure. "Where did Rob score this?"

"It seems Tom's secretary's pictures weren't the only pictures on his computer," John answered.

"Go on, do tell."

"Tom had other interests in the company as well. He had various pictures of him with none other than Amy Howell, doing various things around numerous locations inside the plant."

"Oh my god! You have to be kidding me!"

"Not at all. Somehow those pictures got uploaded to the company's server as well. And let's just say they both got dealt with. Tom's absence allowed the maintenance guys to explore the lab next to ours."

"The one we weren't allowed to go in," Bobby said.

"Yes, that very one. Seems Tom had this equipment the whole time, even though he turned down our purchase requests for this equipment numerous times."

"That dirty rotten son-of-a-bitch..."

"Since we killed two birds with one stone, maintenance decided to throw in a little bonus. If the company didn't know they had this equipment, they won't miss it," John said.

"No, they won't. Will they?"

"We need to upgrade the electric here in order to use all of this though. We don't have sufficient power."

"What do you need? Just tell me and I'll go get it. Bobby wants to play with new toys," Bobby said as he lay atop of the laser cutter, somehow trying to embrace the inanimate apparatus.

"You better wait for Rob. This upgrade is going to be expensive," John informed him.

"I'm not waiting. I'll put it on my credit card. I'll just hide the receipts from Lora."

"Bobby, she will kill you. It's going to cost at least two grand just to get the minimum power we need out here," John warned.

"Don't worry, if she kills me, she can hide the body out here. And nobody will find it." Bobby chuckled.

"She's going to have to dig one big-ass hole."

The men sat down and made up a list of everything thing they needed, and Bobby took off to the hardware store. John needed to get back to cleaning his home. He was on a deadline from the court to get a stable home so that he could see his boys without paying for a mediator. He would need to provide them the same amenities they had when staying with their mother. John had his work cut out for him.

Frank's mother had passed some time back. He told John he could have her furniture. It was just in storage, and he had no use for it. John was sure thankful but not sure that his and an 88-year-old woman's decorating tastes wouldn't clash. But then again, it was free and gave him something to sit on besides a cooler, which often also served as a table-slash-desk-slash-chair.

John, deep in thought and busy with his chores, didn't hear Rob pull up outside. It wasn't until he heard the big rig pulling up the drive blowing its horn that his hypnotic state was broken. Stepping outside to see what the commotion was, he saw Rob directing traffic as the driver backed up to the side of the garage. On the back of the flatbed trailer he saw two small, barn-like sheds. One was for storing fuel, to keep it out of the elements. He had no idea what the other was for.

"Glad to see you finally made it," John said.

"Me too. Almost didn't get that thing up here. We really need to trim down that overgrowth on the drive. The truck just trimmed some of it for us."

"I bet. So what is all this?" John asked.

"Frank didn't tell you?"

"Tell me what?"

"Frank isn't here?"

"How many questions are we going to go through before I get an answer?"

"No more questions, here comes Frank now," Rob pointed out.

As Frank pulled up the drive John noticed he had a passenger. When Frank parked the car, a thin Asian man stepped out. He was dressed grungy; his jeans ripped down to his black Chuck Taylor tennis shoes. He was wearing a black t-shirt with some writing on it about freedom. John couldn't make out the rest of the text due the man's black leather jacket. He couldn't see the man's eyes for the oversize charcoal glasses he wore. The glasses were clearly too large for the man's slender face; he looked like a fly. The bangs of his hair hid part of his glasses, and the rest was pulled back tight into a ponytail that stretched the length of his leather jacket.

"Everybody, I would like to introduce, Mr. Hideyoshi Tatsu," Frank said proudly. The young Japanese man didn't give the traditional bow, but slowly raised his head, nodding at the other two men.

"Nice to meet you," both John and Rob replied.

John leaned over to whisper to Rob, "Who the fuck is this tool-bag?" Returning his attention back to Frank and his friend, he flashed the fakest smile he could drum up.

"Evidently not who I imagined," Rob whispered back. "Frank, can we have a word with you? Excuse us Mr. Tatsu, give us just a moment." Again the tiny Asian man answered with a nod of the head.

As the workers unloaded the sheds, the other three men took refuge in the garage to discuss their new guest.

"Who is this guy Frank?" John demanded.

"He's a hacker friend of mine who needed some work. I thought we could bring him on here, find a use for him," Frank explained.

"Frank you don't make those kind of calls. This is my project, I'm the lead on this!"

"Technically John, it's my project. I'm the one funding it now, right?" Rob said.

"Is that how this is going to be now? Frank, you agree with that?"

"No, but he's got a point John. It is his money, so technically he is the boss," Frank answered.

"Really?" John asked, looking back and forth at both men's eyes. "If this is the way it's going to be, I guess I'm done! Fuck it, I quit! I have too much going on in my life to deal with this!"

John stomped out to the garage and headed back to the trailer, both men in tow pleading his name. "John, John, just listen John!"

Once inside the trailer and cornered, both men barricaded the door with their bodies. "Please John, just hear us out!" Rob requested.

"Hear what? You guys can make all the decisions, you don't need me!"

"There is more to the story than Frank told you. Let him finish John, please let him finish," Rob pleaded.

John was a beaten man. He had already lost everything. And now his project was to be taken away—by his best friends. How much more could one man endure? He hung his head, his heart still pounding as he slumped down onto his cooler-slash-table-slash-desk-slash-chair.

"I'm all ears. Let's hear it."

"John, I won't make any more calls without your approval, but this guy brings cash to the table."

"Lots of cash John," Rob confirmed.

"Millions, once it gets cleared," Frank said.

"What do you mean, cleared?"

"Tell him Frank."

"He and I kind of belong to a little Internet group of hackers. We play some games, share some files, steal some money, talk about hardware and software, do some secret society type stuff," Frank explained.

"Back up. Did you say steal some money?" John asked.

"I didn't steal anything John, but the Dragon did."

"The Dragon? Really? Why do I feel like I'm in a fairytale right now with a money-stealing Dragon?"

"It's not like that, that's his hacker name," Frank proclaimed.

"Great, good for him. What's your name? The Mighty Munchkin? I know what, we all can learn to hack and get cool names. They can call me Broke Dick and Rob can be Captain Pervert!"

"Just let him finish, please?" Rob pleaded.

"Whatever. What's next? I know, is he the pope?"

"Come on, just let me explain," Frank said. "Back in his home country, some of his family members lost their homes to a developer. They took their homes and built a high rise. They forcibly paid those folks a fraction of what the homes were worth."

"I'm sorry to hear about his family," John asked. "But what does this have to do with our project?"

"Those developers were getting ready to do it again with another group of people in his community. So he hacked into their account and stole the funding, leaving the project on hold, and allowing that group to stay in their homes," Frank explained.

"Again, what does this have to do with our project?"

"I'm getting there—hold on a second," Frank stated. "The money is traveling around the world in different accounts and at different times, it is very complex. The money just keeps constantly moving to avoid detection. But when the trail goes cold, he's giving a portion to the families who were displaced, leaving him with a big chunk of change to do with what he wants."

"So why is he here?" John asked Frank. "I've yet to hear why."

"It was getting a little hot back in Japan for him. The developers tried to hire the mob to find him. Since he works closely with them on certain projects, they told him to get out of the country for a while until this thing cools down."

"Okay—it's all crystal clear now. Let me see if I get this right. You have an international criminal with mob ties on the run and you want him to hole up here? So that if they find him—and this is the good part—we all wind up dead or in prison! Am I right?"

"It's not like that. They don't know who he is or where he is," Rob said.

"Well, the mob does. What are they called over there?"

"The Yakuza," Frank answered. "But they don't even know he's here."

"You both know I'm trying to get my kids back? I can see how the judge is going to love this. 'I'm sorry Mr. Kemp, but harboring fugitives is not what we consider good parenting. Do not pass go, do not collect two hundred dollars; it's straight to jail! Enjoy your life!'" John yelled. "Does the guy even speak English?"

"Fluently," Hideyoshi answered. The men were so busy arguing that they didn't notice him standing at the door of the trailer. "May I come in?"

"Yeah, sure," John answered.

"Mind if I sit?" Hideyoshi asked, pointing at the floor in the corner of the room.

"Help yourself, pull up some carpet," John said sarcastically.

"Mr. Kemp—I bring twenty million to your project, in time. I have connections in markets you only dream about. If you want it, I can get it. As for your family, I will not ruin your chances of seeing your children. If in any way, anyone finds my whereabouts, I'll do the honorable thing and disappear. They won't even know I was here."

"No offense—but I just don't know about this," John said.

"I understand your concern. You have my word. I promise that you will not be affected by my actions. Please take some time to consider."

John shook his head yes to the smaller Japanese man tucked in the corner, assuring him he would give it some thought.

Meanwhile Bobby returned from his shopping spree and noticed the new company.

"Who's this fellow?" Bobby asked.

"Shurekku!" Hideyoshi shouted with a smile as Frank and he begin to laugh.

Puzzled, Bobby asked, "What did he just say, Frank?"

"You don't want to know."

"Oh—I want to know. What did he say?"

"Well, he called you Shrek," Frank said, giggling.

"Funny—very funny. You tell him I'm laughing on the inside," Bobby demanded.

"He does not need to tell me. I understand you. My apologies big man, Frank-san said you had sense of humor. He said I should mess with you. You would find it funny."

"Oh he did—did he?" Bobby asked while turning to find Frank, who had already snuck out the door and was in hiding. Bobby stood at the door of the trailer surveying the possible locations of his prankster.

He sent him a warning.

"Fe-Fi-Fo-Fum…I smell the fear of Frank-san! You have to come out sometime Frank! I'll be waiting!"

10

Frank made it through that night—alive. The guys spent countless hours and weeks setting up both the house and the lab. Hideyoshi settled into the other small shed. He turned it into a tiny cabin that he placed behind the trailer. He wasn't much on helping the guys per se, but he was one hell of a watcher. John and Rob performed most of the construction since they had never found another job. Bobby and Frank pitched in where they could, when their work schedules would allow.

Winter was approaching and so was John's divorce hearing. He kept himself busy to keep his mind off of the inevitable. He was finally going to be able to see his kids, but what would they think about the strange Asian man living in the back yard?

"Well guys—we are almost there," Rob claimed proudly.

"It's about time. I can't wait to get started," John responded.

Hideyoshi was sitting in the corner typing away on his laptop as the other men continued stuffing test equipment in every nook and cranny. They saw the finish line, and it pushed them harder. They were so engrossed with the task at hand, they didn't even realize that they had company.

"Rob!" a woman's voice screeched like a banshee, startling the men.

Rob knew that voice; he hadn't heard it at that particular decibel often. But when he did, it typically wasn't a good thing for him. He turned to find Heather standing underneath the open garage door. Although there wasn't much room, somehow the guys found the capability to part like the Red Sea, so that Heather had a clean line of sight on her victim.

"Oh—hi honey—w- w- when, when did you get here?" Rob stuttered.

Heather was holding a couple trays of food wrapped in tinfoil; she tossed them imprudently up on to the laser cutter table.

Then she answered, "I've been standing here long enough to know I didn't give you money for this." She pointed at the laser cutter and jig table. "Why did you spend this kind of money? It wasn't on the list you gave me. That's why I had you make a list in the first damn place!"

"There's a list?" Bobby asked. "I didn't see a list—did you see a list John?"

"I didn't see a list—did you see a list Frank?"

"Well, I definitely didn't see a list," Frank answered.

"Shut it—all of you!" Heather said. "I'm not in the mood for your cute little banter!"

"Honey, let me explain," Rob pleaded.

"Outside, right now!" she demanded.

"Excuse me ma'am. This is my equipment. My apologies for not introducing myself—I'm Hideyoshi Tatsu," he said with a suave, confident smile.

Hideyoshi laid his laptop down, stood and walked over to Heather, extending his hand. "It's a pleasure to meet you," he said.

"It's nice to meet you too," Heather said, reaching out to shake Hideyoshi's hand as he gave the traditional Japanese bow, which placed a flattered smile upon Heather's face.

"Thank you," she said.

"It is my honor," Hideyoshi replied, bowing again.

"Rob, can I still see you outside, please?" Heather asked, still a little red in the cheeks.

"Sure honey. I'll be right back guys."

"Excuse us gentlemen," Heather said, smiling.

Rob scurried outside, following his wife like a good little husband, the guys taking note of his quick surrender to his wife's demands.

"He's whipped," Bobby said.

"Money and good looks—and what are you saying, you're just as whipped as he is," John pointed out.

"Is it just me—or is she even hotter when she's mad?" Frank teased.

"Keep it in your pants Frank," John replied. "That's Rob's wife you're talking about."

"I'm not going to lie. I was turned on," Bobby said. "But then again, I'm married to a mean woman."

John shot Bobby a quick little grin. He walked over and stuck his hand out to Hideyoshi.

"Good save," he said.

"I told you Mr. Kemp. I will be a valuable asset to your team," he said, shaking John's hand. Both men smiled and bowed to the other, and for the first time Hideyoshi finally felt welcomed.

"Yes, you just might. If I give you a list of some materials we need, think possibly you can find them for me?" John asked.

"The Internet is the new black market Mr. Kemp."

"Call me John. I'll get you the list tomorrow."

"John-san it is. Please call me The Dragon."

"No, I don't think I can do that," John replied. "Baby steps—baby steps."

Hideyoshi went back to work on his laptop while Rob was still trying to calm his wife down. John and Bobby headed into the home, leaving

Frank to continue unpacking materials and equipment.

"Bobby, do you think you can call a grown man The Dragon?" John asked.

"I don't see why not. I call Frank the Horny Troll all the time," he answered.

"Maybe that is his hacker name."

"I wouldn't doubt it. But he still hasn't answered that question either."

"No, and he probably never will."

"Let me ask you something John. Do you think we can really pull this off?" Bobby asked.

"We have to. I don't have anything else going. I need this; this is all I've got," John answered.

"I don't want to play devil's advocate, but we've been at this so long. We've only made minor breakthroughs. I'm worried the money will run out before we find it. And it also worries me that this twenty million that 'The Dragon' has— well, I think that's horse shit."

"It is farfetched, isn't it?"

"Come on John, Frank's internet buddy? I'm not buying it."

"I know Bobby, but what else do I have? If this doesn't work out I have nothing."

"There's some talk at work. They may be hiring this next summer. I could put in a good word for you; I'd have to be your boss though," Bobby said.

"Why not? Looks like Rob's my boss out here. I'd work for you anytime Bob."

"I'm going to be honest with you. You're a way better leader than I am. I'm just not boss material."

"You'll do just fine. You can't be any worse than Rob." John laughed.

"Rob's not a boss either. But his wife sure is. I wonder if she's like that in bed."

"I wonder how Rob wound up with her. Just look at her. She's gorgeous."

"That makes two of us. Either he's hung like a mule or she's really into balding, middle-aged, blind, perverted geeks."

"I don't know Bobby, love is a funny thing."

11

"Good morning Jasper," Tom Hawkins said.

"Tom, what are you doing here?" Jasper said, surprised.

Jasper rushed to greet his old boss. He was stunned to see Tom in his lab in Detroit.

"I'm your new expediter."

"You are my what?" Jasper asked.

"I'm your new expediter. If you need it—I will get it!" the once-proud drill instructor said boldly.

"I don't understand. I heard you left the company to pursue other endeavors."

"Well, I'm back!" Tom said as he marched behind Jasper. "And I didn't leave the company. I cannot confirm it, but I think that little band of misfits I fired tried to set me up."

"It will be great to work for you again sir."

"Negative—I now work for you."

It clicked right then for Jasper. With an evil twinkle in his eye and a sly grin, he asked, "I'm sorry—what did you say?"

"I said I work for you, sir! I've been assigned to your team."

"This is interesting. Welcome aboard Tom. You can call me Mr. Van Winkle," the cocky little young man said as he turned his back to his former grizzled patriarch and continued pretending to read emails. He quickly closed down the browser, hiding the fact he was looking at dating sites. He left the crusty veteran red faced, a single vein popping out of his forehead.

"So where do we begin—Mr. Van Winkle?" Tom stressed.

"We are waiting. We have two engineers set to arrive from one of our plants in Germany. And another will arrive from France," Jasper answered smugly.

"Great, two krauts and two fairies. What a team," Tom mumbled.

"What was that, Tom?"

"Nothing, sir!"

"Ease up Tom, I'm sure you're are going to like it here. What did I just tell you?"

"To call you Mr. Van Winkle."

"That's correct. For starters, why don't you find some tools and open those crates?"

"I'm on it," Tom said as he did an about face and headed to the door.

"Oh Tom, again, what did I say?"

"I said I'm on it—Mr. Van Winkle."

"Thank you. You may go now."

Tom exited the lab, his blood pressure through the roof, thinking to himself, *I'm going to kill that little pencil-necked geek when I get the chance!*

Jasper was beside himself with joy. He really was starting to like his new role as the boss. It was up to him to find the best candidates to continue the project. He chose two German engineers, twin brothers, Armin and Klaus Feierabend. Although he wasn't personally familiar with their work, he took recommendations from other engineers in the facility that praised their credentials. His remaining team member was from France. Maurice Bouchard, unlike the others, did not come recommended. Jasper found him in a company directory and thought he would add some class to the team, being French and all.

What Jasper didn't know was that his team would be even more dysfunctional than what he previously thought before. The twins were notorious for arguing with each other, and unlike most twins they didn't get along. Jasper, disliked by his peers, was unaware they had given him bad recommendations. Too lazy to do the work and verify each member's credentials, he took whoever was mentioned. The Frenchman was his own mistake. Maurice was known for being an overeducated slacker. If he wasn't caught sleeping at his desk, he would be found in one of his many hiding places avoiding anything that had to do with work. He was scheduled to be terminated from the company; it looked like Jasper unknowingly saved his job.

Jasper went back to his Internet search for the next Miss Right-Now, unaware he was alone in the lab with Alex Wright, who at that moment was peeking over his shoulder.

"Jasper, what are you doing?"

Quickly fumbling to hide his lack of work, Jasper turned the monitor to his computer off.

"Research Mr. Wright. I was looking for more engineers," he lied.

"No—you were wasting my time."

"I'm sorry Mr. Wright, it won't happen again—I swear."

"Never mind with that, it's not the reason I came down here."

"What brings you to our lab then sir?" Jasper stammered, rising quickly while adjusting his glasses on the bridge of his nose.

"Your old team. Word is they have started to look for sustainability. Word is they are ready to run their own tests as we speak."

"That's impossible sir, there is no way they would be able to secure that kind of funding."

"You calling me a liar?"

"No sir—I wouldn't do that."

"If you know what's good for you, you won't. Now shut up and listen," Alex Wright warned while pointing to a chair for Jasper to sit back down. Alex leaned against the desk, positioning himself over the timid little man, as he looked up cowardly.

"I know for a fact they are—you see, I have a man on the inside. I know every move they make. They don't blink without me knowing about it."

"That's wonderful sir," Jasper praised.

"Just like you, you little worm, I know every move you make," Alex scowled while pointing up to the camera above the door. "They are ready to test samples—and you—you haven't done anything for the last two days but look for the next woman you'll disappoint."

"Sir, I can explain."

"You'll explain nothing. I have approved the transfer requests of your new engineers. They will be here tomorrow."

"Thank you sir. As soon as they get here we are going to get you those test results."

"Don't make promises you can't keep. Do you remember our little talk?" Alex asked.

Jasper nodded yes.

"Then you know I'm going to keep my promise—you at the bottom of Lake Erie!"

Alex Wright left Jasper sitting there stupefied, sick from knowing that his life was still on the line and that his former team was already days ahead of him in research.

Jasper watched as Alex and Tom exchanged pleasantries as they passed each other in the entrance of the lab.

"What's the big guy doing down here?" Tom asked.

"Don't you worry about it, just start opening the crates. I need the lab set up by tomorrow morning."

"Okay, which one would you like to start with?"

"Just pick one and open and damn thing!" Jasper shouted.

"Okay, okay, no need to get your panties in a bunch."

"My panties aren't in a bunch! I need to go home, I do not feel well. I expect you to have this lab set up in the morning. When I return everything better be in order!"

"Yes sir, it will be in order," Tom said.

"Tom how do you address me?"

"Yes—sir Mr. Van Winkle. It will be in order Mr.—Van—Winkle."

"Good!"

I can't wait to kill that little prick, Tom thought.

12

"Dad, how much longer until we get there?" John Junior whined.

"It's just a bit further Little John, calm down. I'm sure you and your brother will like it out here. Plenty of room to run through the woods. We can build a fort if you guys are up to it?" John asked.

"Don't worry Little John, I'm sure Dad is going to protect us from all the zombies out there."

"Thomas, why do you have to do that? Tell your brother there are no zombies," John demanded.

"I'm just kidding bro—there's a witch!"

"Thomas!"

"He knows I'm just playing, Dad."

"Dad, I want to go home," John Junior said.

"John, there aren't any witches or zombies. I'm sorry, but I'm not taking you home. This is the first weekend since your mother and I split that I've gotten to spend with you."

"But Dad…"

"No buts. We are spending the weekend together."

The rest of the trip was silent. The boys clammed up and stared out the windows of the car as John drove. He was hoping his kids would be happy to spend time with him, but it didn't seem like it. He was worried about what picture of him Gloria had painted. How much did she share about the split with their children? *Did she tell them lies? Was Fred taking his place? Were his kids ever going to forgive him?*

They started to turn down the drive as the sun was setting. There was a red glow across the sky, making the eerie drive seem more frightening than it was.

The boys were now focusing on the long driveway, both wide-eyed as the car crept down the path. A coyote howled in the distance, startling the younger Kemp boy. The older was becoming the believer of his own cruel jokes.

"Um, Dad, what's out here?" Thomas asked.

"My home and your other home now," John said as he stopped the car, turning his attention to his boys. His eyes widened and he began to talk in a deep horrifying voice. "The home you will never leave!"

The boys, paralyzed with shock, didn't understand their father was having fun at their expense.

John stomped on the accelerator and laughed out loud as his boys screamed for him to stop.

"Sounds like I have daughters instead of sons. You two are too easy. You both need to lighten up," John said as he slowed the car down.

"I wasn't scared," Little John said with a fake laugh.

"Me either—nice try Dad—maybe next time," Thomas said.

John pulled the old car up in front of the trailer, the boys staring at what would be their accommodations for the weekend. "Well, here we are. It ain't much, but it's home."

"You gotta be kidding me. It's a shithole," Thomas blurted out.

"Thomas, you don't talk like that! Where did you hear that kind of language?" John asked angrily.

"From Fred, Dad. He cusses all the time," Little John said.

"Shut up rat face—you don't have to tattle on everything!"

"Well I don't like it!" John said. "And I don't want to hear it again—from either of you!"

The boys grabbed their bags and followed John into the trailer. John threw his keys on an end table as the boys noticed Hideyoshi standing in the kitchen.

John felt a tug on his jacket as the little boy whispered, "Dad, there is a man in your kitchen."

"I know. He lives here too."

"Who the hell is he?" Thomas asked.

"Thomas, the language!"

"Yeah, sorry Dad. Excuse me, who are you?" Thomas said as he walked over to confront the stranger.

"I am Hideyoshi Tatsu, The Dragon, but you can call me The Dragon."

"What kind of name is The Dragon?" Little John asked.

"It's the name of someone with a lot of video games. Do you like to play video games, little one?"

"I love video games!"

"Good. If you are both nice, I'll get you any game in the world, but you must be nice."

"Deal!" Little John agreed excitedly.

"And you, the one with the frown face?"

"It's a deal—so where are they?" Thomas asked.

"Go out that door to my cabin," Hideyoshi said, pointing at the back door. Before he could finish his sentence the boys were scrambling to see who would fit through the door first.

"Another good save Hideyoshi, thank you."

"Do not fret John-san, they are young and this world is new to them."

"It's a new world to me too."

"Our world is what we make it John-san. Dare to dream."

"My dreams are all nightmares. And now my kids are turning into little nightmares. They never talked like that before," John said.

"Give them time. They will come around."

"I hope," John said. "Care to have dinner with us?"

"It would be my honor."

"I'll get dinner ready. If you want to entertain them until then, I'll call you when it's ready."

And with a nod Hideyoshi was out the door.

It was a long weekend for John; he was happy and sad all at the same time. He enjoyed spending time with his boys, but it bothered him when they acted out, which they had never done before. He didn't know how to cope with it. Hideyoshi was a godsend for John; when they did act out he was able to help smooth out the situation. The boys were fascinated by The Dragon, much to John's surprise. When the boys acted out Hideyoshi would take them to play video games, giving John time to sort out his emotions. He didn't get to see his kids that often and didn't want to spend any of the time yelling at them.

As the boys were saying their goodbyes to Hideyoshi, Heather showed up unannounced.

"Hey John, where's Rob at?" she asked.

"I don't know Heather. I haven't seen him all weekend," John said. He was a little perplexed.

"What do you mean all weekend? I dropped him off here Friday afternoon."

"Who's the babe?" Thomas asked.

"Shut it Thomas, you and your brother get in the car," John said.

"Calm down old man, I was just checking out the babe."

"I'll show you old man, get your butt in the car!"

With the kids finally situated in the car, John turned his attention back to Heather.

"Rob told me you guys were running tests all weekend," she said.

"I'm sorry Heather, but I've had my kids all weekend."

"So where are the other guys?" she asked, her frustration growing.

"They all knew my kids would be here. We all decided to start first thing tomorrow morning so that I could have this weekend with them."

John could see the anger building in the woman's eyes; she was ready to explode at any moment.

"When's the last time you talked to him?" Hideyoshi asked.

"Last night! I could hear you and the kids in the background!"

"John-san, I think I might know where he is. I heard some noises from the garage last night. I assumed it was you."

Hideyoshi walked over to the garage and lifted the door. Sure enough Rob was inside, asleep in a hammock. Heather and John followed, peeking into the darkness of the decrepit old shelter.

"Rob!" Heather yelled.

He did not wake.

"Rob!" John yelled as he kicked the bottom of the hammock, spinning the slumbering man onto the cold cement floor.

Quickly jumping to his feet, Rob staggered to catch his balance, grabbing onto whatever would allow him to continue standing upright.

"Oh, hey everybody, what's up?" the bewildered man asked.

"What the hell are you doing?" Heather asked.

"I'm doing what you asked me to do honey, I got some work done."

At this point everybody was puzzled.

"You've been out here all weekend Rob?" John asked.

"Yeah, I was getting things ready for this week."

"Why didn't you come inside?"

"I didn't want to bother you while you had your kids. Heather said we were taking too long to get this whole thing rolling, so I told her we'd work this weekend—so I worked."

"Oh my god, I'm so embarrassed," Heather said. "Rob I'll see you in the car! John I'm so sorry, I had no idea. Oh my god, I'm so sorry."

Red-faced and angry, Heather stormed off to wait for Rob.

"I don't understand Rob, what the hell is going on? And how come we didn't hear you out here?" John asked.

"She was giving me grief about how long this all took to get started. So instead of listening to her bark at me all weekend, I hid out here. While you guys were sleeping I was working. Check this out," Rob said, pointing towards a centrifuge.

"What's this?"

"I made a plate to hold the test samples using that laser cutter. Now you can mix these fuel samples with a working centrifuge. I've already mixed three batches, one of each sample. It's all ready to go tomorrow."

"I do appreciate it, but I wish you had told me you were here. I feel bad for leaving you out here all weekend," John said.

"Think nothing of it. I had food and a place to crash. I took bird baths in the sink and enjoyed the peace and quiet."

"How did you go to the bathroom?"

"I used a bucket, this one. Don't open it—I'll need to empty it tomorrow."

"That is just so wrong on so many levels."

"I did what I had to do. But I'm still in trouble, as you can see. But she'll yell at me most of the night and then we can have make-up sex, it's the best."

"I hope it was worth it." John said.

"Me too, but I have to be honest. She's been getting a little antsy about this whole project. She's worried this entire investment is going to be a waste."

"All of us are worried, but I understand her concern. She did front the money."

"Don't worry about anything, I was just trying to please her. We should be ready to go tomorrow. I'll see you in the morning."

Rob hurried to receive the tongue-lashing he had waiting in the car. John himself was now late, so he needed to hurry too.

Gloria agreed to meet him at a neutral location. She wouldn't allow him to pick up or drop the kids off at their old home. With this arrangement, he knew time would be crucial or he would have to hear her yelling. He didn't want to have any arguments in front of the kids and did his best to avoid any confrontations with her. But he was late as usual.

13

Finally, John Kemp could get back to work. It had been a long time since he did any work on his project.

He awoke that morning with a little extra pep in his step. He felt good, he felt alive. He was having feelings he thought he had lost; he had found a little purpose in life.

John went to his new lab with confidence that morning. This was his journey. And that journey of finding sustainability was his goal. He fired up all the equipment for the first time, turned on all the lights and stood back in wonder. It was the first time it looked like a lab. Sure the walls were ragged and looked dirty, but the equipment took the focus off the space. He was able to smile for the first time in a while.

"Good morning John-san, how did you sleep?" Hideyoshi asked as he walked through the back door of the garage.

"Considering last night my ex-wife was yelling at me, I slept like a baby."

"That is wonderful John-san."

"Thank you Hideyoshi. Are you ready to get to work today?" John asked.

"Where would you like me to start first?"

"If you found those materials I asked for, when Rob gets here, you two can go pick those up. Right now I'm going to start dividing these test samples, so I don't have anything for you until he gets here."

"Very well John-san, I will be ready."

"Hideyoshi, on your way out can you hit that breaker by the door and turn on the air filtration? It will help me from getting contamination in these samples. Thanks," John said.

"You are welcome. I will leave you to your work and await Rob-san's arrival."

John started taking fuel samples of each mix and dividing them into smaller containers. With new materials and new chemicals, it would allow him to run trials to see what effects would take place. He turned on the radio and settled in, tapping his foot to the music as he proceeded.

John Lennon's "Imagine" came on the radio, a fitting song for John's mood. Imagine that the world was at peace; he was at peace as he sang along with the song. His mind was on his work; he didn't have the millions of thoughts rolling around in his head of what was to be. He was focused.

But John's momentum and the peaceful composition were abruptly interrupted when Bobby showed up. Without warning the large door swung upward, letting in the morning sunlight. John was left squinting his eyes, trying to adjust until the large man's shadow blocked out the rays.

"Shut the door, Shut the door!" John screamed. "Test samples are out!"

"Oh shit, sorry dude," Bobby replied as he quickly slammed the door down.

"We need to nail that door shut or lock it somehow."

"I'll hang a sign on it to walk around," Bobby offered.

"Good idea. And just what are you doing here? Shouldn't you be at work?"

"I took the day off. I wanted to be here for the first day, thought I'd surprise you," Bobby said as he raised up his jazz hands. "Surprise!"

"I'm happy you did, tell you what," John said, "Once you hang that sign, can you hook up the air shower in front of the back door so we don't get any more contamination in here?"

"I'm on it boss man, I'm on it."

They all started filing in. Bobby was first, followed by Rob who had thankfully lived through the night. Frank took half a vacation day and showed up mid-day. It was like they had never stopped; they were working, laughing and enjoying each other's company. They had Hideyoshi come in to be a part of the project, but not before his initiation prank. He was chosen to empty the bucket Rob had left from the weekend.

But this was not the prank; they caught him returning through the back yard from his dirty assignment. John was hidden behind his cabin, waiting to throw a bucket of ice-cold water on him, causing him to lose his breath for a second. Standing there with his mouth wide open, Bobby hit him with a bucket of flour, leaving the poor man white as a ghost.

"Welcome to the club—bitch—now go get cleaned up and let's get to work," Bobby told his victim. "You're one of us now!"

They proceeded to work on dividing the fuel samples. Once they had the first batch split, Rob and Hideyoshi left to get the other materials. Bobby started work, cutting out more plates to add more samples to their centrifuge. Frank started rewriting programs for the test equipment.

"John, I'm going to need better computers. These things are so slow we won't see our test results until next Christmas," Frank said.

"Can you update them?" John asked.

"It wouldn't be much different in cost; new is the way to go. We can't skimp here; we need top of the line systems."

"Here Frank," Bobby said as he tossed him his car keys. "Out in my trunk you'll find what you need, plus some other new toys."

As Frank went to retrieve his new electronics, John asked, "Where you getting all this money, Bobby?"

"I put it on my card, don't worry about it. I'll get the cash back in the long run."

"And if you don't, Lora will kill you."

"Nah, she won't. She might get a little mad. But unlike Rob, I actually like it when my wife's mad. Her temper turns me on," the gentle giant said, giggling.

Frank came fumbling through the door, boxes under each arm, with one stuck under his chin.

"Wow Bobby, this is great equipment!"

"Hang on a second and I'll help you carry the rest of it in," Bobby said.

"John, with these, and when The Dragon gets back to help, we can have everything programmed and running by tonight."

"That's good I guess. It will be just me, Rob and Hideyoshi after today."

"We'll be here on the weekends John, don't worry about it."

"I'm not worried Frank, it'll be all right," John said with a reassuring smile.

With Frank quietly working on his new toys, John felt guilty. He didn't like that Bobby was spending money in light of the potential funding. Heather wasn't handing out cash leisurely, arguing about what was needed and what was not. And as for harboring Hideyoshi, he had yet to provide one nickel for his hideaway in the solemn woods of Ohio. But, here was Bobby, backing expensive purchases without results; he might not have any hope of getting his money back.

"Hey, for old time's sake, why don't we fire up the engine?" Bobby asked.

"Because that would use fuel we have allotted only for experiments," John answered.

"We'll burn a couple gallons, I'll replace it. Come on, I want to hear that bad boy roar."

"Listen to Mr. Money Bags over here Frank."

"I'm with him; I want to hear it too," Frank responded.

"We haven't even verified it's ready to run yet. We can't afford to blow this engine."

"Come on John, don't make us beg," Bobby said. "The exhaust hoses are in place, dummy transmission is installed, what else do you need?"

"Come on Daddy, let the kids play with the engine," Frank whined.

"Yes Daddy, let us play," Bobby said, getting down on one massive knee. He was still almost as tall as Frank. "Please Daddy."

"Okay, okay. Quit begging; go get it ready," John said, giving in.

With both Bobby and Frank still playing the role, they skipped like little kids for John's amusement. Adding fuel to the tank and checking all hookups, they continued the banter of telling John *what a good daddy he was. He was the best daddy in the world*, they kept saying over and over. Winning John's cooperation, they got him to play along. John threatened to ground the two if they didn't straighten up.

As the silly game tired, each started to fall back into a routine. John watched as both men went over every detail; it was like nothing had ever changed.

"We are ready," Bobby proclaimed proudly. "All we need is you at the ignition controls John."

John walked over to look over their work once more, studying every connection and checking every valve.

"Is the pre-task safety check sheet filled out?" John asked.

Bobby turned to Frank, looking puzzled. Frank caught it too, and returned the same glance.

"John, we aren't at the plant buddy, we don't need to do that," Bobby stated.

"Sorry, habit. Lost myself for a second there," he replied. "I was so caught up in the moment, it was like we were back at work."

"Good to have you back captain," Bobby said.

"It is good to be back. Let's fire this engine up!"

With John at the controls and Frank by his side monitoring the dyno program, John turned the ignition, bringing the engine to life. Standing back to listen to the engine rumble, each man felt it in his chest.

"Now that's a moment!" Bobby yelled.

"Sure is. Frank, take the controls and run her though a program, let's see what she's got!"

John walked back to the jig table where he was splitting fuel samples and sat down back on his stool. Frank, at the helm, started to take the engine through its paces.

"How high you want to go?" Frank asked.

"What?" John asked.

"How high?" Frank screamed.

John held up three fingers, indicating three thousand rotations per minute. Frank nodded and carried on with his task. The noise was greater in the little space than their old lab. It had a booth that enclosed the engine, blocking the noise; it was the first time any of the men had been next to the engine as it ran.

Fifteen minutes passed. The noise was becoming unbearable, and the heat from the engine was obvious as the men started to sweat. Each could smell something smoldering, each thought it was the new burning off the engine. What they didn't know was that when Rob installed the exhaust he didn't put in a ceramic tile. He just punched a hole through the side of the garage, allowing the hot exhaust pipe to rest on bare wood. Rob hadn't expected them firing up the engine yet, it was one of the things on his to do list.

"FIRE!" Bobby screamed.

Frank quickly punched the shutdown button, which was in place in case something like this happened. Bobby began searching for a fire extinguisher, frantically pacing back and forth. He noticed one underneath the jig table and leapt for it, bouncing into John, sending him falling backwards off his stool.

Bobby quickly extinguished the flames, but the little garage was left filled with smoke. John was left lying beside the jig table. He twisted to his right, banging his knee on the table; his left hand, trying for something to grasp, smacked a vise installed on the edge. The impact of the blow to his right side on the concrete floor left him gasping for air in the thick smoke.

"Open the door," John wheezed.

Bobby bent down to pick John up as Frank rushed to open the door and vent the garage. With his arm around Bobby's shoulder, he was pulled from the garage into the fresh air.

"Are you okay?" Bobby asked.

John, unable to speak, nodded his head yes. He was struggling for each breath as the men watched over him.

"Call nine-one-one Frank," Bobby ordered.

John immediately waved Frank off, shaking his head no.

"I'll be okay," he said, grimacing. "Just let me sit here for a second."

"I should probably empty that fuel tank before we have a flash up, it got pretty hot in there," Bobby said.

"Go ahead Bobby, I'll watch John."

"I'm okay," John said. "You go help Bobby."

Bobby and Frank went to empty the tank as John was left to lie in the grass. He started to catch his breath, and the cold grass felt good on the back of his neck.

Damn, it was hot in there, he thought.

Staring up the sky, he watched as passenger jets flew by, leaving white contrails behind them.

"How you doing buddy?" Bobby asked.

"I've had better days," John said as he looked up at his assailant.

"Sorry about that. I got scared. I didn't mean to knock you over."

"I know you didn't, but how about helping me up?" John asked.

"Sure thing," Bobby said as he stuck his hands out to pull John from the grass. Taking both hands, Bobby felt something puncture his right hand. "Ouch, you scratched me."

"Good, you deserved it, but I don't know what scratched you."

"Seriously, you scratched me. Look, I'm bleeding."

John looked down at his hands. Did he fall on something that injured him more and now had injured Bobby? He didn't know. He stood there studying his hands until he realized his wedding ring was damaged.

"Look there, it's my ring. The diamond is gone, the setting is bent."

"Damn, that tore your ring up. I'm so sorry John," Bobby said.

"Don't worry about it. You tackled me, I cut you, we are even," John said as he smacked the big man on the back, limping towards the garage.

"We'll help you find it, and I'll even pay to have the ring fixed."

"I'm getting divorced. It won't be that important after this week. Anyway—great first day guys," John said, laughing.

"Here comes Rob," Frank pointed out.

"Bobby, you want to pay me back?" John asked.

"Absolutely."

"Go clean your cut, help Rob unload the car, and then take Rob out in the woods and shoot him."

"I can do that," Bobby said, accepting his orders.

"Frank, let's go take a look at the damage and try to find this diamond, and Bobby?"

"Yes, John."

"Don't really shoot Rob."

"If you say so, but I really want to after that fire."

"No, it's best if we keep him around…for now."

14

It was a late night for the men. They searched for the missing diamond as Rob made repairs to the wall. The diamond was not giving up its hiding place so easily. The search that started inside the small garage was expanded to the outside, but there was still no diamond to be found. One by one the men filtered off as darkness fell on the creepy abode. They would continue their search the next day.

Bobby was the last to leave. He wanted to speak to John alone. It was two days until John's divorce hearing, and Bobby knew it. He had pleaded with John to allow Lora and him to take John out to dinner the night before. John didn't want to go, but Bobby's constant pleas got him to consent.

His second day of work would be different. Now they knew there were several loose ends to tie up, they needed to get busy in order to not have any more hurdles. And there would only be three of them, as Bobby and Frank had to return to their day jobs.

John's second day did not start off as good as his first. His mood wasn't the same. It would be him and Hideyoshi. Rob had called and said he would be late. His wife had an unexpected business trip, and Rob would have to drop her off at the airport.

"Good morning John-san, how did you sleep?"

"I didn't," John grumbled.

"Sorry to hear. Where shall we start first?" Hideyoshi asked.

"Not much we can do without at least one of the other guys, so let's keep looking for that diamond."

As the search continued it took away from the actual research they were supposed to do. Six hours later John had an idea.

"I think we've been looking in all the wrong places," John said.

"What do you mean John-san?"

"Tell you what, go out to other shed and get another metal five-gallon bucket."

John took the remaining samples left over from the day before and dumped them in a bucket underneath the jig table. It looked like a nasty mixture that he wasn't going to stick his hand into.

"Here you go John-san, now what?"

"I want you to hold this strainer over the bucket as I empty this one into it. There's a chance the diamond flew in here."

"What's in this?" Hideyoshi asked.

"It's got about three gallons of diesel fuel combined, what I threw in there and from what

Frank and Bobby threw in from the test tank. It's also got S901, S902 and S903; those are the chemically engineered fuel enhancers we make."

"It does not smell too good."

"No it doesn't, that's from the enhancers," John said.

John began pouring the black concoction through the strainer ever so gently, trying not spill a drop that might contain the diamond. As Hideyoshi held the strainer tight across the bucket he couldn't help but keep turning his head away from the odor.

"Would you look there?" John said as poured the last remnants from his bucket. A solid black stone was lying atop the strainer, no sparkle remaining from its former self, looking as if it was nothing more than a stone found at the bottom of a river.

"Congratulations John-san, you found it."

"Yes we found it. But it doesn't look right."

John went to the sink to wash the residue off of the diamond, but the stone was still jet-black.

"Look at this Hideyoshi," John said, holding the stone in a cloth. "That stuff ate a hole right through the center of the diamond."

"Then what would that do to an engine?"

John didn't even answer Hideyoshi's question. He knew that if his chemicals could eat a hole in a diamond, it would eventually ruin a diesel engine. John realized all his years of research were now wasted; he had been going in the wrong direction.

As Hideyoshi patiently watched, John tried and tried to clean the diamond. Other than his kids, the only thing left from his marriage was his wedding ring. As John became frantic, scrubbing and cleaning the stone, Hideyoshi became worried for John's condition.

"John-san, maybe we can burn it off," Hideyoshi suggested.

Hideyoshi handed John a lighter. He laid the stone on the steel jig table as he tried to put the flame on top of it. It had no effect.

"This is useless. You have any other ideas?" John asked.

Hideyoshi was out of his comfort zone as he looked around the garage at other equipment, "Could you use the laser to burn it off?" he asked.

"I don't know, let's give it a try."

John moved everything off the jig table and set up a smaller laser. He fastened the stone into a harness, setting up reflectors to control the beam.

"Here, put these goggles on, don't want any more accidents."

"Where should I stand?"

"Anywhere but beside the table," John answered. "And if you would, take those buckets out of here first."

"Do we have another fire extinguisher, just in case?" Hideyoshi asked.

"No we don't. Okay keep one bucket and fill it with water, that'll have to do."

John began the procedure of firing the laser. Immediately he noticed the diamond start to glow.

"I think we are on to something here Hideyoshi."

What he didn't expect was the incredible amount of heat it was generating. With each second the laser hit its target, the diamond became a brighter blue.

"John-san, is this normal?" Hideyoshi asked, shielding his face with his hands.

"I don't know, I've never done this before—well, not with a diamond."

"Look John-san, the table is melting!"

From the heat of the diamond, the area beneath started to melt away, dripping onto the floor below. John killed the power to the laser, but the heat was still unbearable.

"It's got to be 2600 degrees Fahrenheit!"

"I don't know Fahrenheit!"

"That's 1426 degrees Celsius!" John screamed, trying to be heard over the popping of the steel.

"That's hot John-san, stand back!"

Before John could stop him, Hideyoshi grabbed the bucket of water and pitched it at the diamond.

"No Hideyo—" John attempted to scream, but unfortunately he didn't get to finish his warning before the explosion happened.

With a forceful rush, John and Hideyoshi were sent flying backwards by the shockwave. John did notice before he was lifted and sent flying that a bright blue light flashed and shot towards the back of the garage. The next thing he could remember was the impact of the door upon his back.

John found his vision hazy as he peered upward through his shattered goggles, looking at what he believed were clouds; he turned his head to find his overanxious helper, wondering what had happened to him. He saw Hideyoshi lying next to him a few feet away in the grass; he had obviously impacted the garage door as well and rolled away once it fell. He was unconscious, but John could see his chest rising and falling; he was relieved that he was breathing. Due to the throbbing pain in his head he could only see a shadow of the fallen man, his vision was blurred, and he was unable to adjust his focus as it kept drifting in and out.

John had the energy to reach up and remove what was left of his goggles, but as he tried to lift his upper body to sit he found that he was too weak to accomplish the simple task. He was finally able to muster enough energy to roll towards his fallen comrade, but to no avail. He fell victim to the same slumber.

It was hours before any help arrived. Rob showed up to the disturbing scene, frantically trying to wake both men. He tried to call for help, but his phone had no service.

"John can you hear me? John can you hear me?" he kept asking over and over.

John responded, his eyes starting to flutter. He could hear a voice, but it sounded so far away. It was Rob's gentle shaking of his shoulder and the pain of his touch that brought him back.

"Please don't touch me," John whimpered.

"Don't worry John—I'm going to get you guys help."

"Just let me get up," John pleaded.

"I can't move you John, you've had an accident."

"Rob, just help me up—please."

Rob gave in and got behind his friend; with his hands placed underneath John's shoulders he lifted. John groaned in pain, his body still stiff from the impact.

"Go help Hideyoshi, make sure he's all right."

John's vision still clouded, he looked around at the carnage beneath him. The door was shattered and mangled beyond repair. Pieces of the wall were still attached at the hinges; the door had totally been ripped away by the impact of the men.

"John-san, you okay?" Hideyoshi asked, his voice weak. He too was struggling to speak.

"I think I'll live," John answered. "You okay?"

"Yes I think so. I'm not sure."

"John, I should really get you two to a hospital," Rob pleaded.

"And how will that work? I have no insurance and he's a fugitive on the run," John said. "We go to a hospital, and they are going to call the police. They will be asking questions, coming out here and snooping around."

"But you two are hurt!"

"Hideyoshi, you got any broken bones?"

"No John-san," he answered.

"Me neither. We are hurt, not injured. Just get us in the house and get us some aspirin. I think we'll make it."

"Hang on John, you need to see yourself," Rob said as he turned and ran to his car; swinging open the passenger door he ripped the sun visor from its holder. He ran back and handed the visor to John.

"Go on, take a look."

John held up the mirror and glanced at the scarlet image that was his reflection. His face had been burnt a solid red while the area around his eyes was still white as snow. His shirt was ripped and tattered. He looked down at his arms and his chest; they were bright red, gleaming like Christmas decorations.

"Me too, I'm burnt," Hideyoshi said. "How does this happen?"

"From a steam explosion," John answered.

"A steam explosion? How did that happen?" Rob asked.

"I'll explain, just get us in the house, and call Lora. She used to be a nurse," John said. "And you better call the guys and get them over here, I got something else to tell all of you."

15

"This lab will simply not do!" blurted the Frenchman.

"How do you say?" Armis asked. "It is sh-e-e-t!"

"I'm sure you mean shit, and gentlemen I assure you this is the best lab the company has to offer," Jasper said.

"When Maurice Bouchard works, Maurice Bouchard works only with the finest equipment. That's why I'm Maurice Bouchard and this lab will simply not do!"

"You should have let us Germans design your lab," Klaus said. "It would be superior. We are the best engineers in the world."

"I beg to diff-e-fer!" the Frenchman said.

Jasper's first day was not what he'd envisioned. He couldn't get a word in edgewise as he listened to his new team argue like kids on a playground. The Frenchman argued with the twins, then the twins would argue with each other, all placing the blame on him. Tom Hawkins was no help as he sat back and watched the group implode, much to his amusement. It was complete chaos until Alex Wright appeared.

"Attention on deck!" Tom announced loudly.

"Good morning gentlemen. How is everyone today?"

"Oh good morning Miz-tur White, it is a hon-ur to meet you," Maurice said.

"It's Wright, not White."

"My apologies sir, it is a hon-ur."

"Yes it is. So, how are the accommodations?" Alex asked.

"We refuse to work under these type of conditions. This lab is unbearable," Armis and Klaus said simultaneously.

"You don't say?" Alex inquired. "Well—let me put it this way so that all of you understand. You will work in this lab, you will get me my results, or all of you are out of a job."

"Sir I assure you, at no..." Jasper tried to interject.

"No, nothing. Do— I—make— myself— clear?"

With a nod of agreement from the dysfunctional group, Alex turned his attention to Tom. "I need to have a word with you. Follow me."

Tom followed the elder statesmen outside of the lab, but not before shooting a gloating smile towards the still-disturbed faction.

Jasper was none too pleased with Mr. Wright wanting alone time with Tom. He was skeptical of Tom's position back under employment with the company as it was. With the lab door shut behind them, Jasper pressed his ear to it so that he could eavesdrop on the conversation. Jasper's attempt to spy was interrupted as the other men began to argue again about who would do what.

"Tom, I've got a special assignment for you. I want you to go back to Ohio," Alex said.

"Ohio, sir? What's in Ohio?"

"I want you to meet with this person," he said as he handed him a card. "Contact this person when you arrive. He'll show you where John Kemp is running his lab."

"Then what?" Tom asked.

"You watch him, you trail him, you find out what he's doing."

"I don't understand sir."

"If he finds sustainability before us, it's over. If he does find it, you steal it and bring the results to me," Alex said. "You do whatever is necessary. They cost you your job once, don't let them cost you it twice."

"By necessary you mean?"

"Kill them if you have to, I don't care. I want my results!"

"Sir, yes sir," Tom confirmed.

"I think I'm going to like having you back Tom. You do this for the company and I'll make sure you never have to work again," Alex said, smiling at Tom. "I might even let you get rid of Jasper when this is over."

"I'd like that, sir."

Jasper found it hard to swallow, hearing this new piece of information. Was Alex serious? Was he going to die when it was over? Had Tom been working against him from the start? His mind was a whirlwind of bad thoughts. He didn't know if he should run and hide, or be the first to find sustainability and save his own neck.

"Sir, I've got one question," Tom said.

"Yes, let me guess. Do I think that group of dipshits in there can find sustainability, is that right?"

"Yes, sir. That would be the question."

"Of course not. They're all a front. They are just filling an empty space to get the stockholders to agree to sign off on continuing the project. Those fucking idiots couldn't turn on a light bulb, let alone invent anything."

Oh my god, they are going to kill me! thought Jasper.

"Once this is all over and they've stolen their fifteen minutes of fame, mark my words, they will never be heard from again."

I knew it...I'm dead!

With an evil laugh, Alex walked away. Jasper rushed to try and break up his team, and put them to work.

"Mr. Van Winkle, I'll be leaving for a few days. The company is sending me out of town," Tom informed the nervous little man.

"Oh Tom, you can call me Jasper. I was kidding about that Mr. Van Winkle thing."

"Anything I can do before I leave?"

"No, just enjoy your trip. We'll see you when you get back."

Jasper was easy to spot. He was quivering, his hands shaking as he waved goodbye to Tom.

"Everything okay—sir?" Tom asked.

"Everything is wonderful, we'll just be here slaving away, me and the guys—right guys?"

The question from Jasper only stopped the others from arguing for a second so they could shoot him a puzzled look. Then they resumed their arguing as if they had never stopped.

"See, it will be just fine—go—go—go enjoy your trip," Jasper said, his voice even higher pitched than before.

As Tom left the lab, Jasper hung his head in his hands, resting his arms on his knees as he sat down, trying to compose himself. He heard the mechanical buzz of the camera turning. He looked up as the lens zoomed in on him.

How can I run if they are always watching me?

16

"I think the two of you will be all right," Lora said. "It's like you've been out in the sun too long. It's almost like a sunburn, a nasty one."

Both men jumped and gasped as she spread lotion over the bright red burns covering their bodies.

"Just keep applying this aloe and you should be fine," she said.

"What about my head?" Hideyoshi asked.

"We'll get you some aspirins. I think we've got some pain pills at home. I'll have Bobby bring them back over tomorrow."

"You look like a red raccoon screwed a Dalmatian," Bobby said as he poked one of John's red spots and watched him jump.

"Bobby!" Lora yelled. "That's not funny, that could have been you!"

"I know, I'm sorry John, just one more time," he said as he poked John again, only to receive a smack on the hand from his wife.

"So what the hell happened?" Rob asked.

"It's hard to explain," John said. "The diamond was over 1700 kelvin. All we did was hit it with the laser, and within a few seconds the table was melting."

"I threw the water on it and that's all I remember," Hideyoshi chimed in. "I didn't know that would happen."

"Well, you do now," John said.

Frank had gone to the garage to survey the damage from the blast. He found the diamond still clamped in its holder. Heat still resonating from the table, he found a glove and a pair of pliers to work with. With the pliers attached to the diamond, he unfastened the clamps. As he pulled the diamond closer, it sprung from the grasp of the pliers. Not even thinking about getting burnt, he snatched the diamond out of the air with his bare hand.

It's cold, he thought.

Frank placed the diamond on his cheek. *I'll be damned, it's ice cold.*

He quickly rushed into the house to inform his friends of his discovery.

"Guys, check this out!"

He walked over and placed the diamond in Bobby's hand.

"What's this?" Bobby asked.

"That's the diamond," Frank answered.

"It's cold."

"That's impossible," John said. "Let me see that."

Bobby placed the diamond in John's palm. Sure enough, he too was amazed by the temperature of the little rock.

"This is scientifically impossible. This should still be warm," John protested.

"I can't explain it," Bobby said. "I've never seen anything like it."

"Why is it black?" Rob asked as he peeked over Bobby's shoulder.

"It was soaking in the waste bucket of samples, but the question is, how did the chemicals eat a hole through the center of the diamond?" John asked.

"Were all the samples in there?" Bobby asked.

"And about three gallons of diesel," John pointed out.

Rob shrugged his shoulders. "I don't get it, this beyond my pay grade."

"I can't believe how cold it is. This is way below room temperature," Bobby said. "I'm going to have to look at it under a microscope to see what's going on."

"I'd like to see that to," Frank agreed.

"Not to interrupt, but I don't think we are going to make our reservations," Rob said.

"What reservations?" John asked curiously.

"Well, it wasn't just me and Lora that were taking you out for dinner. The whole gang was going to go," Bobby confessed.

"Oh shit, I've got court tomorrow, I completely forgot," John said. "I can't go looking like this."

"Can you reschedule?" Lora asked.

"Not this late, I don't think so."

"You guys want to grab some pizzas and skip the reservations?" Frank suggested.

"Hey Rob, would Heather pick them up on her way out here?" Bobby asked.

"I suppose, but when she sees the garage I don't think she's going to be happy about buying dinner."

"I'll pay her back when she gets here. Just give her a call," Bobby said.

"Okay, I'm going to drive down to the road and see if I get any reception from my cell. I'll be back in a few."

Rob was starting to get nervous. He was hesitant to call Heather, because he was hiding a secret from the fellows. Heather was none too pleased with the lack of progress, and money was flying out with no sign of any return. They had started arguing almost every night about how long this project would take. She kept stating that the recession was really affecting their budget, and she didn't know if the risk was worth it without any results. Rob knew that when she saw the damage, she would blow a gasket. It could be the start of World War Three. She might pull the plug on the whole thing.

"I want to go look at the damage," John said, grimacing. "Bobby, can you help me?"

"Haven't you had enough for one night?" Lora asked.

"I'll be fine, you just keep doctoring Hideyoshi. I need to show Bobby something."

"Frank, give me a hand," Bobby said.

"No Frank, you stay and help Lora, I can manage," John said as he slowly lifted his bruised and battered frame off the chair. His bones popped and cracked as he tried to stand upright.

"You going to make it old man?" Bobby said as he offered John a shoulder to lean on.

"Yeah, I'm just a little stiff still," John answered as he painfully lifted his arm up to reach the much taller man's shoulder.

Once outside, John stood in what the remains of the garage entrance. He stood there amazed by the destruction the blast had caused. The garage door was in shambles, and the back door and air shower were completely gone. Test equipment had blown back against the walls, bowing them outwards as if they were molded that way.

"It looks like my new favorite toy took the worst of it," Bobby said, observing the butchered the laser cutter. "It was the one thing I could run without Rob's help."

"Sorry Bobby."

"It's all right. Good thing is that you guys are alive."

"Bobby." John paused. "Sustainability isn't going to happen. If it did that to a diamond, an engine has no chance."

"I pretty much figured that out already, I just didn't want to say anything in front of the guys yet," Bobby said. "So now what? Where do we go from here?"

"I saw something Bobby. I don't if I was dreaming or I actually saw what I saw."

"You did take a pretty good shot to the head."

"But before the blast, I saw a blue flame shoot out the back of that diamond into the back door. I mean, the door was there and then it was gone," John said, "and then I don't remember anything else."

Raising his eyebrows, somewhat disbelieving, Bobby walked over to the door's opening. "Come on John, do you really think that you saw any of that?"

"I'm telling you, I saw something," John said.

As Bobby walked through the opening into the back yard, he stopped dead in his tracks. "Holy shit!" he screamed. "John, hurry, you have to see this!"

John hobbled over behind Bobby.

"Is that your door?" Bobby pointed out.

"Where? I don't see it."

Bobby stepped behind John and used his arm to point outward so that John could follow. The door was hanging in a tree across the back yard. The yard itself covered over eighty yards.

They both stood in amazement as the door teetered back and forth in the wind.

"How high up is that, you reckon?" Bobby asked.

"I'd say about thirty feet, give or take."

"I'm thinking you did see something," Bobby confirmed. "Do you know what kind of force that would take?"

"I don't have a clue, but I think we've discovered something other than sustainability."

"Should we tell the guys?" Bobby asked.

"Not yet. When Heather sees the lab, she might pull the plug. We could lose our funding."

"What about the money Hideyoshi has?"

"Have you seen a dime of it yet?"

"No."

"Let's see what she does first before we say anything to anybody," John insisted.

Heather eventually showed, none too happy. She put on the bitch fit of a lifetime. She lectured anyone and everyone about the money she'd wasted backing up a pipe dream that led nowhere. At one point she went after Bobby when he tried to calm her down. Her ridiculous insults thrown at Bobby fired Lora up. Lora, in return, went ballistic, and at one point the altercation would have become physical if it weren't for Frank jumping in the middle.

Heather left with Rob in tow. Neither stayed for John's final dinner before his divorce. He understood Rob's position on the matter. He was at least going to get to eat and rest his weary body, but Rob was going to be hearing about this for the rest of the night. He didn't know if this would be considered taking one for the team, but he was happy it wasn't him.

"I think I'm going to go to bed," Hideyoshi said.

"Why don't you sleep in here tonight? Take one of the kids' rooms. You really shouldn't be out there all by yourself."

"Thank you John-san, I will accept. Good night everyone," he said, bowing as he turned to limp down the hall.

"Get some rest John, keep putting the cream on, and good luck tomorrow," Lora said. "I'm going to go start the car, I'll meet you outside big man." She smacked Bobby on the behind.

"Okay baby, I'll be right there," Bobby replied before turning his attention back to John. "Listen John, I'm going to take off tomorrow. I'll come pick you up and take you to the hearing."

"You don't have to do that," John said, feeling guilty. "I can manage."

"Don't worry about it. I'm going to be there for you, you can count on it."

"Thanks Bobby, you're a true friend."

17

"All rise! This court is now in session! The honorable Judge Henley presiding!"

"You all may be seated," the judge ordered.

John hadn't slept that night. For one thing, he was too sore, and for another, he wasn't pondering the divorce as most would think. He was still trying to recollect his vision of the blue flame and the diamond. And third, he was wondering how he could recreate it without killing himself, or getting anyone else killed in the process.

"Before we start, Mr. Kemp I need to ask, are you okay?" the judge asked, staring at the defendant's bright red face.

"Yes your honor, I'm fine," John replied.

"Then what is with your appearance, Mr. Kemp?"

"Been playing a lot of golf—your honor."

"If you say so. Let's get on with it, shall we," the judge said, shaking his head. "We are here for the divorce proceedings of one John Edward Kemp and one Gloria Ethel Kemp. Is this correct?"

"Yes your honor, I'll be representing Mrs. Kemp in this matter."

"Cooper, right?" the judge asked. "And you Mr. Kemp, you will be representing yourself?"

"That's correct your honor," John said.

"Okay, who's first?" asked the judge.

"Your honor, Mrs. Kemp requests sixty percent of all marital assets, the family home and fifty percent of Mr. Kemp's retirement."

"Your honor, if I may." John stood up. "She can have a hundred percent of the assets, keep the house and the retirement. All I want is the shared custody that she's already agreed to."

"Mr. Cooper?"

"Just a second your honor, if I may confer with my client," he said as he leaned over to whisper into Gloria's ear. Leaning back up he responded, "Your honor we accept."

"Well, that was easy enough. I hereby declare this union terminated. Good day to you both."

As John stood to leave the courtroom, Gloria confronted him.

"I can't believe it, you've finally lost your mind," Gloria said, indelicately laughing in his face.

"Gloria, get over it. I did."

"Get over what?"

John didn't even give her the courtesy of a response, he just signaled to Bobby that it was time to go and quickly made for the door.

"Did that blast do something to your noodle John? You just gave that bitch everything?"

"Nope, my noodle is just fine. I can see clearly now, clearer than before," John answered confidently. "It just dawned on me what I saw last night. I'll show you when you get me home."

John hurried as fast as his aching frame would allow him. Bobby had to stop and watch the painful hobbler catch up. Although John just came from his own divorce hearing and was battered beyond belief, he was in surprisingly good spirits.

As the two drove down the back road out of town, Bobby couldn't help but glance at his foolish friend. John was attempting to sing with the radio, tapping his foot to the beat and gently rocking side to side.

How the hell is this guy in such a good mood?

"John, I have to ask, what the hell is going on with you?"

"Did you see what that judge was writing with?"

"A pen. What the hell does that have to do with anything?" Bobby asked, getting more frustrated with the car ride quiz.

"Not just any pen, it's like the one you have in your shirt pocket."

"This pen here, the one I got for ten years of service?" Bobby said as he pulled the pen from his pocket, holding it up in front of John's face. "This pen from the dirt bag company that canned my ass last year?"

"That very one," John confirmed, taking the pen from his hands. "It's almost indestructible."

"Okay, dumb it down for me, what are you getting at?"

"It's a tungsten alloy. It has a melting point of 3094 kelvin!" John shouted triumphantly.

"That's great John, I'm so excited." He clapped his hands sarcastically. "It's official folks, he's actually off his rocker!"

"No, no, no, listen, I think I can recreate that blue flame and control it," John said while taking the pen apart and holding up the bottom half. "I'll stick the diamond in here, hit it with the laser and with one of the fuel injectors cleaned, I'll shoot in a drop of water."

"The explosion last night wasn't good enough for you, now you want to go back and finish the job?"

"It won't blow up again, I don't think."

Bobby brought the car to a screeching halt.

"*You don't think?*" he screamed. "John, you're talking about making a pipe bomb—not just a regular pipe bomb—one on steroids!"

"You don't have to be there, I'll do it, and if anyone gets hurt, it will just be me."

"I can't have that on my conscience."

"Bobby, we don't have a project. It's ruined. It was a façade, sustainability isn't possible!"

"But dying is possible," Bobby pleaded.

"We won't die and I won't blow anything else up," John said. "I promise."

Bobby sat there staring at the side view mirror, watching traffic come from behind and pass the men as they sat on the edge of the road. Should he demand they pull the plug and give up? Or should he give into another of John's dreams?

"So what are you trying to accomplish with this?" Bobby asked.

"I don't know Bobby. I don't have the slightest clue what I saw last night. I'm not going to lie to you," John said with a look of despair upon his face. "All I know is that I want to find out. I have a gut feeling it's something great."

Bobby let out a sigh, biting his lower lip as he sat there shaking his head.

"All right. I'm not going to let you die alone, but," Bobby paused, "if we die, Lora's going to kill us all over again."

"How could she kill us if we are already dead?"

"I'm telling you, she'll dig us up and kill us again. That woman's got a mean streak a mile long."

"I'll try not to kill us then." John laughed.

Bobby started the car back up and they proceeded on their way back. As he drove along he kept looking back through his mirrors. Something was bothering him.

"You know anybody who's got a white van?" he asked John.

"No, nobody I know."

"That van has followed us since we left the courthouse. When we stopped it stopped," Bobby said as he adjusted his rear view mirror. "When we took off, it started following us again."

"Speed up or turn off and see if they follow," John instructed.

"Hang on, I'm going to do both."

Sure enough, the van started to match their speed. Bobby took a couple of quick turns without signaling to try and evade the van. Each time the van changed its course to follow.

"Son of a bitch, this guy is actually following us," Bobby said. "Hang on tighter, I got something for him."

"And you're worried about me killing you," John frantically pointed out, clutching the dashboard. "Let's just stop and see who they are."

"What if they are the ones looking for The Dragon? Screw that! We are going corn-fielding! I'm not messing with no Japanese mafia!"

Bobby gave the little car all it could handle, reaching speeds over a hundred miles an hour. Once the van was out of sight, he stomped on the brakes, sliding the car sideways and pointing it towards the nearest cornfield. As the car jumped from the side of the road, each man was thrown about, bumping into the roof of the car. John was twisting with pain as his seat belt rubbed against his steam burns. As the car landed and bottomed out, the impact sent an unpleasant jolt through their spines. Reaching down and grabbing the emergency brake, Bobby yanked it upward, sending the vehicle into a spin. John's headache from the explosion the night before returned as his head banged the window frame. Once the car had come to a halt, they sat watching the roadway for the van to pass by. Each man breathed heavily as the adrenaline flowed through him.

The van was just a white flash flying by. If one would have blinked, one would have missed it.

"Do you think they saw us?" John asked, gasping for air while rubbing the sore spot on his head.

"I don't know. I don't hear any screeching tires, but I sure as hell ain't going to wait until they figure it out and turn around."

Bobby threw the car in gear and took off out of the field, skipping back onto the roadway.

"Well Johnny Boy this is a great day!"

"How the hell is this a great day?'

"Somebody is chasing us, and you want to blow me up. I can't wait to see what tomorrow's fun will be," Bobby said. "Maybe I'll get abducted by aliens."

18

"What the hell happened to you two?" Rob asked as he stood studying the damage on the car. Ears of corn poked out through the grill, and mud caked the car in blots from the front bumper to the rear.

"Nope. It was one of those roadside stands. We didn't feel like stopping so we just drove through it," Bobby answered as he pulled an ear of corn from the shredded metal. "We felt like having fresh corn for dinner."

"So what's going on Rob?" John asked. "I hope Heather didn't take it out on you all night long."

"No she didn't. She left me."

"She what?" Bobby asked.

"Yeah, she left me. She said I was a failure and an embarrassment."

"I'm so sorry," John said. "I never wanted all this to become between you and your wife."

"Oh it's more than that John, all we did was argue," Rob admitted. "We never had sex and when we did, she said I wasn't man enough."

"I don't have the words," Bobby interjected.

"Come on guys, she was out of my league to start with."

"I don't think so," John said. "She was lucky to have you."

"She's gone, the money's gone and all I have is this dump." Rob coughed. "Hello roomy."

"We better get to work then, before it's too late," John said. "And just because we are roomies doesn't mean we are sleeping in the same bed."

"But I like to cuddle," Rob kidded.

"Let's get to work. Can you cut this down to about here?" John said as he marked a place on the pen with his finger.

"This is tungsten, it won't be easy, but I can do it."

"Good, and thank you. Now where's Hideyoshi?"

"Frank brought over an old door. They helped me hang it and I think they went back to his cabin."

"Bobby, follow me," John ordered.

John hadn't filled Bobby in on his plan as they made their way around the house to the cabin, but he was about to call Hideyoshi's bluff. He figured what did he have to lose; he had just been chased by a mysterious white van and survived a face to face with his ex-wife. He was a little bit motivated.

John knocked forcefully on the cabin's door, but no one answered. He waited a few seconds and knocked louder, standing back waiting for the door to open.

"Bobby, kick that fuckin thing down!" John ordered.

Without even asking why, Bobby stepped back and put his size sixteen shoe perfectly next to the doorknob, blasting it wide open. The men inside startled and, now terrified, jumped to their feet. They had been working on the computer. Both men were wearing headsets and could not hear John's knocking.

"What the hell Bobby?" Frank said. "You just scared the hell out of me!"

"You should have answered the door."

"Jesus, you almost gave me a heart attack."

"Hideyoshi?" John called.

"Yes John-san."

"You said twenty million dollars. We haven't seen a dime of that money. You have until tomorrow to show us something, or your ass is out of here!"

"But John, it's not that easy," Frank tried to interject.

"Tomorrow, or his ass is on the street," John said as he pointed a finger at Frank. "You brought him here, you make sure it happens."

As John's eyes darted between the startled men, he thought he made his point very clear.

As he turned to leave the cabin, Hideyoshi called, "John-san."

"What?" John said, whipping back around.

"I cannot have it all by tomorrow, but I can have you something. Also, I will be able to show you where it all is."

"That's good enough. Sounds like you two have some work to do."

John had handily giving his team their marching orders, and he was ready to work. He felt good in spite of his condition.

Rob was cutting down the tungsten as Bobby assisted in repairing the laser table. Frank and Hideyoshi were typing away on keyboards; they could be heard all the way inside the garage.

John had a simple idea. Unlike his previous work, he had no idea if this was going to work. This was uncharted territory.

He started by setting up his clamps to hold the pen cylinder. He was careful to see if the clamps could again stand up to the heat the diamond had put off. He didn't make the connection until now, but those clamps were also a tungsten alloy. Once Rob had finished with his cutting, John had him rig up a fuel injector to spray the water. John's theory was to lead the injector down the cylinder so that it sprayed a drop of water into the center of the diamond. If all worked right, there would be no explosion, just a bright blue flame shooting out the end of the pen.

"Are you sure this is going to work?" Bobby asked.

"It's a fifty-fifty chance, I'd say," John answered, shrugging his shoulders.

"I don't like those odds."

"Me either. Why don't you go get Frank? I need him to work on running this laser remotely."

Rob was tasked with providing the shot of water. He set up his water supply like an IV at the hospital, and the injector would be used to provide the unit of measure.

"I can only get the water to spray about two milliliters," Rob informed John.

"And that means what?" John asked.

"It's about the size of a standard raindrop."

"How often does it spray?" Bobby asked.

"Once you press this valve on the tube leading down from the supply, you get one drop."

"So somebody has to stand in here with it?" John asked.

"It's the best I could do on such short notice with what I've got."

With all the men assembled, John gave his hopefully-not-parting speech.

"I'll stay in here with the diamond and feed the water. The rest of you hide out there behind

Bobby's car. Frank, you have the controls. If something goes wrong, please kill the laser."

"John, one of us should be with you," Bobby insisted.

"No, if this goes wrong, you guys can save me," John said. "You all should back up now— and let's see what happens."

John was beyond nervous as he raised one trembling hand towards the water valve and the other fumbled to lower his goggles. Taking a deep breath, he nodded to Frank that he was ready. Frank gave a short countdown before starting the laser.

"We're hot," Frank announced.

The laser fired its blue-violet stream into the cylinder, hitting its mark. John could feel the heat radiating up towards the bare parts of his face. He took a deep breath and tapped the valve once. He watched as the bead of water traced its way down the tube and disappeared into the cylinder. His eyes were closed tight as he waited for the impact. Gripping the table tightly, he heard a deafening swoosh and a ripping sound that made him weak in the knees.

The bright blue flame shot from the tiny opening of the pen cylinder and blasted the new door. The door, incapable of standing up to the thrust, was sent flying. Rob ran around the side of the garage to see the door hurling through the air, watching as it impacted the other, which sent both crashing to the base of the tree.

John, cautiously opening his eyes, was able to gaze upon the magnificent sight, his fingers sore from still gripping the table.

The bright blue flame was shooting through the opening of the door, twenty feet in length from the tiny cylinder. Constantly it flowed outward from one drop of water; John reached up and pressed the valve again. It changed nothing as the blue stream thundered with the addition of fresh water.

John tried to yell over the roar, "Cut it Frank!"

Franked cupped his ear, turning his head so that he could try and make out what John was saying.

"Cut it!"

"What!"

John raised his hand to his throat, giving the beheading signal to cut the power. As the laser powered down the flame continued to burn; it wasn't exhausting.

John exited the garage to speak. "It's not going out!"

"Cap the end of the cylinder, it could be pulling oxygen!" Bobby screamed in response.

John quickly ran back into the garage looking for something to use. Scurrying about he found a flat metal bracket that he placed over the opening of the pen. The flame continued to burn. John turned and raised his hands. He shrugged his shoulders; he was confused, and he didn't know what to do next. Bobby mimicked John; he didn't know either. This wasn't combustion with oxygen, nor was it nuclear fusion. They didn't know what was occurring.

Twenty minutes passed until the flame ran its course and finally flickered out. Bobby suggested the unthinkable.

"Give it another drop of water John."

"Are you crazy Bobby, did you just see what happened with two drops of water?"

"I've sort of got a theory. I want to see if it's true. Go ahead, hit it one more time."

Shaking his head in disbelief John sulked back into the garage and pressed the valve. With a thunderous roar the flame grew back to life. This time it only burned for eight minutes.

"Heat is the control!" Bobby proudly proclaimed the truth in his theory.

"How's that so, Bobby?" John asked.

"I don't know," Bobby said, gazing over the table. "I don't know what's happening here, and something's going on inside that diamond that is unexplainable."

"We have something here guys, we need to figure this out," Rob interrupted.

"We chemically engineered these samples to match, or changed them to match other fuel sources. We've played with every chemical known to make diesel, carbon, hydrogen, nitrogen, oxygen and sulfur."

"And the diamond itself is a carbon product," Frank interjected.

"Yeah I know, but somehow whatever we changed in the chemical structure, with all the samples, and now the diamond. We've stumbled on to something and what that is I don't know," Bobby said.

"What's that old saying, oil and water don't mix?" John asked.

"That's it!" Bobby said.

"That's what?"

"Water is superheated when it touches the diamond, a chemical change occurs between the two and an exhaust is created, filtering through the diamond!"

"I'm still not getting it guys," Rob said.

"Somehow that diamond is turned into a filter, a super filter," Bobby explained. "I bet if we can control the temperature we can control the thrust or exhaust if you may."

"I see what you're saying," Frank said. "With the laser constantly on we achieved the high temp in the scale. If we could bring the temp up to a certain degree and maintain it, we could control it."

"But how?" Bobby asked.

"I can possibly pulse the laser, link it to a throttle of some sort that you can control."

"We need to control water and heat. I think we really have something here John, what do you think?" Bobby asked.

"I think we got a lot of work to do," John said.

"Bet your ass we do!" Bobby said, smiling from ear to ear.

"Well boss, where do you want to start?" Rob asked.

"Well," John said, looking in the eyes of his happy band of misfits as they waited eagerly for instruction. "I want to start right here, right now. Mark this day. When we started back on this project we were looking for something totally different. We discovered something so much more. What that is, nobody has a clue, but we did it together."

"So what's the next move?" Frank asked.

"We research tomorrow. Tonight, we party. Let's celebrate!"

19

"My god, can't you guys do anything without arguing?" Jasper whined. "This isn't that hard. You two take sample 901, and Maurice you take 902!"

"Maurice wants 903—because— Maurice knows it is the premier sample," Maurice pointed out smugly.

"Fine, take it, I'll take the other, whatever. Just get to work!"

"Why does he get what he wants? We are the better engineers!" The twins spoke in unison as always.

"Take whatever you want, we need to get to work!"

Jasper had lost all control, and Alex Wright was watching.

Sitting behind his enormous hardwood desk, Alex Wright studied the security monitor, watching as the men stood in a circle waving their hands about. It had been the same scene for over two weeks now, and not one ounce of testing had been completed. His frustration was growing by leaps and bounds as his patience grew smaller. He had no expectations of them finding sustainability but at least thought they would attempt some sort of work. He was wrong.

Tom Hawkins, on the other hand, was having more success spying on his victims. He was the man behind the wheel of the van, and he was also the hidden bush that watched as the guys made their discovery. Tom had gone undetected during his surveillance of John's team; it seemed his training as a Marine came in handy.

It would be Tom's phone call that would save Jasper. Alex was ready to head to the lab to shoot them himself.

Ring! Ring! Ring!

"This is Wright."

"Eagle one, this is the flying squirrel, do you copy?"

"What's with the call signs you idiot? I know who this is. Your name comes up on caller I.D."

"Sorry Mr. Wright, thought you wanted to be discreet."

"I thought you weren't a bumbling moron like the other four morons up here, maybe I was wrong. Do you copy now?"

"Yes sir, I copy."

"Listen, this isn't a military operation, you're not taking a hill," Alex instructed, "you're there to give me updates on what those twits are doing!"

"Yes sir, updates on what they're doing…sir!"

Alex's temper growing, he shouted back into the phone, "So what the fuck are they doing, you fucking moron?"

Tom laid it all out for him, giving details about what he saw, considering Tom had no idea what it was he saw. The more he tried to explain the more frustrated Alex became. This little find was something no one had ever seen or even heard of.

"Listen to me, you need to get back out there and find out what they're doing. I don't want any more phone calls until you know exactly what in the hell you saw."

"Yes sir, but one more thing."

"I'm listening."

"Who's your guy on the inside?" Tom asked. "Maybe I can hook up with him in person to get the details of this thing they're working on. We've only talked on the phone."

"If I wanted you to know, I would have already told you who he is."

"But sir, I thought maybe we could…"

"Could what?" Alex interrupted. "Blow his cover? That isn't happening. Do as you're told, and you'll live through this!"

Alex hung up on Tom and threw his phone against the wall.

I'm surrounded by fucking idiots, he thought.

Sitting there, leaning back in his office chair as his fingers thumped the armrests, he turned his attention back to Jasper and his team on the monitor. They hadn't moved since the last time he looked at them. There they still stood, arguing.

He so badly wanted to walk to the lab and slaughter them all. He hated the fact that he still needed them.

Once this is over, I'm going to drink their blood!

20

"Good morning gentlemen," Bobby said as he entered the trailer.

"What are you doing here?" Rob asked.

"Sitting at work I couldn't stop thinking about last night. I wasn't getting anything done."

"So you left and came here?" John asked.

"No, not exactly. I called Lora first. We talked." Bobby paused, taking a deep breath. "Then I quit my job."

"Why the hell would you do something like that?" John blurted out.

"While I was sitting there with a million thoughts running through my head, I realized a few things we could do with this, and I wanted to work on those ideas."

"You could have, but you didn't have to quit your job," Rob said.

"You got bills to pay Bobby, big bills," John said.

"That's why I called Lora. She told me to go follow my heart, and she would support any decision I made."

"You do remember Heather left me, there is no money to give you," Rob pointed out.

"Yeah, she was too hot for you anyway," Bobby said, giggling. "I'm just kidding, it ain't about the money, and I'm sorry she left you over this."

"Agreed. She was hot, but she was a bitch," said Rob.

"What are these ideas? Let's hear what you got?" John asked.

Bobby didn't respond but gestured for the guys to hang on as Hideyoshi entered through the back door.

"Good morning everyone. I have part of your request ready John-san."

"That's good news Hideyoshi, show me what you got."

Hideyoshi handed John a credit card.

"What's this?" John asked.

"It's twenty-five thousand to start. There will be more to come."

John, examining the card, noticed something strange. "It's got Frank's name on it."

"Yes John-san, by his instruction," he respectfully replied. "It can be used to withdraw money from ATM, or make purchases as regular Visa."

"But, why just in Frank's name?" Bobby asked.

"So that if it's tracked it comes back to him and not one of you. Given more time I can create a safer form of withdraw."

"So Frank is willing to take a bullet for us, huh?" Rob said.

"I didn't see this coming," Bobby said. "Old Frank ain't so bad after all."

"Thank you Hideyoshi, and sorry about getting so rough with you," John said, sticking his hand out to shake Hideyoshi's. "No hard feelings?"

"No John-san, no hard feelings."

Hideyoshi bowed and exited through the back door.

"This is a shocker. Maybe we had the little guy figured all wrong," Bobby stated.

"Seems so. Maybe The Dragon is the real deal," John said.

"I'm still not calling him The Dragon," Bobby jested. "But here, let me show you guys my ideas."

Bobby picked up a pen and paper and began drawing out his ideas for the team. He believed with the right materials he could construct an engine with the newfound power source. Possibly powering a small turbine that would use the same concept as an electric vehicle, except this vehicle would use the wattage to power a laser and store very little of the wattage.

His next idea was to use the thrust to power a turbine for flight. Of course this made the guys nervous, as none of them knew the first thing about piloting an aircraft. They all watched intently as Bobby drew out their future. It wouldn't be a conventional aircraft but would solely depend on thrust, much like a harrier jet.

"Let's try the car first, I'm not too sure about flying anything," John instructed.

"Okay then, where would you like to start?" Bobby asked.

"Just write up a list of materials that you'll need and when Frank gets here, we'll start trying to find them."

Bobby's concept was to cast an iron housing, similar to the size of an engine block that would contain the turbine. Using the thrust from the diamond to spin the turbine that would be connected to a shaft that would provide the power source for a generator, which in turn would be the drive source of the vehicle.

"First thing we need to do is run some tests to see how much thrust we have," Bobby said.

"How the hell do we do that?" Rob asked.

"We un-lag the table and attach it to a scale, fire the diamond and see how much the table moves."

"Oh it's that easy...not!"

"It's the same way they measure thrust for an airplane. Of course, we would have to build everything from scratch," Bobby said.

"Did you not see what happened to the doors?" John asked.

"That's why the scale will have to be heavy duty."

"We're going to have to take all that test equipment out just to test this—aren't we?" John asked.

"None of this is going to be easy, finding someone to cast the housing, getting all the materials to build the scale and figuring out how to not burn down the vehicle once the engine is fired."

"Okay Bobby, this is your baby, draw up the plans and give them to Rob, I'll go with Hideyoshi and find a casting company that will accept an open print," John instructed. "Then I'll start throwing out the test equipment to free up some room for us to work."

With marching orders in hand they each began their tasks. It would only take Bobby a couple of hours to draw up what he needed, given that Frank would arrive soon. Each man found work a little easier. Things began to flow and fall into place; it was a pace that each enjoyed. They felt they had a goal that was finally attainable.

Bobby had been given the honor of dragging his favorite toy to its doom. With the laser cutter un-repairable they hooked up a chain and used John's car to pull it from the garage. Everything was placed in a junk pile to use for spare parts if needed.

The men continued to work throughout the night, losing track of time. It wasn't until the sun came up that they realized this.

"It ain't pretty but it will do," John stated.

"Nope, it ain't. All we should have to do now," Rob said, "is lag and weld this frame to the ground and test her."

"Oh shit!" Frank said, realizing the hour. "I'm late for work."

"Yeah you better take off, we can finish this up Frank," John said.

"Screw that, you're not doing this without me—watch this," Frank said as he pulled out his cell phone and placed a call. "Mr. Johnson, Frank Henry here…I quit."

Frank began waving off the intrusions of his friends as they coached him not to quit.

"Yeah, I quit and by the way, I slept with your wife," Frank bragged as he hung up the phone. "Yep, I did her, I did her good."

"You really didn't, did you Frank?" Bobby asked.

"No, but now you guys can't ask me to go back. I mean you got to quit your job."

"But did you have to tell the guy you slept with his wife?" John asked.

"Not really, but the guy is a dick. He was always picking on me about my height."

"You're an idiot Frank, but you're an idiot we love," John said.

The men got back to work welding the frame of the scale; even Hideyoshi came out of hiding to assist. It was one happy bunch, working and joking as they finished.

"Do we want to rest first and fire up later, or do you guys want to do it now?" John asked, but he didn't need to. He was surrounded by eager men who wanted to see it now, and the yeses flooded the hollow garage.

"Same as before, you guys get out there, and I'll press the valve."

Frank fired the laser as once more John carefully pressed the valve. Again with a thunderous roar the diamond ripped to life, sending the table crashing back towards the backstops of the scale. What was different this time was the vibration. The table was violently shaking. Not only was the table a scary situation, but the valve that sent water was now malfunctioning. The vibrations had caused the valve to stay open, and a steady stream of water was impacting the diamond. The table itself began to tilt upwards. Frank shut down power to the laser but it was too late, the diamond had reached max temperature.

John pulled out his pocketknife and cut the water supply, letting the hose drip the excess water on the ground, and then he retreated. It was too late; the table rose upright as the flame impacted the roof of the garage, sending boards and shingles flying into the air.

"Holy shit!" Rob yelled.

"Good thing we lagged the scale frame down, but who didn't fasten the table to the scale?" John asked.

Each man pointed at the other, leaving John without answers.

What was supposed to be an easy experiment would now be a long wait for the flame to extinguish. Time ticked away but the flame only shortened. John walked over to the laser and powered it back up.

"What the hell are you doing?" Frank asked.

"The flame is shrinking, the diamond is cooling off. Heat the diamond back up and it should burn off that water quicker!"

"Will that work?" Rob asked.

"I don't know, I'm just guessing here!"

It worked. It only took another ten minutes for the flame to disappear. The roar quieted, and the men could once again hear one another.

"I hope you got some data out of all that," John said as he studied the new hole in the roof.

"It's off the charts," was Bobby's answer.

"What do you mean off the charts?"

"Well, before the table tipped over we passed 60,000 pounds. That's more than an F/A-18 hornet, and it was still climbing."

"So what's your best guess?" Rob asked.

"Calculating the speed the table went back, the fact that it broke every weld on the frame and crushed both rams, I'd say we are in the neighborhood of about 100,000 pounds of thrust."

"Technically guessing then, we've been in danger this whole time," John said. "Those original lag bolts wouldn't have held much longer, would they?"

"They shouldn't have held at all—just saying," Bobby pointed out.

At this point, Tom Hawkins turned off his camera as he snuck away from the house. It wouldn't be long before Alex Wright would see this footage.

21

With the team's secret out it would only be a matter of time until Alex Wright came calling. If they only knew this, they could be prepared. Tom spent days peeking into the garage from his wooded seclusion, gathering more valuable intel.

Bobby drew up the design for their engine. The only problem that he encountered was getting the parts made with tungsten. The team, however, agreed to disagree; they needed to lean on Hideyoshi and his contacts to get several parts made. Not only did that put Hideyoshi at risk, requesting such things from the United States could get them visits from certain organizations wanting to know what they would be doing with such materials. They had to roll the dice and take a chance if they wanted to continue.

Hideyoshi had the parts delivered to Frank's residence. They took turns trailing Frank back to the garage, watching for tails. It wasn't only an adventure to discover such a power source, but to play spy and protector on top of it gave a little mystique to the journey.

John's loaner car from Bobby was the sacrificial lamb. The consensus was that if they were going to burn up a car, why not an old Ford

LTD? Rob gutted the vehicle of its drivetrain completely, leaving nothing but the interior and shell. Everything else would be new, from the diamond power source to the rear axle. They fitted the trunk with a fifty-gallon water tank, which Rob filled up with a hose he ran to the kitchen sink, hillbilly engineering at its finest. Under the hood, it looked like a big black box that only housed the laser and turbine set up. Alongside the fender wells Bobby installed batteries to store the extra voltage supplied; this way they could power up computers and test equipment from inside the car. The main concern was the heat. They took precautions to protect and insulate everything they could, but the uncertainty of whether it was enough was always the question. Everything plastic inside the engine compartment would be removed and replaced with heat-resistant materials.

"It looks like the same car, but it's not," John said.

"The computer will comp everything from acceleration to readings," Frank stated.

"What do you mean?" John asked.

"I've programmed the laser to respond to the pressure on the accelerator along with lowering the water injection. I can tweak it as we go, if need be."

"What about the exhaust? Even at low usage the heat will burn up anything behind us."

"Well John, I ran the exhaust to point straight at the pavement. Bad news is," Rob was saying, "it's right below the engine. We didn't calculate how much pipe it would take until we went to install it. We forgot that detail."

"Won't that blow out the tires?" John asked.

"Hope not. Only one way to find out," Bobby said. "Let's go for a ride."

All four men climbed in. John got behind the wheel, and Bobby took shotgun. Frank got in behind Bobby to man the computer that was installed behind the seat.

"We have a problem," John said.

"What?" Frank asked.

"Where is the ignition? This key does nothing."

"Put it in gear, and that'll fire the laser. It's all controlled by the pedals."

John pulled the lever down, putting the car in drive, and gently pressed on the pedal. The car drifted slowly forward until Bobby helped. The large man placed his foot atop John's.

"Give it some gas, I mean water, you puss!"

The car shot forward and raced down the old driveway. It was all John could do to handle the vehicle and make a few of the turns. Bobby laughed hysterically as the two men in the back started to scream. Finally John was able to remove Bobby's foot and stop the vehicle just before he reached the main road.

"Damn it Bobby!" John screamed. "Have you lost your mind?"

"Never had it to start with. Let's see what this thing will do."

"We left a big black streak down the driveway," Rob said as he looked out the back window. "We better get on the pavement."

John continued and pressed the accelerator again, turning down the main road and heading further out of town. It wasn't as loud as he expected, but much like a typical vehicle, the faster he went, the louder it got.

"Good idea John, keep us out of town and away from other vehicles," Frank said.

"Unless we get behind a hay wagon we should be okay," John said.

"Levels look good, water consumption is minimal, heat is steady and the laser is firing normally."

"But it's getting hot in here. Everybody roll down your windows," John ordered.

"Hot?" Bobby said as he readjusted in his seat. "I think my balls just got stuck to the seat!"

"If we don't catch on fire, next step will be to provide some sort of air conditioning in here," Rob said.

With the windows down the men found some relief from the heat, although it was still hot enough to make them sweat. They didn't stop until they wound up in front of the main highway.

"Should we?" John asked. "There's going to be more cars up there than we would like."

"Go for it, readings still look great," Frank pointed out. "We haven't spiked anything since we've started, we should be okay."

As John took off he checked his rear view mirror and noticed a white van tailing them.

Is that the same van? he thought.

He didn't want to alert the guys in case it wasn't, so he kept watching to see what the van would do. He changed lanes several times, going around slower vehicles; each time the van would follow. He would slow down and so would the van; each time he sped up the van matched him.

Okay…this guy wants to play.

John stepped on the accelerator and took off, the engine humming even louder. He watched as his speedometer climbed.

"That's it Granny, about time you learned how to drive," Bobby said.

"If that's not your granny behind us, that van is back and following us again!" John said.

The guys turned and looked as John increased his speed even more, the van still in tow.

"Come on John, let it rip! Lose this guy!" Bobby demanded.

John started reading the speed out loud, "Eighty…ninety…one hundred…one hundred and ten…one hundred and twenty…it's buried, I've lost the speedometer!"

"Just concentrate on the road John, I've got your speed back here," said Frank.

The van had started to lose ground. John and the boys were making a clear break away, and then the cops showed up.

"One thirty-five…John!"

"We got cops!" John said.

"Just keep going!" Bobby said.

"One forty-five!"

"We got a vibration. I don't think this old car can handle it!"

"One fifty!"

"One sixty!"

"Cops are gone, I think they got him. I'm going to find a place to pull off and hide for a while."

John exited the highway and found a do it yourself car wash they could duck into. He pulled the car into a stall and threw it in park, killing the laser. The guys sat there, each with eyes fixed forward as their chests heaved. Sweaty from the heat, no one moved.

"We really need to fix the suspension on this thing," John gasped.

The men turned and stared at each other before Bobby's laugh broke the silence, the others joining in.

"What was the top speed Frank?" Bobby asked.

"One sixty-three and temp is normal, water usage...is...we've used," he answered, staring at his computer screen. "You won't believe me if I tell you."

"What, Frank, what?" John asked.

"Less than an eighth of a gallon. This is unbelievable."

"We need to do a check. Check everything over for damage before we head back," John ordered.

The men checked the vehicle and found minor damage. The tires were worse for wear, either from heat or speed. They didn't know at this point. John would nurse the vehicle back at home.

"Well John, what do you think?" Bobby asked.

"Need to fix the suspension, get some air in that thing and find some tires that can handle the heat."

"Now, do you think we found the next fuel solution?"

"We need more testing. We have something, but next solution? I'm not sure yet."

"Guys, check this out," Rob said.

He had lifted the hood on the old car and raised the lid on the turbine case to check the laser and diamond. He pointed at the white residue surrounding the diamond.

"It is calcium and lime residue, common from tap water," Bobby pointed out.

"Those injectors won't last and will eventually clog. We'd have to stop so often to clean them, once the engine cools down of course," Rob said.

"Salt water won't do that," Frank said.

"Good idea, salt water is a great idea," Bobby said to Frank with a slap on the back.

"Where are we going to get salt water?" Rob asked.

"The ocean, dummy," Bobby smirked. "I think I know what we are doing next."

"Road trip. I'm sure he wants to take a road trip," John said.

"Hey, you want more testing and I could use a few days lying on the beach. It's a win-win."

"I got my kids this weekend Bobby, and I doubt Gloria will let me take them to the beach."

"I'll tell you what, we'll fix the suspension and the air, and you ask her," Bobby suggested. "The worst she can say is no."

"I don't know about this. My kids in the car? What if it catches fire?"

"It won't. Don't worry about it, you just go make the call."

Bobby pushed John in the direction of the house, coaxing him to walk on with a hand motion.

"Okay boys, let's get this thing fixed. Bobby needs to be on the beach with a margarita in his hand!"

22

Alex Wright didn't appreciate having to send someone to bail Tom Hawkins out of jail, but he did appreciate the video he was watching. As he sat watching in amazement, he realized sustainability was no longer the goal. The car chase would be all the proof he needed to pull the plug on Jasper's team, but they still needed to be the scapegoats. He wanted that new power source. So he would send Jasper and his dysfunctional team to assist Tom in attaining the source.

John was in heaven. He would finally get to spend some quality time with his children. Gloria agreed without question; she quickly passed the kids off without John having to beg or ask twice. She had come to find out raising two boys gave her little time to herself, and Fred was no help at all when it came to dealing with children.

To deal with the heat issues, Hideyoshi commandeered an experimental heat shield material that was once rejected by NASA. The guys fastened it under the car to help keep it from roasting them. With an abundance of electricity, Rob was able to install a cooling unit to bring some comfort to the cabin. They placed a beefed-up suspension under the old jalopy that was capable of handling all the weight and decreased the vibrations once they had gotten up to speed.

"Where do we sit Daddy?" Thomas asked.

"You sit in the back with Rob and Frank, Little John can sit up here between me and Bobby."

"Great, eight hours in a car with these freaks," Thomas griped.

"Be nice Thomas, don't make me tell you again," John ordered the young man.

"Don't worry John, he whines one more time and I'll strap him to the roof of the car," Rob said with an evil grin as he stared down at the boy.

There wasn't much room for luggage. Everyone had to pack light in order to fit everything they needed in the car. Thomas had to prop his feet up on some of it.

"My god, it smells like balls in here already," Thomas said.

"Hang on guys. Rob, let him out of the car," John said as he flung open his door and slammed it behind him. "Thomas, come here!"

Thomas huffed and puffed as he made his way out of the car.

"Listen to me, you can lose the attitude right now. You're not going to ruin this trip for everybody. I don't get to see you two that often, and it's important for me to spend time with both of you," John said. "Any more crap out of you once we get started, and I'll pull this car over and put you over my knee!"

"I'd like to see you try," the arrogant boy blurted out.

John grabbed the boy by the collar and pulled him close, lifting him up onto his toes. "You want to try me right now?"

"No."

"No...what?"

"No sir. Can I get in the car now?"

John nodded for him to go on and took a minute to calm himself. As John walked back around the car Rob patted him on the back.

"Kids. They're great, ain't they?"

"When they're asleep, maybe," John answered.

"Come on, let's hit the road."

It was a quiet start to their adventure except for Little John; he was wide-eyed and curious about everything. Thomas sat in the back sulking; John would look in the rear view mirror, and the boy would be looking back, staring with hateful eyes. It broke John's heart to see him act out this way; he needed some way to connect with him.

"Daddy, can I play a CD?" the younger boy asked.

"Sure. Do you need help or can you figure it out?

"I got it," he said as he fumbled through his backpack, pulling apart the case and inserting the silver disc into the player, smiling as the music came on.

Bobby's chin dropped open as he stuck his fingers in his ears, a look of pain across his face. He moaned, "Oh my god what is this? It's…it's hurting my ears."

"It's Justin Bieber, goofy," Little John answered.

"Let me see it," Bobby said as he hit the eject button to remove the disc. He gently took the case from the boy. Placing the disc back in its case he studied it for a few seconds and pitched it out the window.

"Hey, that was mine!"

"Here, let Uncle Bobby show you what real road trip music is," Bobby said as he reached into the glove box and retrieved a new disc, handing it to the young man. "Put that in. That's real music."

Little John fumbled with the case before he could get the disc out. He pushed it in the player and sat back. As the music started to play he began rocking back and forth to the beat.

"See, real music," Bobby said, placing his arm on the seat behind the boy. "Now it's an official road trip."

"I like it." Little John smiled up at Bobby and then turned to his dad. "I like it a lot."

"I knew you would, that's the Doobie Brothers."

"Daddy, what's a doobie?" Little John asked.

With lips pursed, shaking his head in disbelief at Bobby, who had his face in his hand, trying to hide his snickering, John answered, "It's Scooby Doo's older brother."

The four men erupted with laughter as the little boy joined in, unaware of what he was laughing at; he was just part of the group. Even Thomas eventually joined in, not so much for the joke, but because of Frank's laugh. Frank laughed like a hyena on helium.

"Okay Frank, let's get down to business. How are the readings?" John asked.

"Everything looks good. We need to test for vibration so you'll need to speed it up a tad."

"Thomas, why don't you watch what Frank's doing, so if he falls asleep you can take over."

"Really?" Thomas perked up. "I can do that."

"Good, that way you can be my copilot."

"Cool. Teach me, Frank."

"My pleasure, young man, my pleasure," Frank said, offering his terminal to the boy.

"Daddy, where are we going again?" Little John asked.

"Myrtle Beach, Johnny boy, we are heading to the beach."

All seemed well in the world at this time; if only the guys knew they were being followed again. Jasper and Tom were right on their tail, and they didn't even have a clue.

23

With the others sleeping, John and Bobby sat quietly staring out at the ocean. The moonlight danced gently across the water and white caps crashed on the shore, sending a relaxing echo hurling back at them as well as the accompanying breeze.

John had driven through the night, only stopping once so that the kids could have a bathroom break, and finally found a place to nestle into south of Myrtle Beach. It was Garden City, south of the pier, where he found a small parking lot so they could catch their first view of the ocean.

Bobby looked down at Little John resting so peacefully, stretched out between them in the front seat, his head resting on his father's lap while his legs stretched out across his own.

"He's a good kid."

"Yes he is," John said as he brushed the youngster's hair away from his eyes. "They're both good kids, when they're not fighting, awake or, well, let's keep it at awake."

"You know, Lora and I both wanted kids. But it just wasn't meant to be."

"I think you'd make a great father Bobby." John smiled. "When do you guys plan on trying?"

"She'll kill me for telling you this, but we try all the time," he answered. "Trying's the easy part, actually conceiving is the hard part. Lora needs a surgery to correct a birth defect of her own. We just haven't had the money."

"Won't your insurance pay for it?" John asked.

"Not all of it. It's an expensive procedure, so until then, we just try and pray for a miracle."

"Wish I had the money to give you, or the power to grant you a miracle."

"Thanks bubba, but if it happens, great." Bobby shrugged his shoulders. "And if it doesn't, it's okay too. Lora is the miracle in me. If it weren't for her I don't know where I'd be today."

"Hopefully this thing pays off and we all have a miracle to enjoy," John said, pointing towards the engine compartment.

"I hope so."

"So do you think we should wake them up and try to get a hotel?" John asked.

"Let's just crash here, it's only a couple of more hours until sunrise," Bobby answered. "We can look at test results, and then drive up to Myrtle and find something."

John nodded in agreement and both men laid their heads back, shutting their eyes and letting the sounds of the waves rock them to sleep.

What they should have done was notice the other vehicle pulling into the lot behind them across the street. Tom and Jasper had found their resting place.

"What are we doing?" Jasper whined, "Let's go up there and take them now!"

"Calm down princess," Tom commanded. "Let's wait until sunup. I'll block the exit and then confront them."

"But...but...what if they get away?"

"They can get away. That car ain't going anywhere."

"Mr. Wright isn't going to like this, we should be taking it now!"

"Listen up Jasper!" Tom said as he reached across the vehicle and poked the frail man in the chest. "He ain't here, and I'm running this operation, you little shit!"

Tom leaned back in his seat, pulling back his jacket and showing Jasper the handgun tucked into his pants. "If things get out of hand, I've got it covered."

Jasper sat straight up in his seat and stared out the window at the old car in front of them, his eyes shooting a glance in Tom's direction to see if the Marine was still staring at him. Not only was he scared to confront his old team, now he was scared of the armed man sitting next to him.

I didn't sign up to kill anyone, Jasper thought.

What was only two hours seemed like an eternity to Jasper. He grew more nervous by the minute. Between his fears and the pungent smell of Tom's cigar, he was getting sick.

"Wake the others up," Tom ordered Jasper. "I'll be right back."

Tom opened his car door and quickly trotted across the street.

Jasper watched as the man snuck up to the old car, surveying the situation. He watched in horror as he shook the twins and the Frenchman. Tom was getting awfully close and risked being discovered.

Tom stood there, glaring through the driver's side window as John and his crew slept. The sun was rising, shooting a red glow across the morning sky. Jasper watched as Tom pulled the handgun from his waistband and pointed it at John's head. His eyes wider now, he watched as Tom simulated an execution; he could even see him mouth the word *bang*.

With an evil grin, Tom tucked the pistol back into his waistband and returned to the vehicle.

Once inside he laid out the game plan. "Listen, I'm going to block the entrance. Once I do that, all of you sneak up and surround the car.

But be careful, that car is humming and I don't know what that is."

John had forgotten to turn the car off before drifting off to sleep, so the laser and diamond were still fired up.

"Humming? How does a car hum?" Jasper asked.

"It's clearly not the engine. That old V-8 would be louder than that. It sounds like an air conditioner," Tom said. "But that's not the point. Just surround the car and I'll do the rest.

With everyone in place, Tom tapped John on the forehead with his pistol, stirring him. Still groggy from his nap John tried to focus with the bright morning sun in his eyes. Tom reached in and tapped him on the forehead again, this time bringing John to life.

"What the hell?" John said, alarmed. He reached over to shake Bobby. "Bobby, Bobby, we got company."

Bobby awoke, looking at John only to see Tom standing there with his pistol. He turned to his own window to see Jasper standing beside him with his arms crossed. He was standing next to someone Bobby didn't recognize, but he didn't care who he was. He flung open his door and the mammoth of a man stood up, towering high above Jasper and the Frenchman.

"Sacrebleu," the Frenchman gasped as he sized up the giant.

"Tom, you shoot me in the back I'm going to come around there and shove that gun up your ass!"

"Don't do nothing stupid Bobby, and I won't shoot you," Tom said.

Bobby stood there, sizing up his opponents.

"Tom, what the hell are you doing? I got my kids in the car," John said.

"We just want the car. If you cooperate then they won't see you get shot today."

Little John started to stir; the commotion had woken him. "Daddy, where are we?" the little boy asked.

"Don't worry about it John, just stay down," John ordered, placing his hand on the child's head, holding him down. "Bobby, get back in the car!"

"Don't be dumb John, don't make me do this!" Tom yelled.

"Bobby!"

Tom hadn't realized that while John was calming the child, he had placed the vehicle in drive.

Bobby threw a quick right jab, knocking Jasper unconscious, and then he quickly snatched the Frenchman up off his feet. He turned, using the man as a shield between himself and Tom. The Frenchman dangled high above the ground, helpless.

The others in the back seat had been woken by the commotion as well, as they heard Tom yelling at Bobby.

"Put him down now!"

"You come get him!" Bobby ordered.

With the gun pointed at Bobby, Tom walked behind the car, still barking orders to lower the man. Once in range, Bobby did as he was ordered, and he flung the man at Tom, sending both men crashing to the pavement. The twins took off running back towards the street, as they wanted no part of Bobby.

Bobby dove into the car headfirst, landing across the laps of Frank, Rob and Thomas.

"Go...Go...Go!" Bobby screamed.

John floored the accelerator, sending the old car jumping up on top of the curb as the tires squealed. Salt and sand sprayed back into the faces of the would-be car thieves. The car crashed through temporary barriers, knocking over fence posts and dragging the bright orange net underneath their car as they careened onto the semi-vacant beach. Bobby was flailing about, crushing those in the backseat as they yelped in pain.

"Head for the pier!" Bobby screamed.

The car was halfway up the beach before John saw another parking lot and turned to crash into it. Slamming on the brakes, he brought the car to an abrupt halt.

"Get back up front Bobby!" John ordered.

With the kids crying, Frank and Rob still confused by what had just happened, Bobby crawled into his own seat. John took off again, flying down the sand-covered stretch of road.

"Are they following us?" Bobby asked as he belted himself back in.

"I don't think so," John answered.

"Probably still scraping Jasper off the cement. Damn, that felt good!"

"Wait a minute," Rob interrupted. "What the hell just happened?"

Everyone in the car started asking questions at the same time, freaking out, scared and puzzled.

"Shut up!" John screamed as he whipped the car into a convenience store parking lot.

Throwing the gearshift up into park, the car rocked back and forth before settling. John turned, placing his arm on the back of the seat so that he could address everyone. "They wanted the car, plain and simple. I don't know how they knew about it or how they found us. I'm pretty sure they're the ones who've been chasing us, and I'm pretty sure they will try to find us again."

"So what are we going to do?" Frank asked.

"First off, call and see if Hideyoshi's all right. If so, tell him to check into a hotel and take the bucket of chemicals with him," John directed.

"Tell him we will come get him when we get back into town. Tell him to lay low."

"Daddy, I want to go home," Little John cried.

"Listen, I need you to be my big man right now, okay?"

"But I'm scared Daddy."

"Don't worry, Little John, I won't let anything happen to you," his brother said.

Giving his older son a wink while mouthing *thank you*, John knew he needed that support from his older boy. He reached back and patted him on the leg. He appreciated that the older boy was willing to take on the role of protector to comfort his brother.

"Bobby, get that map out and find us a place close to the ocean, someplace not so populated."

"On it boss."

"Rob, take the card and the kids, and go get us some supplies and food."

"Yes, sir."

With everyone on their assigned missions, John had time to sit and plan his next move. Although only a few minutes earlier he had a gun to his head, all he could think about was the diamond and its newfound power source.

"Found something," Bobby proudly announced as he jumped back into the car. "It's not the beach, but an inlet that we can pull straight up to."

"That'll work. How far is it?"

"Just a couple of miles up the road. It looks like a park of some sort."

Frank finished his phone call and returned to the car. "Hideyoshi is fine, said he would call me back when he gets to a hotel."

"That's good to hear," John said, relieved.

With Rob and the kids back in the car and breakfast being passed around, John drove to the park. It wasn't busy, but there were people around; if anything else was to go down he felt comfortable enough that they would be all right. He found a parking spot close enough to the water that they could possibly exchange water sources without people asking too many questions.

"Frank, Thomas, how much water did we use, what's our reading?" John asked.

Frank pointed at the computer screen. He nudged Thomas, urging him to answer.

"We've used," Thomas paused as he studied the screen before answering, "two gallons, two point three gallons."

"What kind of mileage is that?" John quizzed them.

"Let me take this one," Frank said to Thomas. "Okay then. We traveled six hundred and thirty-five point five miles. That gives us…two hundred seventy-six miles per gallon… give or take a few ounces, I'd say we've done it."

"Holy shit," Bobby said.

"Holy shit is right," John agreed.

"Dad, language. You said we couldn't cuss," Thomas pointed out as he tapped his dad on the shoulder.

"Okay, okay, just this one time. Everybody, same time."

"Holy shit! "

The team got quickly back to work, draining the tap water from their tank and resupplying it with fresh saltwater. They took their time cleaning the injectors to rid any foam build up so that when they got back home they could verify the differences.

Once everything was squared away, John set a course for home.

"Daddy," Little John asked. "Can we say it one more time?"

To the giggles of his friends, John answered, "Don't push your luck little man."

"I'm not, Uncle Bobby made me ask," Little John said as he began poking Bobby in the ribs, laughing and carrying on.

"You sold me out, you little rat," Bobby teased.

"It was easy," Little John giggled.

"Okay, okay, both of you, one more time and don't ask again," John agreed.

"Holy shit!"

24

John had only slept a couple of hours out of the last twenty-four, but he wasn't tired. He kept thinking about the possibilities of their new discovery. The mileage was amazing, but what were the other possibilities? Could he use this power source to fly, and would it be conventional flying or could he do what so many have failed to accomplish—hover.

As the others slept, John was at peace with his brainstorming. It allowed him to imagine all the wonderful scenarios he could dream up. Flying, orbiting the earth or possibly visiting other planets we could not get a man or woman to yet. His fantasies were endless.

"What time is it?" Bobby slurred as he stirred from his slumber.

John, looking at his watch, answered, "Quarter after five."

"Want me to take over so you can get some rest?"

"No, I'm good, just been thinking, enjoying the ride."

"Has anyone been following us?" Bobby asked.

"Nope, ain't seen anybody behind us for hours," John answered. "I think we lost them."

"That's good. I think I've had enough excitement for a while."

Bobby began sorting through items and bags on the floorboard, his mouth dry from his slumber. Finally finding a Coke to drown his cottonmouth he took a big gulp and belched out the window.

"Classy," John said.

"I know, I'm the regular king of etiquette."

"King of something. Etiquette? Nah, I wouldn't go that far."

"Well, thank you very little." Bobby toasted John before he took another gulp.

John reached up and turned the radio down, turning the knob so that the only sound was the wind howling through the windows.

"Bobby, let me ask you something."

"Sure, what's up boss man?"

"You ever wanted to fly?"

"Like fly a plane? Or fly like Superman?" he jested.

"No, like into space."

The question caught Bobby a little off guard. He hadn't given that question much thought ever. He was curious what John had on his mind.

"Space? Can't quite say I have. Only time I've ever flown in anything was when the company sent us to California," Bobby said. "But I can tell you this. I didn't much care for the whole flight experience thing. Turbulence was horrible, they stuff you in one of those little seats, and they feed you cardboard disguised as chicken."

"Yeah, can't say I care too much for commercial flying either," John agreed.

"So what's on your mind, John?"

"It's crazy. I was just thinking…no, never mind, it's just silly daydreaming."

"No seriously, tell me. What are you thinking?" Bobby asked.

"When you drew up that turbine idea, it got me thinking." John paused a few seconds. "I want to do that. I want to fly. I want to see if we have enough thrust that we could lift an aircraft."

"Lift as in like what the Air Force tried?"

"Not like a saucer, but if we built it, could the thrust possibly maintain altitude, direction, control?"

"An aircraft solely dependent on turbine thrust?" Bobby asked.

"Yes, exactly."

"I'd have to read up on it. I've never designed an aircraft, let alone anything with wings," Bobby pointed out.

"What I've pictured in my head wouldn't need wings. We could use the thrust to accomplish everything, complete control."

"Do you know how many turbines that would take, not to mention we only have one diamond? This could get very costly. We are talking spending hundreds of thousands of dollars, possibly millions."

"Well, if Hideyoshi actually has the money, that shouldn't be a problem, now should it?" John asked.

"If he doesn't, I'm knocking him out next. I'll knock him all the way back to Japan!"

"We're here. Let's get the kids up so I can drop them off."

John pulled up in front of his old house. He noticed the grass hadn't been cut in some time, the bushes were unkempt, and the flowerbeds were overgrown with weeds. As Bobby was waking the kids up John ran to the front door where he found a note attached; he thought it could possibly be a foreclosure notice. As he began to read it, he realized it wasn't a notice at all but a letter from Gloria; she had taken off. Her letter asked John to watch after the kids. Fred had left her and gone back to his wife, and she needed time to find herself. And that she would call when she found a place to settle. John knew in his heart she wouldn't call, she just ran out on her own children.

This was the hardest thing John had ever faced. How would he tell his kids about their mother? Would they hate her or him for all of this? The divorce had already taken its toll, would this now strain their relationship further? His heart was breaking as he broke the news to his two young boys.

The ride back to John's was quiet, neither child saying much of anything. Each man grieved for the children in their own way. Even Bobby found it hard to hold back tears as he sat with his arm around Little John, trying to comfort him. Thomas crawled back into his own awkward shell, refusing to speak one word about how he was feeling. He sat with his head against the back of the seat as his eyes stared at the roof of the car, and John knew Thomas wanted to cry, but the young boy was too proud. He wasn't going to show his vulnerabilities.

Arriving at the trailer, they found the other cars broken into. Glass was smashed and personal belongings hanging from open doors. The trailer door was swinging in the wind, and the windows were broken as well. Test equipment from the garage was strewn across the yard.

"Guess they know where the lab is at now!" John said, slamming his hand against the steering wheel.

"I need to call Lora," Bobby said.

"We need to get out of here, find a place to stay," John said.

They spent a few minutes trying to salvage what they could and headed to Bobby's place. Lora said it was fine and that no one had shown up; she was at the store and would meet them there. They soon found out their home wasn't safe either. It was in shambles, much to Lora's disgust; she hadn't been gone long. As Lora packed up what clothes and valuables she could, the men attached a luggage carrier to the top of the car. None of them thought their little discovery would bring this, until reaching Frank's house, which was by far the worst.

"We need to go to the cops," John said.

"And do what?" Bobby asked. "Tell them we found the next great fuel source with stolen money while possibly harboring an international fugitive? Yeah, we'll all look great in prison orange."

"What stolen money?" Lora asked.

Bobby had just let the cat out of the bag, now he hoped Lora would understand. Both stood outside the vehicle arguing while Frank tried to contact Hideyoshi.

"Will you two get back in the car?" John tried shouting over the fighting couple.

"Yes we will, but we will be going to the police," Lora shouted as she sat back in the car, pointing her finger in John's face. "You are taking me there now!"

"Hideyoshi's not answering, we need to go find him," Frank said.

"Fine, go find your friend, then you're taking me and Bobby to the police station.

Twenty years of building a home down the fucking drain! Bet your ass you're taking me to the police!"

John nodded yes; it was all he could do to satisfy the angry woman.

The whole car spent the next twenty minutes listening to Lora and Bobby argue as they drove to Hideyoshi's hotel room. They wouldn't even stop as they all loaded into the elevator to reach the floor his room was on. It wasn't until they reached his room that the couple took a break from the screaming.

Hideyoshi's door was ajar. Peeking into the darkness through the crack, Bobby tried to locate him. John slowly opened the door, only to see the room fully intact with no Hideyoshi. As they all gathered in the center of the room, Rob checked the window to see if it had been tampered with. Bewildered, they stood in the silence until a familiar voice spoke from the doorway.

"Hello everyone, hello little ones," Hideyoshi said, startling the group.

Little John ran and hugged him, almost knocking him down. He was relieved to see his friend.

"Thank God you're all right," John said.

"Why wouldn't I be John-san? I was just at end of hall getting chips."

"Grab your things, we need to go. We'll explain in the car."

With the car loaded and everyone stuffed inside, they sat there. They had no place to go.

"Lora, if we go to the cops, we all go to jail," John confessed.

"Honey, we can rebuild everything, just give us some time to figure this all out," Bobby begged.

"And why should I? Why should I when we just lost everything we ever worked for?" she asked.

"Because we found something so much more, none of us will ever want for anything ever again. Trust me Lora, let me prove it to you," John said.

"I'll give you two weeks…that…is…it!"

"Thank you Lora." John smiled. "Okay, we need a place to go. Anybody got any ideas?"

"I got an uncle who lives just east of Tucson. He's got a ranch up in the hills, I'm sure he'll take us in," Bobby suggested.

"Will he let us work in his garage?" Rob asked.

"No garage, but he's got several barns. I'm sure he won't mind. I'd give him a call but he doesn't own a phone."

"It's worth a shot. How far is it, and how much water do we have left?" John asked.

"Forty-five gallons and it should be somewhere around 1700 miles…should be a great test run if nothing else," Frank said.

So they set course for Tucson and away they went. Even though the car was larger than most modern cars, it was still cramped with four and a half adult-sized men, two children and one tiny angry woman that they tried not to infuriate any further.

25

Twenty-eight hours, sixteen arguments and eight pee breaks later, the team on the run had their patience tested to friendship-breaking extremes. If you want to test friendships then take a long road trip, just like our team was doing.

It was midday when they arrived at the ranch. There wasn't a soul in sight, and Bobby didn't even know if his uncle was still alive. Lora had never met him. He was a recluse who valued his own way of life, which meant he didn't visit you and you didn't visit him.

Hot, sore and sweaty, they all climbed from the rusted chariot to stretch their legs and get some fresh air after being cramped in the car for so long. The fresh air wasn't the greatest; it was hot and windy, dust and sand blowing about as tumbleweeds danced across the crusted ground. The house look deserted, as if time had given up on it; drapes covered the windows, and the white paint was dulled from numerous sand storms. It was dingy and rundown. There were no livestock in the corrals, not even a single chicken pecking at the earth.

"Are you sure your uncle still lives here?" Lora asked.

"Are you sure your uncle is still living?" John butted in.

With a smirk Bobby answered, "I'm sure if he passed I would have heard about it, but then again I haven't been here since I was a teenager."

"Shouldn't you have told us that before we traveled this far?" Rob asked.

"Probably, but it was the first place to pop into my head. Let me knock on the door and see if he answers."

Bobby strolled up to the front door and knocked gently. He paused a few seconds and gently knocked again. John motioned for him to knock louder. Nobody answered and nothing happened, so Bobby knocked even louder.

"I think we drove all this way for nothing Bobby!" Lora said, her tone impatient now, her frustration starting to show again.

A lone dinner bell sat at the foot of the steps off the porch. It was the only thing remotely clean of sand and dirt.

"Somebody's been here. Looks like they keep this old bell clean. Let me ring it and see if I can get someone's attention," Bobby said.

There was a leather strap hanging from the clapper of the bell. Bobby reached up to grasp it, but before he could the bell rung and swung on its own, startling him. Pulling back his hand quickly, he was more startled when he heard gunfire in the distance. Everyone was sent ducking and running for cover. It was a bullet that rang the bell, much to everyone's surprise.

"Somebody doesn't want us here Bobby!" John yelled.

Bobby had hidden behind the fender of the car. He peeked over the hood to see a dust bowl coming down from the hill in the distance, traveling their way.

"Bobby, where the hell did you bring us?" Frank asked as he lay behind an empty water trough.

"I don't know Frank. Why don't you walk over here and we'll discuss it?"

"Screw that, you come over here," Frank responded.

The dust bowl coming towards them was a jeep. John watched as the vehicle drove up behind them, parking next to a fence leading into the property.

"You folks are trespassing, you've got one minute to get off my land or I'll shoot every one of you damn taxmen," the elderly man said as he hobbled from the jeep to the porch. "I've told you for the last time, you ain't taking my land!"

"Uncle Garrett! Uncle Garrett, don't shoot, it's me, Bobby!"

"Bobby White? My nephew? So now you want to pretend you're my family. I should shoot you right now!" he said, pointing the rifle at Bobby.

"Please Uncle Garrett, don't shoot, it's really me," Bobby said, climbing up onto his knees.

Lora wasn't going to stand for any more of this. She came from behind the old man and snatched the rifle from his hands.

"Give me that. You ain't shooting my husband. If anyone is going to shoot him it's me. How dare you point a gun at your own family member? What the hell is wrong with you?"

"Lady, put the gun down now," a young man said from the jeep, standing up inside as he pointed his rifle at Lora. "Don't make me shoot you."

"Shoot me? Young man, don't make me come over there and shove that gun up your…you know what!"

"Atsa, put your rifle down," the old man said, waving for the young Indian boy to comply. "I don't think these are them there taxmen."

With sighs of relief and the wipe of a few brows, the team crawled from their hiding places.

Garrett White was a salty old codger, an old war veteran, one of those who would rather live alone than to grow with society. He didn't have much use for the government or any type of authority figure. He had been locked up a few times for shooting at unwelcome visitors. He looked a little frail, slumped over in the shoulders from time. He walked with a limp and squinted to see, probably because he was too cheap to go see the eye doctor.

He was accompanied by his only friend, a young half-Navajo man named Atsa, who like Garrett had a dislike for the modern world himself. He had recently gotten out of the army. He was of average height but he was fit, narrow at the hip and broad in the shoulder.

"Is this the way you treat company?" Lora barked at the old man. "You could have shot one of us, for God's sake. We are family."

"I didn't shoot at you," the old man said, chuckling. "But that boy did. Ex-army sniper, he's one hell of a shot. That must have been five hundred yards."

"Six hundred," Atsa proudly corrected the old man.

"Well, it doesn't matter how far, you could have killed one of us!" Lora said as she wagged her finger in the face of the old man.

"Bobby, you better get hold of your woman, before I put her over my knee," Garrett huffed. He was old fashioned and didn't think it was a woman's place, although he had never met a woman like Lora.

"Oh, I'd like to see you try, you old buzzard!"

John quickly stepped in to drag Lora away before she handled the old fella. If she did get a hold of him they'd have just driven 1700 miles for nothing.

Bobby attempted to explain their situation without giving too many of the bad details, but the old man had an eye for bullshit. The more Bobby poured it on the more holes the old man shot through his story.

"Stop right there," Garrett said. "Why don't just tell me you need a place to hole up? It won't be the first time somebody hid out here from the law."

"It ain't the law that's after us sir," John said. "It's some people wanting what we've got. To tell the truth it's something that we built."

Now that he had gotten the old man's attention, dollar signs began to roll in his eyes.

"Well, since you two are kin," the old man paused a few seconds as he pointed over towards Bobby and Lora, "I suppose we could work something out."

"That would be great Uncle Garrett, it would be much appreciated," Bobby said.

"Hang on now. You all willing to pay?"

"Sure," John said. "How much are you figuring?"

The old man scratched his head, looked up at the sky as if he were actually calculating in his own mind. "I owe that damn tax man, five thousand three hundred and seventy-four dollars, so I reckon I'll charge you fifty bucks a month rent for that old barn over there."

With a sigh of relief John said playfully, "Well sir that's awfully steep, but I think we can manage it. Right guys?"

"Absolutely," Frank agreed.

"Yes, I believe so," Rob chimed in.

"So them two kids there, Bobby and that little loudmouth woman can bunk in the house, you others will have to sleep in the barn."

"Really, loudmouth?" Lora chimed in.

Bobby was quick to calm her. "That'll be fine Uncle, thank you, thank you."

"Of course she'll have to do all the cooking and cleaning. I like my morning coffee at five and my breakfast on the table at six sharp."

"Oh you do, do you?" Lora spouted off.

"That'll be fine Uncle Garrett," Bobby said as he shushed Lora.

"But I'm not too sure about that Chinaman," the old man said, pointing at Hideyoshi, who was quietly typing on a computer as it lay on the hood of the car.

"I'm Japanese, China is a different country, but as far as your taxes go sir, they have been paid in full," Hideyoshi said as he turned the computer around so the elderly gentleman to see the screen.

The old man squinted his eyes, his face crinkling up. He couldn't see it if he wanted to. But he shook his head as if he did.

"Thank ya—Chinaman. Now why can't she," Garrett said, pointing at Lora, "be as nice as old Hop-Sing there."

"I'm going to kill that old bastard in his sleep," she mumbled.

"What she say?"

"She said she'll try to be nicer Uncle," Bobby fibbed.

They settled into the barn. It wasn't much better than the old garage they started with; in fact, it was worse. It had no electricity or running water. Rob had to rig up the car with some old electrical cables he found to provide lights to their temporary home. The car still had plenty of water, somewhere around forty-two gallons, but this wasn't its typical use. Now the car was a generator that would hum through the night.

26

It was probably the worst night's sleep John had ever had in his life. The ragged, time-worn sleeping bag the old man had lent him was infused with the smell of mothballs and rat droppings. It was a stench that would stay imprinted in his mind for years to come.

His back sore, legs stiff and his neck wrenched, he sat upwards to take in his dim surroundings. Propping himself on his arms, he tried to roll his neck in circles to rid the cramping sensation he was feeling.

Staring up through a hole in the old barn roof, John took in the view of the morning stars as they sparkled. He was interrupted by a sound he had only heard in movies and on television. This was the first time he ever heard it in person. The sound came closer.

"Rattlesnake!" John screamed as he jumped to his feet. The others stirred, all weary-eyed, as they watched as John ran for the barn door.

"Rattlesnake…Rattlesnake…get out of here!"

The others, jumping and stumbling, followed John out of the barn. John flung open the door only to find the old man sitting on the trunk of the car laughing. They tripped over one another as they all tried to exit the barn at the same time. They found themselves crashing together and falling in a pile for the old man's amusement.

"You city boys never have been in the desert before, have you?" Garrett chuckled. "Welcome to the home of rattlers and scorpions."

Atsa walked from behind the barn shaking a rattler toy made from an actual snake. With a smirk on his face he said, "Good morning."

"What kind of sick joke is this?" John grumbled.

"Not a joke, a wakeup call. Breakfast in thirty minutes. You boys go get cleaned up before breakfast," Garrett said as he slumped down off the trunk and hobbled back towards the house. The guys still lying in the dirt could hear the old man laugh as he walked with Atsa in tow.

"I think I broke my toe," Rob said.

"I think I pissed myself," Frank said.

Cleaned and ready for breakfast, they joined the others in the house. Both Thomas and Little John fell asleep at the table, only to be woken by the old man smacking his cane on the leg of the table, urging them to wake up and sit up straight.

Bobby and John spent breakfast informing the old man of their situation, talking about the discovery and who had been chasing them. He sat intently listening, pausing to sip his coffee and clear his throat. He wouldn't speak but only grunted as if he understood.

Lora worked around the bunch, placing food in the center of the table and helping the kids prepare their plates. She actually enjoyed taking care of the kids, but wouldn't dare admit it to any of them. She didn't mind the men, except for Garrett, who no matter what he said rubbed her the wrong way. He was stuck in an era of times past. Women had long ago burnt their bras for equality; she wanted to place hers on his head and light it.

Taking a break from the men, Lora retired to the front porch where she found Atsa keeping watch of the territory.

"You should go in there and get some breakfast before they eat it all," she said.

"No thank you Ms. Lora, I've already had breakfast," he answered.

"Well, aren't you the polite one?"

"Yes ma'am. Please don't let the old one get to you," Atsa said quietly. "He wasn't always like that. When Ms. Lucy was alive, she wouldn't let him act like that."

"Who's Lucy?" Lora asked.

"His wife. She passed sometime back."

"You mean somebody actually married that old codger?"

"Yes ma'am. She was a wonderful lady." Atsa smiled as he spoke of her. "She helped my people a lot. She was a nurse who volunteered at our reservation. She helped deliver most of us who live there now. She was a mother and a friend to us all."

"So what did she see in that man?" Lora asked as she pointed back towards the house.

"She saw the good in everybody. At times you can see her in him."

"You're a good man for putting up with him." Lora smiled. "Come on in, at least I can pour you a cup of coffee."

Returning the smile, he followed her back into the house. John was still trying to explain the diamond to Garrett.

"I can show you, I think that's the best way to explain it," John said.

"Daddy, can I see it too?" Little John eagerly asked.

Shushing the boy, John whispered in his ear, "Finish your breakfast, let the adults finish talking."

The boy nodded his head yes, grinned and went back to work on a piece of bacon.

"So you boys want to build a plane, go flying? You even want to become astronauts, huh?" Garrett scoffed in amusement.

"That's the general idea Uncle Garrett," Bobby said.

"Not me, my ass belongs on the ground," Frank chimed in.

"I'd have to be drunk," Rob said. "Only space I want to see is the one between a woman's…"

"Rob!" Lora shouted, pointing at the boys. "We have children here!"

"Sorry, wasn't thinking."

"I'm with chrome dome here on the woman thing," Garrett said. "Speaking of women, sugar britches, can you open that cupboard and hand me that bottle?"

Although disgusted by the old man, Lora complied and retrieved the bottle from the cupboard. Handing it to him she said, "And my name's Lora, and if you want anything else you're going to have to learn to use that name. Do I make myself clear?"

The old man looked up at her, shocked and wide-eyed. She stood over him, hands on her hips, waiting for his reply.

"I'll work on it," he said sarcastically.

"And don't you think it's a bit early to start drinking?"

"Darlin, I'm 81 years old. A little snort to start the day won't kill me any faster than time's been doing all these years," Garret scoffed.

"Too bad then. If it sped up the process I'd say take two shots."

Leaning back in his chair he watched as the little woman grinned and started to clear the table. He actually liked her peppiness, spunk and attitude. It did remind him of his Lucy. Uncorking the bottle he tipped it back, gritting his teeth and wheezing out a burning breath as the liquor made its way down his throat.

"Now we are ready to start the day," Garrett huffed as he held the bottle up, offering it to his visitors. Each graciously declined with a simple headshake.

"Pussies," Garrett said, smirking. "Eat a man's food but won't drink his liquor."

The young Navajo man reached over the older man's shoulder and took the bottle. Taking a sip, he offered it up next to Bobby. One by one the bottle made its way around the table until each had been bitten by its burn. Even Thomas tried to grab the bottle until John snatched it away from him.

Lora rushed the kids off to change their clothes as the men made their way outside to look at the car.

"So you boys want to build a plane out of an old Ford?" Garrett asked. "No wonder people are chasing you. They want to lock you up in an insane asylum."

Bobby grinned at John as he opened the car door and released the hood. John raised the hood. He immediately had to stand back from the heat. The diamond hadn't cooled down enough yet from running all night. Frank opened the trunk and retrieved the insulated glove. Once fitted he popped the latch on the case, lifting it, and exposed the turbine.

"What the hell is that?" the old man asked, Atsa peering over his shoulder in amazement. "That itty bitty thing drives this old car?"

"Yes it does, and that, sir, is the future," John said. "Fire it up Bobby, let them see what it does."

The two men stood amazed as the turbine lit up and started spinning. They had never seen anything like it. Each man had to take a step back as the heat hit them in the face.

"She gets pretty warm. How do you stand being in there?" Garrett asked.

"Insulation and multiple cooling sources. Don't worry, it won't catch on fire," Rob answered.

"Damndest thing I've ever seen. What about you Atsa, you ever seen anything like this?" Garrett asked.

"No sir, but I like it."

Bobby shut off the power source as the two men watched the blade from the turbine start to slow.

"Is it going to stop?" Atsa asked.

"When the water burns off, it'll stop. Takes it a few minutes," Frank answered.

"Well boys, you can stay, build your flying thing or whatever you want to call it," Garrett said. "You won't be bothered out here. Atsa will keep an eye on you from those hills. Anybody comes out here he'll let you know by ringing that bell, I'm sure you all remember that."

"Thanks Uncle Garrett."

"Not so fast," Garrett said. "You'll need to head in to Tucson, up that way, get a camper or something to stay in. Wasn't really joking about the rattlesnakes, this country is loaded with them. Sleeping on the floor in that barn won't do. Atsa will take you into town so you don't get lost. I'm sure you can find something cheap."

"If this pays off Uncle Garrett, we'll make it worth your while, I promise," Bobby said.

"Just bring me back a bottle of whiskey every time you go to town. I'm 81, my while ain't worth much anymore. And pick up a nice dress for that woman in there; just don't tell her it's from me. Don't want her getting any ideas."

27

Time ticked away. Things were different for everyone as they settled into a new life, a new home and a whole new world. Hideyoshi stayed true to his word and provided the team with the financial resources to continue their project. They found themselves becoming more than a team, but a family. They enjoyed sitting down for meals as Garrett would tell old war stories. Everyone took care of the kids and helped them through their troubled times, easing the pain.

Atsa provided security from afar, proudly watching from the hills, only coming down to join the team for dinners. Other meals Lora would take the four-wheeler up to meet him. As he ate they talked and got to know each other.

Garrett became used to having others in his home; although he wouldn't admit it, he really enjoyed the company. He became fond of the children and liked to watch them play in the yard. Sitting for hours just watching them reminded him of his own youth when the world was a simpler place. He continued to verbally poke at Lora to get a rise out of her; he enjoyed watching her get all fired up. Every time the guys went to town for more supplies or equipment, he made sure that they brought her something nice back, but he still insisted it wasn't from him. She eventually caught on and played along by keeping his wishes a secret. But what started as a rocky introduction between the two was now more of a playful wordplay she continued to keep the old man on his toes.

Although Lora was heartbroken about losing all her possessions, her old life and everything she and Bobby had built for so many years, she found comfort in caring for the boys. She loved them. She looked at all the men as belonging to her; they were her family and children. She did a fine job of keeping each one in line, and not a one dared cross her, even Garrett. She ran a tight ship. When it was time to eat they came and ate or she was coming to drag you to the table. If one were feeling sick, she would care for them only as a mother could. She was the glue holding the team together in this new chapter of their lives.

The team worked day and night building what they thought would be an acceptable aircraft. Frank spent hours reworking anything and everything he thought would not be safe. Rob could be depended upon to do most of the assembly, welding, running cable and fabrication of parts they could not find. Bobby designed several sizes of turbines; Hideyoshi was tasked with getting them made in Japan and shipped in, and his only problem was getting them past customs.

John had the toughest task of all. He was now the lone parent in his kids' lives, and the leader of a group of outlaws on the run. If it weren't for everybody's help, he didn't know how he would have pulled it all off back in Ohio. He waited for Gloria to call and check in on the kids, but she never did.

Still waiting on parts, they took a final evaluation of what was left to do. Standing back and looking over the craft, John marveled at its presence. It was around eighteen feet long and six feet high. The bottom of the craft housed sixteen slots ready for turbines, the roof was ready for eight and the sides would carry ten each. At the nose there was room for an additional six; they intentionally tapered the nose down to an off v-shaped slant. It was narrower at the bottom with a long slant at the top that housed three four-inch thick bulletproof windows. Bobby had insisted on the glass due to a fear of hitting a bird or anything else. Looking over the back of the craft, everyone was excited about the eight huge turbines that would propel it forward; of course the others were for lift and direction. But these would be the power source for speed. John imagined when fully lit, the craft would be one big blue light traveling through the sky.

"Well, she ain't an airplane," John said.

"Nope, but with that black paint, she looks like a flying grill," Bobby pointed out.

"What other color would you want?" Frank asked. "Blue to match your eyes?"

"I was thinking more pink, to match your panties Frankie," Bobby playfully responded, punching Frank in the arm.

"Counting them up, it's going to take fifty-eight diamonds to fly this thing," Rob said. "Anyone got any ideas?"

"We'll have to visit a jewelry store, find a good necklace, and with any hope they have the one we need," John said.

"Hideyoshi, do you think you can find us something in town and clear up some money for it?" Frank asked.

"Turbines will be delivered tomorrow in town, we will need to pick them up. And the diamonds. I will have payment for both waiting," Hideyoshi answered. "I'll go find a store now."

"Thank you Hideyoshi." John smiled.

Without anyone paying attention the old man crept up behind them.

"What the hell is this?" he spouted. "You all do know this is UFO country. If that thing actually makes it in the air, you'll have every nut from here to California looking for you."

"It won't be anytime soon. We have to get five hundred gallons of salt water here to fuel it," John said.

"Saltwater? Why saltwater?" The old man asked.

"It contains no calcium or lime. Only build up on the injectors we get is salt, which eventually blows off through the exhaust," John answered.

"Bull butter," the old man scoffed. "Around here we use well water, none of those silly chemicals in our water. Hell, we have it tested every so often to make sure of it."

"I'm not sure we want to do that Uncle Garrett."

"How the hell do you know it won't work if you don't try?" Garrett said, raising his voice to make his point. "Go get a bucket and fill it up at the pump at the side of the house."

"It's worth a shot," John said. "Rob and I will drain the tank while you fill up."

Following the old man's orders, they gave it a shot. Frank jumped in and cleaned the injectors while everyone was busy draining and filling. Once Bobby filled the tank, they tried her out. It would be the first time Garrett took a ride in the newfangled contraption, as he so lovingly called it.

"See, told you," he bragged. "Well water wouldn't hurt your precious clunk of junk."

"Actually Uncle, we won't know until we stop and check the injectors."

"Let's make a bet then?" Garret offered. "I'll bet you five dollars big man."

"Okay, you're on."

"No offense Garrett, but you don't really know that value of the dollar today, do you?" John asked.

"Don't you sass me pretty boy. Now stomp on that thing, and let's see what this jalopy can do!"

"Yes sir, but be careful of what you ask for."

John took off like a bat out of hell, laughing with the old man as he got more excited with each straightaway and every turn. John took the car up through the hills and down across the desert flats, enjoying watching the old man hoot and holler.

Finally returning to the ranch, the old man just sat in the car with a smile on his face.

"Reminds of me when I was seventeen years old, my daddy bought a 1950 Chevy Fleetline. She was dark blue and ran the hills of Kentucky like a dream. I remember him tanning my hide when I snuck out one night and took her for a spin. Was this cute little girl who lived a couple of hollows away. I met in her in school and told her I had my own car. Knowing that, she agreed to go on a date with me."

The guys sat and listened intently as the old man reminisced.

"We went flying all over those hills, finally found a place to park and you know, fool around. We were getting pretty hot and heavy until my daddy snatched me out of the car. I didn't know he had found me, for all I knew, Bigfoot had gotten a hold of me. There I was screaming like a little girl in front of this angel until I figured out it was my father."

"What happened to the girl, Uncle Garrett?"

"I married her." Garrett smiled. "She was my Lucy, my best friend since that day. Oh well, you boys check those injector thingies out, I'll be back. Need to go take a piss."

"What the hell? That's how you end a story, I need to go take a piss?" Rob asked.

"What more you want?" Garrett replied. "You want to know how the piss turned out, I'll be right back to tell you, you fruit."

With everyone in the car teasing Rob, they waited until the laugher died before getting back to work, checking the injectors. Still too hot to continue, they just lifted the case and let the air cool it off.

"You ain't done yet?" Garrett asked as he returned.

"Nope, still too hot," John answered. "How was the piss?"

"Good. I may go back and do it again. At my age that's every fifteen minutes."

"It's going to take some time for this thing to cool off," Frank pointed out.

"Ever thought about hitting it with a little liquid nitrogen?" Garrett asked. "Instant cool."

"That never crossed our minds," Bobby said. "Thanks Uncle Garrett, we'll have to give that a try."

"Son of a bitch," John said. "How did we not think of that?"

"Wouldn't take much. A drop or two would cool that right down," Rob said.

"Boys, I can't do all your thinking for you. Buy you books and send you to school, what do you all do? Eat the teacher!" Garrett said, mumbling as he walked away, leaving each to stare at the other in amazement. Another item they would add to their list. Hideyoshi would earn his keep once again finding liquid nitrogen somewhere in Arizona.

28

"Lora, Lora, throw me the ball!" Little John yelled as he stood jumping, waving his hands in the air.

"Here it comes, can you catch it?" Lora said, leaning way back and tossing the football as high as she could. Little John ran in circles trying to get underneath it, jumping up just in time to quickly clench his arms tight, securing the ball.

"Atta boy!" Lora cheered. "Okay, that's enough for me. You two are simply wearing me out. I need a break," she gasped.

Walking over, she plopped down on the top step of the porch, still waving her hand at her face, trying to cool off and catch her breath. John had been watching as she tossed the football around with the boys and joined her on the step.

"You're good with those kids Lora."

"It's not hard to do. They're good kids. Part of me wishes they were mine."

"They are. You're just as much a part of their family as anyone else," John said as he reached over and gently squeezed her shoulder. Appreciating the comment and gesture, she reached up to pat his hand.

"Thanks John. It's amazing what you've done with those boys. They're turning out to be such great kids. One day Bobby and I will have some of our own."

"Yes you will, and you'll make a wonderful mother."

"Hey, you trying to hit on my girl?" Bobby interrupted as he rushed through the screen door, sitting and nudging his way down between both of them as he placed his arms around their shoulders, pulling them both in tight.

"I tried," John laughed. "But she said I wasn't as pretty as you."

"That's true." Bobby pondered for a second. "When you're this sexy, life just ain't fair. I mean there's me and there's Fabio. What's a guy to do?"

"Okay Fabio Junior, get your big log off me, I'm too hot and sweaty," Lora said.

The screen door swung open and out walked Garrett, wearing his Sunday best. His hair was trimmed and his face cleanly shaven. His gray flannel suit looked a little aged for the time, but he wore it well. String tie lying around his neck and his fedora hat tipped slightly to the nose, he proudly walked out on to the porch.

"My, my, my, doesn't someone look handsome?" Lora teased.

"If you would be so kind young lady, help me fix this tie," Garrett grunted at Lora.

As she adjusted and straighten his tie, Lora said, "You know if I wasn't married to your nephew and you were twenty years younger I might give you a shot at the title."

"Even twenty years younger I'd still be too old for you," Garrett responded. With a sly little grin he leaned over and gave Lora a quick peck on the forehead, stepping back to admire her as she blushed.

"Hey now, don't you go trying to move in on my girl too," Bobby laughed.

"Don't you worry about that, now days anymore…it's just like Brylcreem?"

"Brylcreem?" John said confused.

"Yeah Brylcreem, it was hair product back in my time. Their slogan was a little dab will do ya." Garrett chuckled. "I'm thinking she would need more dabs than I could handle."

"Garrett!" Lora gasped. "You dirty old man."

With a smile on her face and a giggle in her voice she walked past the old man, playfully swatting him on the rear end as she passed by before entering the house.

"Okay boy, let's head to town," Garrett ordered.

"Wait, let me get the guys," John said.

"Yeah John—about that, I kind of promised Uncle Garrett just he and I would go. He wanted to go to the VFW for lunch and a quick drink. But I promise I'll pick everything up, no worries."

"Are you sure?" John asked. "That's a lot of stuff for one guy to load. And the diamonds. Diamonds are the key to this whole thing. I mean, you'll have to pick those out all by yourself."

"Don't worry, I got this. We'll take his old truck. I've even thrown some tarps in the back to cover everything up so no one will see what I've got."

"I guess it's all right then. We all trust you, so no worries here. You gentlemen enjoy lunch. We'll see you when you get back."

"Adios amigos. See you in a few," Bobby said before hopping into the truck.

Atsa watched through the sight on his rifle as the truck left the ranch, a trail of dust billowing in the air behind it. Turning his attention back to the house he saw John start passing the ball around with his boys. Rob was laying on a swing behind the house taking a nap, as Frank and Hideyoshi were hard at work in the barn, programming the controls and equipment for the aircraft. He slid back behind his rock and resumed staring at the horizon, once again waiting for any unwelcome visitors.

Lora made lunch for everyone. Eventually she took her daily trip up to Atsa to deliver his meal so that once again they could have their daily talk.

"Hello, Ms. Lora, how are you today?"

"Believe it or not, I'm actually starting to like it here, but don't you tell anyone," she said, laughing.

"Never Ms. Lora, your secret is safe with me."

Atsa helped her up the last little hill, climbing through the rocks to his nest. Sitting down, she took her scarf from her neck and wiped the dust off her face. Raising her hand to shield the sun from her eyes, she looked out at the horizon. The red glow of the sun against the backdrop of hills and valleys, with a slight breeze making the dust dance in tiny whirlwinds, made her smile.

"I could never get tired of this view," she stated.

Atsa smiled at her, watching the breeze blow through her hair as she marveled at the view.

"It's peaceful up here, isn't it?" he asked.

"One day we'll have to change jobs. You cook and I'll keep watch. I could get used to it up here."

"I don't think they would like my cooking Ms. Lora." The two shared another smile.

"Can I ask you a question?"

"Of course Ms. Lora."

"How do you tolerate that old man?"

"He's my friend."

"I see that, but he's a caveman. He thinks women should be barefoot and pregnant in the kitchen serving him like a master. He's often somewhat racist, downright ornery, not to mention he can be a complete pain in the ass," Lora pointed out. "So how is it...he likes you so much, because...you...you...know?"

"I don't understand Ms. Lora, what do I know?"

Carefully thinking about her next words, Lora blurted out, "Does he know you're gay?"

With his chin dropping a mile, Atsa stuttered, "But...but...but, I'm not..."

Tipping her head and smiling, looking over top her sunglasses, Lora cut him off. "Really?"

Shocked and still hesitant he asked, "How did you know?"

"I'm a woman, honey. For a man who spends his days in the desert hills, you color coordinate way too well."

Seeing that she made him uncomfortable now, she felt as if she had overstepped her bounds. He became quiet and reserved, sitting back watching the house, he didn't respond to her.

"I'm sorry, I didn't mean to offend you. I promise I won't tell anyone."

Still not looking at her, peering out in the distance he said, "I'm not offended. I'm proud of who I am. The old one doesn't know. I ignore his jokes because I know who he really is, and I tolerate his views because they change often."

"I'm so sorry. I shouldn't have asked, I shouldn't have brought it up."

"It's fine, for some reason I feel relieved that someone knows. It does worry me that if Garrett knows he will disown me. My father worked on the trains that came through town. He wasn't married to my mother, but when he found out about me he never returned. Garrett and Lucy helped raise me when my mother became heartbroken. She would sit and stare at the railroad tracks waiting for him to return, but he never did. Every day she would go and sit by the tracks until her heart couldn't take it anymore. Eventually her heart gave out and she passed away."

"Oh my god, that's so sad. I'm so sorry Atsa," Lora said, tears welling up in her eyes. "If I had known, I'd never have said anything. I feel so horrible for making you feel uncomfortable, for even bringing it up."

"Who's uncomfortable now?" Atsa laughed, finally turning to face Lora. "My mom lives at the edge of town, and she owns a beauty shop."

"Excuse me?"

"For one, yes, I am gay. For two, the old man does know and for three, he just says those things to get a rise out of you all."

"You asshole! You really had me going!" she said, picking up a small pebble and playfully tossing it at Atsa, hitting him in the arm. "I should strangle you!"

"Bitch, you can try," he said, gigging.

So Lora jumped up and tackled him, poking and tickling. The two snickered like schoolchildren as they rolled around in the dirt.

Out of air and gasping, Lora sat up, dusting the sand and dirt from her blouse and arms. She mischievously smacked Atsa's leg before jumping to her feet.

"You know, he's not as bad as you think he is."

"I do now, but you, I'm not sure about now. You really had me going."

"Thank you Ms. Lora."

Puzzled, she asked, "Thank me for what?"

"For being a friend." He smiled.

"Anytime. Come here give me a hug. I need to get back down there before the kids tear the house down. You know you can't leave John, Rob and Frank alone for a minute."

After a welcome embrace, Atsa carefully watched as she rode back to the house.

29

"I think they'll approve of the necklace," Bobby said confidently.

"They should, it damn near cost enough," Garrett said as he climbed into the rickety old truck, slamming the door. "Should have got two for the price they charged for that one."

"Nothing's cheap anymore. If you'd get out more you'd see that."

"That's why I don't get out."

"I'm sure that's the reason," Bobby said, smirking. "Okay, only one more stop before we head back. Looks like we'll need to get some gas."

"Gas, I already got gas," Garret said, lifting his left leg and leaning towards the door. "Yep, nothing like a VFW fish fry and some draft beer."

"Jesus, do you have to do that in here?"

"I'm too old to jump out of the truck and run alongside. Take it all in big boy, I got more where that came from."

Bobby whipped the truck into the nearest gas station. Jumping out, he gagged from the stench the old man shared with him. Garrett was amused as onlookers stopped to stare.

"Well boy, I feel like a soda pop. A root beer. Yep, a root beer sounds good, might settle my stomach down. Can I get you anything?"

"Yeah, a gas mask if they have one."

"Want a root beer too?"

"No thank you, I'm good," Bobby gasped.

"Suit yourself," Garrett said as he hobbled from the truck and headed towards the store.

As Bobby was pumping the gas, the old man fumbled around the store searching for his beverage of choice. He stopped to take in the magazine rack, then pretended to read the ingredients on a bag of chips he couldn't actually see. He watched as two men entered the store, both dressed in black suits wearing sunglasses. Hair slicked back, small but mean looking. Both were Asian, carrying a picture. He watched as they started showing the picture to other shoppers and asking questions. He thought it was time to pay for his soda and get out of there.

While standing at the cash register as the clerk rang up his order, he was approached by one of the men, who smugly said to him, "Excuse me sir, have you seen this man?"

Garrett fumbled with the new glasses the team had bought him, peering down his nose through his bifocals. He studied the picture for a minute. "Nah, can't say that I have. We don't get too many of you fellows around here."

"So you've never saw this man before?" the smug man insisted on asking again.

"Nope, can't say that I have. But seen a few look like him when I was overseas. I'd probably do what I did over there if I saw him."

"And what's that?"

Garrett stuffed his change back in his pants pocket. Turning to face the man he pulled his suit coat back to expose his .38 revolver strapped to his belt. "I'd shoot him. Now if you'd gentlemen would excuse me, you're in my way."

Watching the Asian man step to the side with a sarcastic smile on his face, as if he was amused by the comment, Garrett quickly exited the store. Once the door was closed behind him he attempted to sprint to the truck, but his tired legs only let him jog. He was doing the best he could with old legs.

"Get in the damn truck," he demanded. "Get in the truck now."

"What's wrong Uncle Garrett?"

"Just get in the truck and let's get out of here before we get shot!"

Bobby quickly fumbled with the gas cap, trying to hurry at the urging of his uncle.

"Go boy, and don't look back!"

Bobby started the truck and took off out of the gas station parking lot. Confused and somewhat worried, he had no idea what his mischievous uncle was up to.

"What's gotten in to you?"

Checking his mirror, turning and looking back to see if anyone was following, Garrett just kept his focus on what was or wasn't possibly behind them.

"Uncle, what the hell's wrong with you?"

"There was a couple of those Asians in there with a picture of your friend. They was asking questions, wanted to know if I'd seen him."

"What the hell? What did you tell them?"

"Well," he huffed, "I didn't tell them nothing, I'm not going to do that."

Worriedly shaking his head as he drove, Bobby made for the ranch.

"We got to get back, warn the guys."

"Don't you worry. If they come a calling, we'll be ready, you can count on that."

Bobby drove as fast as the tired old motor would let him. He knew this wasn't good. He was worried about how anyone found them. Frank and Hideyoshi had both ensured that their tracks were completely covered. This wasn't good. They were so close to launching, and this could throw a wrench into everything. Especially since all of the money they used to build with was stolen.

Thundering down the lane to the ranch, dust was blowing high into the air, and Bobby was laying on the horn, trying to get everyone's attention. Atsa squinted as he looked through his scope. He saw Garrett with his hand out the window, waving him down. Before Bobby could bring the truck to a stop, Atsa was already heading down the hill, creating his own rooster tail in the dirt.

John and Lora ran out of the house to see what all the commotion was about. Frank and Hideyoshi stood at the doorway of their camper, peeking through the foggy pane of glass.

"Is everything all right, is Garrett okay?" Lora asked, imagining the worst.

"He's fine baby," Bobby answered. "But we do have a problem."

Bobby ran to the other side of the trunk to help his uncle out as Atsa pulled up to the house. Everyone gathered around Garrett.

"What the hell is going on?" John asked.

"There's some guys in town asking about Hideyoshi," Bobby said.

"What guys?" John asked suspiciously.

Frank and Hideyoshi slowly walked up, joining the panicked group.

"What's going on?" Hideyoshi asked. He too was hesitant as the group turned its attention towards him. "Did I do something wrong?"

"Those friends, the ones you said couldn't find you, well, they found you, and they're in town right now!" John said.

"Yakuza?" Frank asked.

"It ain't the Mickey Mouse club," Bobby spouted off.

"Hideyoshi, you assured us that nobody could find you. The money was untraceable and that these so-called friends were holding off the people you stole from so you could get out of the country," John said. "Then why are they here?"

"I would assume they raised the bounty on my head John-san. They have to find me now. I'm guessing they have hired another hacker to track me. It must be from the credit card transactions or shipments from Japan that they have found our location."

"So now we're out of money?" Rob asked.

"Not necessarily Rob-san, but the card can only be used one time. And then you'll only have minutes, maybe seconds to get away before they show up. Once the card is used it will be tracked instantly, by who I do not know, but I will find out."

The team started arguing with one another as they all realized the dream might be over, who was to blame, their world turned upside down again, their new home compromised and now this little hiccup could bring the whole thing crumbling down.

"*Stop it!*" Garrett screamed. "Nobody has seen me with him. They can't make the association, because we have never been to town together."

"That's true Garrett. They might know he's close to here, but they don't know exactly where at," John said.

"So with that said, Hop-Sing you're confined to the ranch, so no more going out in town. Atsa, you get back to your post, Bobby and I will relieve you at dusk. I can't see and I'm pretty sure his big ass can't stay awake. John and Rob, you'll relieve us at one in the morning, and Frank and Hop-Sing will relieve them at four in the morning and wait until Atsa gets back." Garrett firmly laid out the orders. "Lora, you just take care of them boys, keep them in the house for now and don't let them outside. If you ain't standing watch or sleeping, you'll work on that flying contraption until it's finished, and then you'll get the hell off my ranch. I've made it this long in this world, and I'm too old to get shot now."

"Thanks Uncle Garrett, thanks for not running us off and letting us finish this thing," Bobby said politely.

"You're all my family whether I like it or not, but as long as you have that whatever you call it here on my property, ain't none of us safe. So, let's get this finished, and when it's safe and ain't anybody hunting any of you, you're welcome here anytime. But if we don't make it, and the shootin starts, they need to shoot Frank first."

"What? Why me first?"

"So the rest of us have a chance to get away," Garrett said as he playfully poked Frank in the stomach. "We still have a chance in life…to sleep with a woman we didn't pay for."

"Aw, that's just wrong," Frank replied.

30

The first night's watch wasn't as successful as Garrett had planned. Garret and Bobby were late to relieve Atsa by thirty minutes, and in turn John and Rob followed suit with their late arrival to relieve them. Other than Atsa, no one was accustomed to standing watch in the hills. It was eerie and quiet at times; coyotes would howl, breaking through the silence, startling anyone not used to those types of sounds. Traffic on the main road in the daytime was sparse as it was, and the road was even less traveled at night. A simple whisper would echo loudly through the valleys, so talking was kept to a minimum.

Frank and Hideyoshi were the last watch of the night. Although they were the first to arrive on time, it would be them who would eventually drop the ball. It wasn't even an hour into their watch when they drifted off to sleep in the cool morning desert air, leaving the others vulnerable as they slept. This was a horrible mistake to make, as visitors would, in fact, come calling.

Garrett was sound asleep in his bed. He awoke when the unexpected visitor pressed the cold barrel of his pistol against Garrett's forehead. Although groggy from his slumber, he still knew not to yell or jump up. He looked up through foggy eyes as he tried to focus on his assailant. The visitor cautioned him as he reached for his glasses, slowly, he motioned. He grabbed a fistful of Garrett's pajama top, pulling him from his warm bed and walking him towards the hallway. At the same time they entered the hallway, he saw another man with a pistol at Bobby's head. Lora was in front of him, whimpering as they were ushered downstairs.

Shoving the old man onto the couch, the visitor instructed his partner, "Tie them up. I'll get the others."

A few minutes passed, then the man came walking back down the stairs. His hand firmly squeezed Thomas's neck as he guided him; he was carrying Little John in his arms, who was still half asleep and not aware of who had him. Bobby was infuriated, noticing that the man had the pistol still in his hand as he carried the child.

"Where are the others?" the first visitor asked.

Nobody answered. They sat quietly watching the pair as one placed the sleeping child across Lora's lap and pushed the other child down on the couch between Garrett and Bobby.

The second visitor quickly hit Garrett across the head with his pistol, cutting him above the right eye. He raised his voice. "He asked you where the others are!"

"Stop it!" Lora pleaded.

"If I ask you again, one of you will die," the first visitor said.

"In their trailers, beside the barn," Bobby confessed. "Just don't kill anyone."

He nodded to his companion to go and retrieve them as he stood watch over the already captured victims. Within a few minutes he would return with John and Rob. As he reentered the house he said something in Japanese that they couldn't understand.

"Where is The Dragon?"

"I don't know, "John said.

He too received a pistol-whipping for his answer. This time the first visitor made an example out of him as he hit John over and over, almost making him lose consciousness.

"Stop it dammit! Stop it...they're on the hill!" Lora screamed. Both children started crying for their father, as he lay huddled on the floor at their feet.

"Show me," the visitor ordered.

Lora rose. Walking over to the window, she leaned over and pointed towards the hill with her eyes. Again the man nodded to his partner.

He was gone for what seemed like an eternity. They all heard scuffling out on the porch and with a loud boom the front door blasted open. He tossed Hideyoshi helplessly into the room. He landed on his right side, bloody and battered. It was obvious that he had not gone quietly.

"Where's our money Dragon?" the first visitor asked as the second kicked Hideyoshi in the ribs, laughing evilly as his blow lifted the defenseless man off the ground.

John had scooted himself towards the couch and was trying to sit upright as the first visitor pointed his gun at his head.

"I won't ask again, Dragon, where is our money?"

"Don't…don't…please don't." John gasped for air. "He'll get you the money…don't kill us."

"I will—I swear it," Hideyoshi pleaded.

"We are not here for negotiations. You took money from our client and they want it back!"

"Just listen to me, for the love of God just listen," John begged. "I have something more valuable than any amount of money on earth. Just let me show you, don't kill us and it's yours."

"And my client's money?"

"He'll get you the money…just don't hurt anyone…if you let us live you can have it all."

The two visitors talked. Hideyoshi understood, but the others were worried. Was this it; were they all going to die?

The first visitor started to walk towards John. He flinched as the man reached down to pick him up.

"Show me. If you are lying, I'll kill you where you are standing."

They returned sometime later. The other intruder was still keeping watch over the team as the morning sun broke through windows. He shoved John, who fell on top of Bobby and Thomas, who wrapped his arms around his father's neck, sobbing and thankful for his return.

The man jerked Lora up from her seat and cut the rope from around her wrists.

"Take the children and feed them. Go now!"

Garrett was still bleeding badly. He needed medical attention as much as Hideyoshi and John. Everyone was worried about Frank, who hadn't been brought down from the hill. They prayed he was still alive.

"Where's our other friend?" Bobby asked.

"So there is another?"

"Shit," John murmured. "Damn it Bobby!"

Once again the man nodded to his companion to retrieve the last remaining team member. As he pulled the front door open with a loud bang, the second visitor fell to his knees, and then he slowly fell onto his face. His own partner had raised his pistol and shot him in the back of the head, instantly killing him. They heard Lora scream from the kitchen in horror, but they were too shocked to respond as they watched the blood stain the sun-dried wood planks on the porch.

He turned and walked towards John, cutting him free and handing him his knife. John quickly cut the others free as the man retrieved his partner's weapon.

"What the hell just happened?" Rob asked.

"I don't know," John said.

Cutting Bobby free he tried to go after the man, but John and Rob had to restrain him. Lora and the kids were crying in the kitchen. It was obvious the man didn't want them to see what was about to happen.

"Please forgive me," the visitor bowed. "I am sorry that all of you had to see that. I beg for your forgiveness."

"Where's the other one, where's Frank?" John asked.

"He said there was no one else in the hills, so I was sending him to look again."

"But did you have to kill him?" Bobby growled.

"If I did not, he would have killed all of you. He would have taken everything you have and finished his mission without concern."

"I'm still fucking confused," Rob said.

"You can call your friend down from the hill, and I promise no harm will come to any of you."

Frank had awoken and gone to take a leak. When he was returning he saw Hideyoshi being dragged towards the house. Scared and not a fighter, he hid, waiting for Atsa to return so that he could inform him. Atsa returned but did not have a weapon now; he was plotting how to get to the house without being discovered.

Bobby and John went outside and rang the bell, calling their friends down from the hills, waving to them that all was clear. It took some time before either would come down, cautious that they were being set up for capture.

As they waited Lora started patching up the others. Hideyoshi would require medical attention she could not provide, but he refused. He wasn't about to let anyone else know his whereabouts.

"How did you find me?" he muttered painfully.

"We have your brother," the visitor answered. "He is well. He's in a car down by the highway. If I am safe to retrieve him I will do so now, if you wish?"

"Yes, go get him," Lora ordered the man.

"As you wish."

Everyone still had a million questions. Who was this man? Atsa and Frank were filled in as much as they could be; there were too many holes in the story for it to make sense to anyone at this point.

The man returned, driving up to the house in a long black car. Hideyoshi's brother, Yuuki, sprinted from the car to check on his brother's safety.

John, with bandages half hanging from his head, stopped the man at the porch.

"Why'd you do that? Why'd you help us?"

The Japanese man paused. Stepping back, he again bowed to John. "Allow me to introduce myself. My name is Shou Shin. I am the son of a former Yakuza family boss."

"Okay, but that doesn't explain what just happened here."

"Can we walk?" Shou asked.

"Sure, hang on a second," John answered before calling into the house. "Bobby, walk with us!"

John wasn't feeling all that safe considering that the man just killed someone. He didn't like the odds of being alone with him.

As they all started to walk the man explained his story.

"I was born into the Yakuza. My father wanted something more for me so he sent me to private schools and later made me join the Japanese military. He wanted me to be a pilot. I only returned to help my father when he became ill. He has since passed."

"Go on," Bobby insisted.

"I've not always approved of my life, but it was my duty to honor my father and his legacy and his name. He did not want me to return to the Yakuza, but I did, as many threats were placed on his ailing condition. I made sure he died of natural conditions."

"You mean natural causes," Bobby corrected.

"Yes natural causes, my apologies, English is not my first language."

"Yeah, we get that," John said.

"When I saw what you had discovered, I felt life again."

"Alive?" Bobby asked.

"Yes, alive. You have discovered alternative energy. I did not think it wise that it be in the wrong hands, it would be very dangerous."

"So you shot your partner?" Bobby asked.

"I've killed many men for my job. I do not want to kill again, and I despise it. But if I don't kill, they would kill me for losing honor. When you showed me your aircraft, I found purpose."

"What do you mean you found purpose?"

Stopping in front of the barn, Shou studied the aircraft.

"If you fly this craft, you will die."

Bobby was insulted by this comment, considering he was the designer, although in actuality it was the first aircraft he had ever designed.

"I mean no offense. But clearly you have no experience in air flight. The airframe is too weak for the thrust load, it will fall apart shortly after takeoff."

"Bullshit, it's designed to go into space!" Bobby was clearly offended.

"Again, my apologies, but as a pilot you'll be exposed to radiation, and you do not have enough protection to prevent it. First you must master flying this craft in our atmosphere. You have the power but not the…how you say…structure?"

"Hang on Bobby, let's hear him out. He did just save our lives."

"He came here to kill us. If it weren't for this we'd be dead!"

"Exactly. This has changed all our lives, why not his? Let's hear him out."

"I can help you design a craft that will achieve your desired goals. It would be my honor. And give honor to my family name."

"What do you suggest?" John asked.

"Stronger airframe, titanium alloy covering and the correct avionics to fly both in space and in the earth's atmosphere. I offer my services as a pilot with expertise and knowledge of aircraft. It will be safer to fly. I will guarantee that, if you allow me to help you?"

"How do we know we can trust you?" Bobby asked.

Shou removed his pistol from underneath his suit jacket and handed it to Bobby.

"What's this for?"

"I place my life in your hands. I will not dishonor any of you, or you may take my life in return. You have my word."

"We won't go to those extremes," John said.

"Maybe not, but I'm still hanging on to the gun," Bobby said.

"And it was not as hard to find you as you may think. You should not have supplies delivered so close to your location. I will work with the brothers to correct this problem. You will be pleased with my service, I promise."

31

As much as the team hated to admit it, Shou was right. The craft's airframe was weak. They had calculated enough thrust to launch six aircrafts at the target weight ratio. In their defense, how would they know? This was all still new to them.

Shou also corrected the tracking issues; credit cards were used once and disposed of. They would have shipments sent to different cities, Flagstaff, Phoenix and Prescott. They even used out-of-state cities like San Diego, Los Angeles, Las Vegas, Albuquerque and Las Cruces, anywhere they could drive to pick things up that wasn't currently in their own back yard.

They pulled the original power source from the old car and placed the drivetrain under Garrett's old truck. With a hitch installed they could pick up more supplies pulling a trailer than they could with the old car. They were starting to become more efficient under Shou's advisement.

Yuuki, who was used to hack his own brother, became part of Frank's team, as he had almost the same skill set as his brother. Shou worked close with Bobby on design; Bobby was still in charge and had the final say, which at times left the two to clash. John tried to balance them all. What started out as a ragtag team of four was now a ragtag team of twelve, with two kids who were more than willing to help.

What used to look like a vacated old ranch now looked like a fully functioning junkyard. There were scrap parts lying about, and the sounds of grinders and saws filled the valley air. There was the occasional fire due to the natural learning curve of building an aircraft.

"How much longer do you guys think? You know, until we can test her out?" Garrett asked.

"About a week. We need to convert the diamonds. Get those in the turbines, and then get those suckers installed," John answered.

"What you going to name her?"

"I was thinking we'd let you have that honor, Garrett. You did take us all in and give us a place to do this, so we'll let you pick the name," John said as he smiled at the old man.

Garrett scratched his head as if he was pondering hard. He stood up and crossed the porch to take a seat next to John on the steps. He looked up at the night sky and smiled.

"You see that star right there?" he said, pointing straight up.

"I see a million stars." John laughed.

Lora was giggling at the conversation from the porch swing, where she sat hemming a pair of pants for Little John.

"That one there." He pointed again. "Watch it, it will twinkle every few minutes."

"That's Venus, Garrett," John pointed out.

"Nope, that's Lucy. When she passed sometime back, I'd come out here and sit. I imagined every time I looked up there, that was her winking back at me."

"That's so sweet, Garrett," Lora said.

"You hush back there," he growled.

"Aw, you did ask the wizard for a heart," she said as she stuck her tongue out at the old man.

"Shut it woman, but anyway," he said, turning his attention back to John. "I want to give her that name."

"Venus?" John kidded the old man.

"No you jack wagon, Lucy, I want to name her Lucy."

"I know, I was just playing. Lucy it is."

Rob came strolling up to the porch carrying the bucket of mixed samples.

"Where you want to do this?" Rob asked.

"Garrett, you care if we do this at the kitchen table?" John asked.

"Suit yourself, just don't spill that concoction in there."

John had promised that if the boys behaved they could help place the diamonds in the samples. He took apart the necklace as Rob filled each sample dish with chemicals, then each boy took turns placing a diamond in the dish. It made both men feel good that the kids were interested in the project, except every day when Little John would ask to fly the craft, and he was relentless.

"Okay twenty-four hours from now, we should have diamonds for each turbine," John said.

"Hey Dad," Thomas called out, "then can you fly it?"

"No, we'll need to install them into turbines, then install those turbines into Lucy."

"Then can I fly it?" Little John said, jumping up and down in his chair.

"Not before me," Thomas said.

"Yes I will!"

"No you won't!"

John had to step in and separate the boys as a shoving match started.

"Nobody is flying it until they hit the proper age to do so, and I'm setting that age at," John paused, "I'm setting that age at thirty!"

"Dad!" Little John said.

"Don't Dad me. Now both of you go get ready for bed."

John watched as the two took off running for the stairs, elbows flying as they competed to see which one made it up the stairs first.

"Well John, where you want to store these?" Rob asked.

"Place them in the cupboard. That should keep them out of the way until tomorrow."

"I'm on it."

Twenty-four hours came and went. Everyone had finished supper and eagerly waited to see the diamonds. This time John wasn't just going to be hounded by two kids. It seemed that every man was now six years old as they pestered him to take the diamonds out.

"Come on John, let's see them," Bobby said.

"No kidding, I'm dying here," Frank joined in.

"Okay, okay, you bunch of whiners. Settle down, and everybody get a chair."

Everyone gathered around the kitchen table in anticipation, even Garrett. One by one John opened each sample as if it was Christmas morning. But this time, not all the presents were good ones. The first seven he opened all turned out fine, but it was number eight that made them realize they had a problem.

"Uh-oh, this doesn't look right," John said, holding up the diamond. It was hollowed out like the others, almost. It was hollowed out from the top to the side.

"Might be a fluke, keep going," Bobby urged.

John was starting to get nervous as more and more of the diamonds turned out flawed.

Under Shou's new design he would need twenty-seven good diamonds. It wasn't looking good.

"Good one."

"Bad one."

"Bad one."

"Good one," John said, his frustration growing.

"Last one," Garrett said. "Cross your fingers boys."

"And we have…a bad one…damn!" Rob said as he watched John pull the Diamond from the dish.

"I don't understand it. That's sixty diamonds, and we only have twenty good ones," John stated as he leaned back in his chair, rubbing his temples.

"What do you think happened?" Frank asked.

"John-san," Hideyoshi called. "Look at this."

Turning his laptop for the men to see, Hideyoshi was looking through pictures of diamonds he found on the Internet, ones that were magnified under a microscope.

"I believe John-san, it is clarity that would be the issue."

"That's interesting, look at these," Frank pointed out. "The ones here you can see clear through to the point, this one here, you can see a heavier grain boundary."

"So what are you saying? The fuel sample eroded, flowing down the boundary?"

"It's possible," John said.

"We may need more diamonds," Frank pointed out.

"You boys are going to pay top dollar for those kind of diamonds," Garrett said.

"We paid a lot for our wedding rings, it was one thing Gloria insisted on."

"How many more do you need?" Garrett asked.

"Seven Uncle Garrett," Bobby said, "Seven, and possibly more. We haven't even tried them out as a power source yet."

The old man motioned for them to hang on as he made his way towards the stairs.

"Where you going Uncle Garrett?"

Again the old man motioned, this time was a tad more firmly. Up the stairs he went and returned a few minutes later carrying a diamond bracelet. Holding it up in the light he studied the diamonds it contained.

"What do you see?" John asked as he stood beside him.

"Not a damn thing with these old eyes. Here, take this and tell me what you see. Tell me how many are there?"

John counted up the diamonds. "Twenty-one," he announced. Trying to look for clarity he held them as close to his eyes as he could before his vision blurred. "I can't tell if it's what we need."

Yuuki, Hideyoshi's brother, reached into his pocket and pulled out a jewelry loupe. Yep, one of those little magnifying glasses that jewelers use. He took the bracelet from John's hand and studied it, slowly going over each stone before handing the bracelet back to John. He held up nine of his fingers, indicating how many candidates he found for clarity.

"So nine?" Bobby asked.

Yuuki shook his head yes in agreement.

"Can't you speak?" Rob asked.

"Not well Rob-san, he does not like to speak English as he just started learning."

"So where did he get the little glass thing at? Does he always carry one around?" Bobby asked.

"Yes Bobby-san, like myself, he does not always get employed on the proper side of the law."

"Well boys, you can have that bracelet. Take what you need and give me back the rest. It was Lucy's. God rest her soul, I don't think she'll miss them, but the bracelet at least can stay in her jewelry box. I'm pretty sure she wouldn't mind donating to the cause."

John had Yuuki mark the diamonds he suggested. Removing those, they soaked them in samples for another twenty-four hours and found another key to the puzzle as they all turned out to be acceptable. Each was perfectly hollowed out, creating the funnel similar to the first diamond. Now it was Rob's job to get them installed into the turbines and tested.

32

Looking scraggly and unshaven, Tom Hawkins was driving somewhere to nowhere outside of Salt Lake City, Utah. Unwilling to give up searching for John and his team, he pressed hard, wearing down his band of opposing engineers. The longer they searched, the more dysfunctional they became.

Jasper had lost his phone somewhere around 1500 miles into their search. He was no longer communicating with Alex Wright, who in return had become infuriated, thinking they had run off into hiding.

"It's been awhile since we checked in, do you think we should call Mr. Wright?" Jasper asked.

Not wanting to give up in defeat, Tom Hawkins agreed to contact him at the next stop.

"If he fires us, I'm shooting every one of you!" he stated arrogantly.

"We are not defeated," Maurice proclaimed proudly.

"For your well being, you'd better hope so. And can you two shut the hell up, quit arguing for one damn day!"

33

"Yes…Yes…Yes!" Rob screamed.

The others watched as he ran out of his trailer, his hands twirling in the air as he spun in circles, dancing around on the dusty lane in front of the house. A smile as wide as the Grand Canyon showed upon his face.

"This is unbelievable!" he shouted.

Running around frantically, he hugged them all one by one until he got to Bobby. Rob stretched his arms wide around the behemoth, trying to lift him off the ground and failing. Not losing heart, he continued dancing and shouting.

"What the hell has gotten into him?" Bobby asked.

"I don't have a clue," John answered.

"Rob!" Bobby shouted.

Rob would not answer; he was too busy dancing.

"Earth to Rob Yarborough, come in Rob Yarborough!" John shouted.

Rob finally stopped, turning to face them all. His chest heaved from his play as he tried to catch his breath. Still smiling as if he had won the lottery, he stared back at them, not saying a word.

The two German brothers argued the entire search, from the time they left the beach to the very minute Tom called them on it.

"We can stop in Provo, I'll call from there," Jasper said as he folded the map.

They had searched high and low for John, but there was no sign or trail to be found.

Finally finding a motel next to the highway outside of Provo, Jasper made the call he had been dreading.

He wondered…*As we are looking for them, does Alex Wright have someone looking for us? This could be bad.*

Jasper found an old payphone next to the lobby of the motel and made his nervous call. He wasn't well received.

"You twits finally check in to tell me you still don't have it!"

"But Mr. Wright, it's…"

"I don't give a fuck what it is, you're wasting my money and my time because you're incompetent!"

"Let me explain Mr. Wright!"

"You'll explain nothing! Where are you?"

"Please Mr. Wright!"

"Please nothing! Where are you?

"Outside Provo, Utah sir," Jasper sighed.

"Utah? What the fuck is in Utah? Don't answer that. You stay put. I'm sending back up. I'll find out where they're at, and you'll go get them. You'll bring everything back to me, and I mean everything!"

"I'm sorry Mr. Wright, I'll fix this."

"You couldn't fix a hole in your blow up doll with ten rolls of duct tape. You couldn't catch an STD in a whorehouse with a fistful of hundred dollar bills. I've never seen this much incompetence in my life. I'm disgusted with you, you're lucky I don't have someone come end your miserable life right now!"

"Again, I'm sorry Mr. Wright," Jasper pleaded.

"Stop sucking up, you little sniveling worm. This is what you're going to do. Go buy another cell phone, and you're to call me twice a day. And don't miss a call or I will send someone to kill you. Do you understand me?"

"Yes sir," Jasper answered as he heard the click on the other end of the line.

Jasper returned to the rooms to explain the situation to the others. Everyone but Tom was relieved to not be traveling anymore. Tom wanted to keep searching; he didn't like the idea of sitting and waiting, playing the puppet.

Alex Wright had devised another plan to find them. He had lost faith in Jasper but still needed him to be the scapegoat in finding sustainability. Once that purpose was fulfilled, Jasper was finished and so was his team.

As things were falling apart fo team, John's team was still having w things happen every day.

"Okay, now you're freaking me out," Frank said.

Rob took off running towards John, stopping just before knocking him down. He grabbed his shoulders and began shaking him.

"What the hell is wrong with you Rob?" John asked.

"She wants me back," he answered as he wrapped his arms around John in an embrace. "She really wants me back."

"Heather?"

"Yes, she just called. Said she's sorry and she's miserable without me!"

"I'm happy for you. Can you quit hugging me now?"

Rob pulled away from John, reaching up to help adjust the shirt that he had just messed up.

"Sorry about that, I got a little excited."

"Do you think?" Bobby said. "I thought you were going to pee on my leg!"

"Sorry about that too," Rob said. "Can't help it, I'm so excited. I'm beside myself!"

"So what are you doing? Are you leaving to go home?" Frank asked.

"No. I was thinking I could bring her here, that's what I was coming to ask of you all. What do you think?"

John turned to look at the others. He didn't know what to say, so he shrugged his shoulders.

He was somewhat happy for his friend, but part of him was jealous. Gloria hadn't called since they left Ohio, and here was Rob with his wife wanting him back. He didn't want to say no, so he looked at the others for answers. Garrett would be the one to save him from the uncomfortable situation.

"Yes she can come here, but how do you plan on getting her here?"

"I haven't had time to give it much thought. I can have her fly in," Rob said as he snapped his fingers.

"Not to Tucson son," Garrett said. "If someone is watching her, they can follow her. And that's how we got these other two yahoos. Not to mention that one buried out there in the desert."

"I'll tell you what Rob," John chimed in. "Why don't you fly her in to Vegas? You can take the truck to pick her up. If someone is following you can at least have a chance to lose them."

"That's not a bad idea John," Rob said.

"If you'll give me my weapon back, I'll go with them just in case they can't get away," Shou offered.

"Whoa, wait a minute, I don't like that idea," Bobby said.

"Bobby please, he's proved himself," Lora said. "There's no reason why you shouldn't trust him. He's helped you all build that thing out there, and he's kept you out of trouble since. Give him back the damn gun and let him help Rob."

Bobby wasn't sure for all the right reasons; he did watch the man murder another in cold blood. But not agreeing would ruin Rob's happy day. He conceded and didn't interfere, promising to give the man's weapon back.

It didn't take long for Rob to run off and make plans. He had Heather book the first flight she could get. Before everybody realized what had just happened he was headed to Vegas to repair a part of his life. Shou, now armed, was literally riding shotgun. The rest of the team went back to work preparing the craft for flight.

Heather arrived around midnight, ushered in under a veil of secrecy. Hellos were short as they quickly tossed her luggage into the back of the truck, shoved her in the cab and took off with Shou at the wheel. Not even a simple introduction as to who the stranger driving them was. And the truck was way below her typical standards; as it rattled and shook, she could feel every bump in the road.

"I'm so sorry for everything Heather," Rob said.

"Don't apologize, it was both of us. It was just a bad time, I just want us to work through this."

"We will baby, I think you'll be happy with what we've done."

"What you've done, what you found it? You guys did it?"

"We didn't find sustainability. But we found something so much more exciting. I can't wait to show you," Rob said as he pulled her closer, planting a kiss on her forehead.

"So you picked Vegas to live?"

"No," Rob said, laughing. "We have a ways to go to get to the ranch."

They joked and laughed as Shou drove. He kept his attention on the task at hand, watching in front of him, checking his mirrors for potential followers. He wasn't going to let anyone interfere; he wanted to prove his loyalty to the others.

Heather watched as they drove, exit ramp after exit ramp. Gas stations flew by and not once did they stop. Rob explained a little bit about their discovery but didn't divulge too much information; he didn't want to ruin the surprise for her. Six and half hours later they finally pulled up back at the ranch, as the morning sun broke over the hills.

Heather watched as Rob climbed from the cab and walked to the front of the truck. He lifted the hood and motioned for her to join him. She stood in confusion. This wasn't an engine she was looking at.

"What is this?" she asked.

"It's our discovery."

"But what is it?"

"We haven't actually named it yet. But this," he said as he placed on the insulated glove and lifted the cover, "got us from Ohio to Tucson on six gallons of water."

She stepped back from the heat.

"Wow. I still have no idea what it is, but it's amazing, I guess."

"See, the money you spent wasn't wasted. We just needed a little more time to show you some results. We just drove four hundred miles on not even a couple gallons of water."

"Oh my god Rob! That's amazing!"

"Everybody should be getting up, let's go in and join them for breakfast. You can say hi to everyone. And I warn you now, there's more of us."

And off they went. She was welcomed with open arms. It took the entire breakfast to explain their journey to her. The only part they left out was the shooting; they didn't want to freak her out too much. But they took the time to explain the entire discovery. They let her know her investment wasn't a total waste, and she let them know how sorry she was for pulling out early.

John was still a little jealous, but he had to put his own personal feelings aside and join in

Rob's happiness. He wanted to show his support. It was awkward at first, but he eventually pulled it together.

34

Lora already had the role of wife, surrogate mother to the kids and house mom to the men wrapped up. The team all had their specific roles they were accustomed to. Heather found it hard to fit in and spent most of the time in her trailer waiting for Rob to return. They all offered to include her, but she wasn't interested in the tasks that were asked of her. Getting dirty wasn't her thing and household chores, well, she was used to paying someone to do those. She was just looking to find her niche.

Test day was around the corner. Loose ends had to be tied up in order to pull it off. Long hours and more money were inevitable.

Frank and Shou went over the flight controls with John.

"Okay John, get up there in the cockpit," Frank instructed.

John climbed in and took his seat. Standing outside the craft, Frank motioned for him to place the headset on so they could communicate.

"Okay, what you got?" John asked.

"All right, see the joystick on your left? That controls your altitude; it'll take you up and down. Want to go higher, you pull back, lower push down."

"That's easy enough."

"Okay, the one on your right, that's a little different. That controls direction and pitch. Want to turn or raise and lower the nose of the aircraft? This is the joystick you'll use."

"Okay, got it."

"See the pedals on the floor?"

"Yep, I got them," John answered.

"This is simple, the one on the right is the gas."

"And the one on the left is the brake or reverse, is that right?"

"That's right John-boy, you're a quick learner," Frank teased.

John took a few minutes, playing with the joysticks as if he were actually flying the craft.

"Are you done playing John-san?" Shou asked.

"Yes." John laughed.

"We simplified your avionics, looking at the monitor between your legs shows your altitude and flight path. The small monitor, shoulder high to your left, shows your airspeed. Center will be your communication panel and to the right, that monitor will be the radar and global positioning system. And you'll also get temps and fuel usage from that monitor."

"What are these panels to my left on the bulkhead?" John asked.

"Yes John-san, those are for your programs. If need be we can take over control of your craft and fly it remotely. We can calibrate your joysticks for more feel or less feel. However, you'll need to land for us to calibrate. Calibrating while flying will cause you to drop like a stone."

"Let's not do that, if it's okay with you guys," John kidded.

"The bank of switches below that fires all your lasers," Rob said.

"So that's how I start this thing?"

"Exactly. It also has one that controls all your systems, life support, equipment and such. It will be part of your pre-flight start up. Bobby will also have access to those features."

"How do I know if this thing is calibrated right?" John asked.

"You don't. We guessed based on Shou's experience flying jets. We don't want you to press a joystick and go flying straight up, losing consciousness. That would be bad."

"Too many Gs, got it."

"Yes we need to calibrate the G-force load, so that you don't have an accident. You'll need to take it easy so we can get some readings of how much to add or take away from your joysticks and throttles," Frank said.

"I have a question."

"Go ahead John-san."

"If you guys guess wrong, how hard will it be to land this thing?"

"Honest answer?" Frank asked.

"Yes, give me an honest answer," John demanded.

"Extremely. You have a fifty percent chance of crashing," Frank said.

"Sorry I asked."

John climbed down from the craft. He watched as Bobby took his climb into the craft. John giggled as Bobby barely fit through the hatch. Bobby would ride right behind John as the navigator and engineer. He would have all of the maintenance controls, communications support and overrides.

"Hey Shou?" John called. "What about flight suits? We can't actually wear our street clothes in this thing."

"No worries John-san, I have proper flight suits coming in tomorrow."

"Are those masks going to be enough?"

"Not if you're serious about flying to space. We'll need proper suits and that will raise concern. Those are not items you get on black market."

"But can you get them?"

"Yes John-san. But they will be old and will need much work. And will cost much money."

"Let's see if this thing even flies first," John said, patting Shou on the back.

Lucy had an entirely different look then what John had first imagined. The nose was slenderer, with a sharp edge extending down both sides. Three small turbines peeked out the nose for braking power. Shou insisted on two small wings on each side for balance and lift; they sloped evenly with the bottom of the craft. Instead of the former boxy design, the top now had a rounder appearance, and just above the wing were three more boosters needed for turning the aircraft. The tail still had six enormous boosters for driving the machine through the air. John lay down underneath and looked at the retractable landing gear; no wheels, just pads to rest on. Eight retractable turbines peeked out from their sheaths for lift. John marveled at the engineering feat they had all pulled off. It still had room to carry five hundred gallons of water and if need be up to a thousand. It was truly impressive to look at, but everyone had their concerns. John himself kept asking himself the most important question of all... *Will it actually fly?*

"She's long and lean, ain't she?" Bobby said as he squeezed from the hatch and jumped down, landing right beside him.

"She's heavy," John answered.

"You remember what that first one did to the slide. She'll have enough thrust to get off the ground."

"I'm not worried about lifting the aircraft," John said.

"Then what are you worried about?"

"I'm worried about it lifting your big ass."

"Funny, very funny."

John held out his hand for the big man to lift him up. Bobby accepted graciously despite his best friend's insults.

"Let's go get a beer big man."

"Hell, let's go get two, three, or more."

Lucy was almost ready for her maiden voyage; there were just a few loose ends to tie up. Prepping everything and everyone on controls, tracking and the most important thing of all, safety. They had come this far and jumped every hurdle; the last thing they wanted was to have someone lose their life. They had already seen one unfortunate soul come to this fate.

What John didn't realize was that everyone was still in danger. Alex Wright was on his trail, and he was coming. There was still a fox in the hen house. And they would bring Alex knocking on their front door.

35

"This suit's a little tight," Bobby said as he walked out of the bathroom.

Tight would not be the right way to describe what our team was seeing. Bobby's flight suit didn't fit at all. It was six inches short in the leg; he looked like he was afraid of high water. The front of his suit wouldn't zip, it was open from his neck to his navel.

"I don't have the words for what I'm seeing," Rob gasped.

Cell phone camera flashes started going off like fireworks.

"Putting that in the old scrap book," Frank spouted off.

"Come on guys, give him a break." John stepped in, standing in front of Bobby.

John's flight suit fit like a glove. He actually looked like a pilot. He stood there looking rather dashing as he came to Bobby's defense.

"Lora, could you do something with his suit?" John asked.

"Sure, you boys go take those off, I'll cut up another one and fix his. I'm going to add something else to them too. It's a surprise."

"We only ordered three. If you cut it up no one else will be able to fly," Shou stated.

"Just order some more," Rob said.

Shou looked to Hideyoshi for approval. He wasn't going to say it, but he really wanted to fly too.

Hideyoshi immediately started typing away, looking for more suits, which brought a happy grin of satisfaction to Shou's face.

"Okay, now everybody go get cleaned up for dinner. I, with the assistance of Garret, made something special for tonight in honor of tomorrow. So now go on, get!" Lora ordered, watching as the men scurried away.

Garrett had roasted a pig in the ground, something he learned to do as a child. The boys had helped him dig a hole and line it with stones. In the bottom he placed charcoal. Placing the pig on top, he covered it up with dirt, allowing it to roast all day. Lora made all the fixings to go with it, baked beans, coleslaw and greens. It wouldn't be the feast of a king, but it would be the best meal they'd had since they left Ohio and started this journey.

Lora was hoping the fine dinner would turn the conversation to something else other than work talk, but this wasn't to be. John insisted as they ate they go over their flight plan one more time.

"Boys, enough is enough," Garrett interrupted. "Save it for tomorrow."

"Thank you Garrett," Lora said.

"I know it ain't Thanksgiving, but I'm thankful all of you are here," he said, leaning back in his chair and smiling as he looked around the table. "You've brought a little excitement to the old man's life. I'm grateful."

"Thank you Garrett," John said.

"Oh, don't thank me. Why don't we go around the room and everybody say something? What are you all grateful for?"

John started off. He was thankful for his children and his team. The boys were thankful for their new family, as strange and weird it was. Rob was thankful for Heather, as she was for Rob. Frank also called out his friends. Hideyoshi was grateful for being a part of something, as was Yuuki. Shou was humble; he looked forward to a new life without having to do horrible things, and he had a direction of his own now. Atsa was gracious; he thanked everyone, one by one. Bobby was Bobby and started off being thankful for his beer, but he acknowledged them all, especially his Lora. Lora made it very clear she loved all of them, but she was going to show Bobby just how much tonight. This brought laughter to the room as they continued going around, each comment getting sillier and more foolish.

They laughed and joked up into the wee hours of the morning before turning in. Fat, dumb and happy, they all eventually headed for bed.

Bobby, getting up, noticed a tube of Lora's hand cream. Picking it up, he handed it to Frank.

"You're going to need this," Bobby teased.

"You're laughing now, but it ain't a bad idea. Perfect end to a perfect night," Frank responded playfully.

"Gross, let's go to bed before that vision imprints on my brain. Come on Bobby darling, take me to bed!" Lora said.

"You heard her boys, it's Bobby time!"

Cheering him on as he scooted up the stairs after Lora, they all retired one by one.

Only a few slept that night. John spent most of the night staring at the ceiling. Partly nervous and partly excited, he kept going over the mission in his head. Daydreaming about the kids, Gloria and how they all came here, to Arizona.

Bobby slept like a log, leaving Lora to sew the flight suits. She placed a simple patch on one sleeve. It read 'S2706,' and she wanted to see if the guys knew what it meant.

Since John couldn't sleep, at sunrise he made his way to the house. He just sat beside his children, watching them sleep and waiting for the others to rise. He lovingly watched as they slumbered. Being a father made him doubt flying the aircraft. Their mother was gone and if something was to go wrong, he was worried about who would look after them. Second thoughts were running through his mind now. But would his kids understand if he pulled out of the mission? They were so proud that their dad was doing this. He was at a crossroads.

John heard someone in the hallway. It was Lora heading downstairs, so he gently closed the bedroom door and followed her.

"Good morning John. Did you sleep well?"

"Not really," he sighed.

"Uh-oh, I know that face. What's wrong?" she asked, placing a cup of coffee in front of him.

"It's nothing, I don't want to bother you with it."

"Bother me with it." She laughed. "I've lost my home, my belongings and everything I've ever had. Yet, I'm the happiest I've ever been in my entire life. I don't think there is anything you'd say that would bother me."

"I know I shouldn't think this way, but just in case something goes wrong today, terribly wrong, would you take care of the kids for me?"

Lora realized at that moment there was something that could be said that would bother her.

"John, don't talk like that. But of course I would take care of those boys, I love those boys.

But understand this, the man I love is going up there with you. You will bring him home to me."

"I know it's stupid, but I can't help but think about it."

"Don't think about it, you'll be just fine."

"Okay," John agreed as he got up and hugged her. "I'm going to go wake the others."

Before leaving the kitchen Lora stopped him.

"John," she called. "I promise you this, everything will be fine. You guys are doing something great today. And nobody can take that from you."

John gave her a smile and wink, and headed on his way to wake the others.

After breakfast, Lora had the men try on the altered flight suits before they prepared for takeoff.

Bobby emerged looking as dashing as John, finally. His suit fit, and this time, it at least zipped.

"Great job honey," he said, leaning down to give her a kiss.

"So you like?" she asked.

"Just like you, I love it."

Strutting his stuff down the center of the living room like a model on the runway in New York City, Bobby acknowledged the catcalls from his teammates as John made his way in to the room.

"Lora, what's this patch?" John asked.

"You really don't know? Think about it John."

"I get it," Rob said.

"What? I don't get it," John said.

"It's what got us here. It's the fuel samples added up." Rob pointed to the patch. "S2706!"

John glanced back down at his patch. "That's what we'll call it then. Great job Lora."

"Well boys, what time you going to fly that thing?" Garrett asked.

"We need to get the aircraft fueled up, hook the truck back up to Frank's trailer so he can fire up all his systems, and then we should be ready to take off," John answered.

"Let's get to it!" Bobby shouted.

Their brief moment of excitement turned into fear as the bell outside the house rang. Everybody was silenced as it rang again; Atsa was firing warning shots at it. This was what they all had feared. Somebody was coming.

36

Atsa watched through the scope on his rifle as a long black limousine accompanied by two black sedans barreled down the drive towards the house. He fired a final warning shot at the house, trying to alert them.

"Yep, I'd say we got company," Garrett confirmed.

"Do you think it's Tom and Jasper?" Rob asked.

"I don't know who the hell it is," Bobby answered.

"You all stay down and hide. I'll go out there and see who it is," Garrett said as he grabbed the double barrel shotgun sitting beside the door. "If something happens and shooting starts…run!"

Garrett pulled the door closed slowly behind him. He walked out on the porch with the shotgun hung over his forearm. His handkerchief in his hand, he blew his nose as he watched the caravan of vehicles stop in front of the house. He casually leaned against the porch post, waiting for someone to emerge.

A tall man with a fine suit stepped out of the limousine. Garrett watched as the outsider smiled and walked to the front of the vehicle to confront him.

"Mornin. Can I help you? You lost?" Garrett asked.

"No, I'm not lost. I believe this is exactly where I'm supposed to be," Alex Wright said, smiling smugly at Garrett.

"You sure? We don't get to many fancy suit-wearing folk out here."

The question only made Alex laugh louder.

"Holy shit, that's Alex Wright," John said as he peeked out the window.

"What the fuck is he doing here?" Bobby asked.

"I have no idea, but I bet he didn't come to offer us our jobs back."

They watched as Alex motioned towards the caravan. Tom, Jasper and about ten other men they didn't know all stepped out of the vehicles, carrying weapons.

"You boys looking to go hunting, ain't much out here but rattlesnakes," Garrett said.

"Shut up old timer, or I will put a bullet in your head. Best thing you can do to stay alive is tell John Kemp to come out here!"

"John who? Never heard of the man."

"Really? Never? I don't like being lied to," Alex said.

Garrett watched as the man quickly pulled a pistol from underneath his suit jacket, firing a single shot that lodged in the porch only inches from his foot.

Garrett didn't even flinch. He just looked down at the hole and back towards Alex Wright.

"You missed. Not much of a shot, are you? Here's what a good shot looks like." Garrett raised his hand in the air to signal Atsa.

Nothing came, so he raised his hand in the air again.

"You waiting for that Indian in the hills to shoot me?" Alex asked. "He won't be assisting you today."

Garrett started to raise his gun. His fury over what might have happened to Atsa caused him to think irrationally.

"I wouldn't do that old man, these boys will cut you down before you even fire a single shot," Alex warned him, brazenly turning his back towards Garrett. Again he laughed, as his posse now had its weapons drawn on Garrett.

Garrett hung his head in shame as he heard the door open behind him. John came out with his hands in the air.

"Don't shoot!" John called.

"Well Mr. Kemp, you are here."

"What the hell are you doing here Wright?" John asked.

"You have something that belongs to me. Well, it doesn't actually belong to me. But I'm going to take it anyway."

Garrett and John watched as two men pushed Atsa towards them. He was holding his hands behind his head; blood trickled down the side of his face. He'd obviously been hit with the butt of a rifle; they must have ambushed him.

"How'd you know we were here? How'd you know he was up there in the hills?" John asked.

"Oh John," Alex sighed. "I've known where you were the entire time, from your dinky little shack in Ohio, your adventure to the Atlantic Ocean and now to the dust bowl of a living hell!"

"But how?"

"In due time John, in due time. Now everyone in that house, come out here. Or I'll start shooting your friends one by one!"

Alex watched as they followed his commands. With an evil smile he gestured for them to step out in front of the caravan and face him.

"You see John, this is your team. Your family and your friends, but are they?"

"What are you saying?"

"You're an idiot John, to think they have your back. One of them actually works for me. You want to know how I found you, this is how I found you," Alex said.

"Somebody sold us out?" Rob asked.

"They sure did!" Alex Wright, with his smug little smile, ordered them once more. "Keep your hands on your heads. Don't anyone make another move, or these gentlemen behind me will tear you down! They'll shoot you to shreds!"

John looked at Rob, then at Bobby and Frank.

"Guys, why?"

Little John started to sway, catching Alex's attention.

"Boy," he said, leaning down to look the child in the face. "I'll kill you too, if you move again. Move one more muscle, and you're dead."

"You son of a bitch!" John yelled as he lunged at Alex, only to be knocked to the ground by a quick punch.

"God you're weak Kemp!" Alex gushed with satisfaction at seeing his nose bleed.

"John!" Lora screamed.

"Pick him up." Alex motioned to Bobby.

"Bobby, is it you?" John said, puzzling over Bobby responding to Alex's orders.

"It's not me John, I swear," Bobby whispered as he lifted him.

"Alex, we at least deserve to know who sold us out," John said in pain.

They watched as Alex Wright folded his arms, a devious smirk upon his lips, tilting his head to the side.

"You're right. It's the least I can do before I kill all of you. I mean, I did have a guy on the inside the entire time. I infiltrated your ranks, and that was the easy part. For this ruse to go on this long, why not?"

The others looked around, waiting for someone to move, anger building up from lies and betrayal.

"Oh for fuck's sake, come here Robert," Alex ordered.

"Bobby?" Lora screamed. "Why?"

"It's not me, I don't know what the hell he's talking about," Bobby confessed.

Silence fell on the ranch as the team watched Heather emerge from behind the crowd and walk towards Alex.

"Please allow me to introduce to you Robert Blair," Alex said.

"Heather?" Rob asked. Now he was confused and dazed.

The others stood just as shocked as they saw her turn and smile back at them, snootily turning her nose up towards them, listening to her sickening laugh as she stood next to Alex.

"Okay, I'm thoroughly confused now," Bobby said.

"You said a guy?" John asked again.

"She was at one time," Alex answered, mocking his question.

"Dude! You married a dude!" Bobby shouted, causing a few of the others in Alex's posse to laugh.

"Silence!" Alex screamed. "How about I kill you first, big man?"

Rushing towards Bobby he placed the gun at his forehead.

"I do not think that is wise," Shou spoke up.

Alex stepped in front of Shou; looking down at him he placed the pistol to his chest.

"You don't think it's wise, do you? Okay, I'll kill you first!"

Before anyone could blink, Shou had disarmed Alex and was now holding the pistol underneath his chin.

"No, it is not wise."

Alex's men panicked, each trying to reposition to get a shot on Shou, who had now gained the upper hand.

"You don't know who you're fucking with little man," Alex said, grimacing as Shou pressed the pistol deeper into his chin.

"No, you don't. I am Shou Shin. Third generation Yakuza, and you are threatening my family. Tell your men to lay their weapons down or I will kill all of you!"

"Don't listen to him," Alex ordered.

Shou quickly spun the larger man around, dropping him to his knees and bringing him down to size as he placed the pistol to the side of his head. With his arm wrapped around Alex's neck, he pulled back the hammer on the pistol and waited.

"I will count to one and then I will kill all of you!" Shou shouted.

John and others started backing away, not knowing if the shooting was actually going to start.

"Ready?" Shou asked.

"Drop your damn weapons!" Tom Hawkins screamed.

No one had to tell Jasper twice; he had dropped his weapon and was running back down the lane just as fast as his scrawny legs would carry him. The others laid their weapons on the ground as Atsa and Garrett started to collect them. The whole time Shou held steady with the gun pressed to Alex's head.

"What are we going to do with these guys?" Frank asked.

"Do you want me to kill them John-san?" Shou asked.

"No, we aren't killing anyone," John answered.

"I got an idea," Garrett offered.

Garrett's idea was to do the unthinkable. Shou, Atsa and himself would take the gang out to the desert, strip them naked and let them try to find their way out. No one argued with the idea, considering Alex Wright had come to kill them. Anyone who would threaten to kill a small child deserved what he got.

They set their vehicles ablaze when they dropped them off. Shou gave them one warning. If they made it out alive, don't ever return or he would kill them, and nobody would ever find the bodies.

Rob insisted on accompanying them to drop them off; he had unfinished business. Before he turned Robert Blair over to the rest of them, they had words; nobody knew what those words were, and nobody asked. The only thing that would be shared from then on out went unspoken, was that he dropped him like a sack of potatoes with a haymaker punch. He then offered to help him up and in doing so, dropped him again.

Jasper they never heard from again, nor did they give chase. The opinion was he wouldn't fare too well hitchhiking; he was a tender boy to start with. They were certain life would deal with him, hoping he hitched a ride with the wrong trucker.

With the first day of testing now ruined, they had to regroup and re-plan. It's not everyday someone actually comes to take your life. It made them all realize what they invented would bring others calling.

Yes, originally Alex Wright wanted sustainability, which was a pipedream at best, but the diamond, this was alternative energy that used man's life source and the most abundant compound on earth, water. Every government in the world would want this technology, being capable to power cities on a few hundred gallons a year, and yet they haven't learned its full capabilities. Secrecy was now crucial. Maybe they shouldn't have let Alex and the others go, but nothing is worth the loss of a human life.

37

"Okay, we have satellite and ground capabilities. We are ready for ignition," Frank said.

"Wait a second, we don't have satellites," John said over his headset intercom.

"We sort of do. Hideyoshi and Yuuki hacked into the Air Forces'. They technically don't know we are there, we are just piggy backing."

"Frank, you sure that's a good idea?" Bobby asked.

"Don't worry boys, they'll never know we're there. And if they see you, we'll know they are coming, and we can get you down quick as possible."

"I'm trusting you on this Frank," John said.

"And you should. Have I ever let you down before?"

"Yes Frank you have, should we start counting off how many times?"

"No you don't." Frank laughed. "Just sit back, relax, and enjoy the ride."

They pulled the aircraft out behind the barn in which it had been built. It was the only flat spot far enough away from the house that it wouldn't cause any damage if things went wrong.

"Okay boys, the plan is to do a small altitude test, twenty feet up. We'll go a bit higher if that works out okay. Then we'll let you try to navigate around the valley for a few and eventually work on a landing."

"And if doesn't work out?" John asked.

"We'll switch controls back to down here and Shou can land it remotely."

"Won't that crash us?"

"Only if we try and calibrate, switching to remote, you should be okay," Frank said.

"Let's stop using the word should," Bobby said.

"Okay, okay, no problem."

John spoke to Bobby off radio. "You ready to do this Bobby?"

"Too late to turn back now, just don't kill us John. Just don't kill us."

"I'll do my best." John flipped the switch back on to speak with Frank. "Okay, we're ready."

"Roger that, I'll be Control. You'll be Lucy, just in case somebody is listening, copy?"

"Copy."

"Lucy you're go for ignition in three...two...one....mark!"

John started flipping the switches up on the panel to his left, the bottom eight turbines roaring to life. The others just sat dormant.

"Control, I've only got eight functioning," John said.

"You're okay Lucy, the others will respond when you call on them by using your other controls. You're okay to lift. Pull slightly back on the joystick until you feel lift."

"Copy," John said, pulling back on the left joystick.

The turbines were kicking up dust. The team watched as dirt billowed out from underneath the craft.

John and Bobby could both feel the craft teeter back and forth on the three skis. John pulled back more as the craft started to lift off the ground. Leaning to its left, John used the joystick on his right to correct it.

"Whoa, she's bit touchy!" John shouted nervously. "Or sluggish, I don't really know what I'm feeling right now."

"Want to set her back down and calibrate some of that play out of it?" Frank asked.

"No, it could be just me, let me take her a bit higher and see if I can get a feel for her."

"Roger that Lucy. Watch the screen between your legs for roll, pitch and yaw. Take her on up to ten feet."

"Copy," John answered as he increased the lift. Slowly they watched as it climbed and the craft became more unstable. John quickly lowered the altitude until the aircraft was back on the pad.

"Shut her down," Frank said. "What's the problem, what are you experiencing?"

"It's sluggish, it's not responding in time. There's a hesitation in the controls."

"Copy that, shut down the turbines and leave the battery on, I'll add ten percent more control."

John flipped the switches off as Bobby wiped the sweat away from his eyes.

"Hey Frank?" Bobby called.

"Control...Control...Control...don't out me!"

"Whatever. It's ten degrees cooler in hell than in here. Can we get someone to open the hatch and get some fresh air while you calibrate this thing?"

"Control to Shrek, you're sitting in the navigator seat, look up at the panel to your left. Did you turn on the cooling system?"

"No I didn't, and if you call me Shrek, does that make you my jackass?"

"Negative, and that would be Donkey. Watch the movie!"

"I did watch the movie, and you're still a jackass!"

"Chill out boys, get this thing calibrated and let's go again," John said.

Hideyoshi ran the program, adding ten percent while John and Bobby waited, finally getting cool air in the hot compartment.

"While we're doing that, what do you guys want your call signs to be?" Frank asked.

John didn't wait long to answer. "I like Big Daddy and Jethro!"

"Let me guess who Jethro is?" Bobby asked.

"That'd be you, big boy. Hey, are we ready yet Control?"

Hideyoshi gave the thumbs up.

"You are now, kill the battery and count to fifteen and re-fire. It will reboot your onboard computer with the new settings in place."

John flipped the switches, waited and fired it back up.

"Control, we got power, firing turbines."

"Roger that. Proceed on your own mark. Jethro, watch all your gauges, you got temps, fuel levels and of course those creature comforts."

John increased the power, lifting the craft off the ground. This time he had responsiveness. It took a few moves of the joystick to get a feel for how quickly they responded. The others watched as the craft steadily climbed; this time she wasn't swaying as much. The calibration must have solved the teetering issues.

"All right Lucy, how does she feel?"

"Much better Control, taking her up to twenty feet."

"Copy that, proceed."

John pulled back on the joystick too hard, and the aircraft started flying upward past twenty feet. Nervousness took over, and John completely let go of the joystick as she leveled out at fifty feet.

"Okay Lucy that's okay, get a feel for it. Letting go of the stick won't send you crashing down. But it will level you off due to a built-in safety. Play with it, and you'll feel a click about one quarter's throttle. The computer kicks in and helps maintain altitude."

"Will the computer help change my shorts?" John asked.

"We could see about adding that. Not sure we have the technology, but we'll see." Frank chuckled in the headset microphone. "Let's do some turns, right and then left."

"Copy, I'm on it," John said, calming down as he began spinning the aircraft.

"John, this is a bad time to tell you, I hate the teacup rides at the amusement park, I throw up every time!"

"Sorry buddy," John said. "Okay Control, going to take it around the valley."

"Copy that, now don't get too high. Davis-Monthan Air Force base is northwest of our location. You get too high and you'll come up on their radar. And trust me, they will come and pay us a little visit."

"That wouldn't be good," John replied.

John turned the aircraft right as it hovered over the pad. Slowly he pressed the right pedal, pulling back on the right joystick to keep the nose up. The aircraft started taking off towards the hills in Atsa's direction. John could see Atsa waving from outside the cockpit window.

The others watched as John flew the craft from side to side in the valley, watching as he became more confident in his ability to control it. From each end he would accelerate and stop and turn and head back the other way, each time getting faster.

"Control, I think I have the hang of this," John said proudly, with a big old grin on his face.

"Roger that. How's your readings Lucy?"

"Everything's good. Very little water use, temps look great," Bobby said.

"Think I'm going to really take her for a spin," John said.

"Negative Big Daddy, we don't have a chase vehicle. If something should happen it would take some time to get to you for a rescue."

"We'll be fine, see you in a few."

Ignoring the response, John took off, climbing the hill south of the ranch past Atsa's location. He could hear Bobby behind him wheeze and grunt every time he banked the vehicle. Amused with Bobby, John picked up even more speed. Forgetting the altitude rule, John tilted the nose up and took off up into the sky.

"Control to Lucy!"

"Go ahead Control," John said. "This is one fun ride!"

"Fun's about to stop, we got traffic that you've been spotted as an unidentified flying object. Not to mention you just crossed into Mexico, and that's an illegal border crossing to boot!"

"What do we do?" Bobby asked.

"Get low and get back here before they get to you!"

"I'm on it," John said.

"Good job John, first flight and they think the aliens have landed," Bobby said.

"Yeah, I got a little carried away."

John turned the vehicle and set course back towards the ranch. What he didn't know was the Air Force had already launched and was heading his way. And they were coming fast.

"Lucy you got visitors approaching, they just flew over us!"

"Shit!" John shouted. "What do we do now, I can't fly by them!"

"Lucy this is Grasshopper, put your masks on."

"Who? Who the hell is Grasshopper?"

"That's Shou," Bobby pointed out.

"Put your masks on, turn on the oxygen system. You'll need to run!"

John could see two planes approaching, too far yet to make out, but he didn't wait around to see. Banking right, he lifted the aircraft and smashed the pedal. Both men were tightly pulled back into their seats as the G-forces started to weigh on them.

"Lucy you have two F-16 Fighting Falcons on your ass, those things are supersonic. I don't think you'll outrun them!" Frank shouted across the radio.

"Don't know unless we try," John responded. "Hang on Bobby!"

Considering John started at such a slow speed the Falcons were gaining on them. The more the G-forces pulled on them, the more tempting it was for John to take his foot off the accelerator. But he wouldn't; he fought through it and continued accelerating.

"They're still closing, you'd better move it!" Frank said.

"We're gaining speed," John said, grimacing.

The view from the cockpit wouldn't allow John to look behind him and see the other two planes. What he didn't realize was, not only was he accelerating, but he was climbing as well.

Instead of watching his monitors he kept his eyes fixed out through the window.

"I think I'm going to puke John!"

"Hang on Bobby, hang on!"

John pressed the pedal as far down as he could, sending all the power to the rear turbines. Not being an experienced pilot he didn't realize how fast he was going until Frank came back across the radio. His communication was broken up.

"You're supersonic!" Frank screamed. "But so are they!"

Hardly making out what Frank had said, John didn't let up. The aircraft was now approaching forty thousand feet and was close to breaking Mach two.

"Lucy you're losing them, back it off!" Frank pleaded.

John watched as a commercial airliner flew below them, passing by like it was standing still, just sitting there like it was floating in air. Looking down at his monitor he realized that he was sixty-two thousand feet. He released his pressure on the pedal.

"Bobby look at this!" Bobby didn't respond; he had passed out long ago from the G-forces. "Bobby?" John heard nothing. "Bobby! Lucy to Control, Bobby's passed out. Are they still chasing me?"

"Lucy they've turned back. But look at your GPS."

John looked down to find that he was halfway across the Atlantic Ocean.

"What the hell happened?" Bobby said groggily.

John started to descend the aircraft before answering. He also had to turn it back in the right direction. Fear had taken over, and he had taken them somewhere they had no business being.

"You were just taking a nap, the excitement wasn't enough to keep you awake, big man."

"Damn, I feel dizzy," Bobby said as he tried to adjust his weary eyes, still overcome from passing out. "Where are we?" Looking out the window all he could see was water as they broke through the clouds.

"Control, how do we get back home?" John asked.

"Get to about five thousand feet, set your altitude. Set course for the Gulf of Mexico, somewhere in the middle of it. I'll get you a course home, standby."

"Roger that Control."

John had to take the long way around to get home, zipping across Florida and hitting altitudes as low as five hundred feet at times. Frank had plotted a course that should keep them off of the radar, but made them an easy target for anyone looking up. He had them enter through Mexico and work their way up back to Arizona, trying to avoid any major towns or cities. What should have been a simple test flight turned into a six-hour joy ride. And they still had to land, something they haven't done yet.

Luckily John had a better feel for the aircraft, and although he didn't get her to land exactly where he wanted to, he got her down safely.

As they exited the aircraft they could hear the cheers from their team. Not sure he was due a hero's welcome, John wasn't sure how to accept the praise.

"Oh my freaking God!" Frank said. "Do you know how fast you were going?"

"Not really." John shrugged him off.

"Dude, you almost hit Mach three. Only a Blackbird has done Mach three point three!"

"We wouldn't have done it in the first place if I wasn't being such an idiot."

"John don't beat yourself up, for a first test flight…wow…you just outran two F-16's…Fighting…Freaking…Falcons!"

"Sorry Frank, I'm just mad at myself," John responded sadly as he removed his flight gear.

"Don't be mad at yourself, that was simply freaking amazing!"

John noticed Shou standing by the craft, hands on his hips and shaking his head as he inspected the aircraft.

"What's wrong Shou?" John asked.

Turning to look at John, "We didn't have the right material to fly at that speed. It's charred," he said, pointing at the wing's edge. "Any faster the friction would have torn you apart."

"Holy shit, would you look at that," Rob said.

"What?" Bobby asked.

Rob was looking at the front turbines. They all gathered around him to see the damage. All three turbines were ruined. It was why John couldn't set the aircraft down where he wanted.

"They couldn't handle the speed either, airflow going back up into them may have torn them apart, or you hit something. Possibly a bird?"

"You can still land it and slow it down by pitching the nose up. We won't need the front turbines. But we will need some sort of heat shield and protection from the friction. I will look for something," Shou offered.

"Not tonight you won't. Whether anyone likes it or not, this test was a success," Frank said. "So what do we do after we have a success?"

"We party," Rob answered.

"Exactly," John said, finally smiling.

"I'll party after I go puke," Bobby butted in.

"Poor little guy," Frank kidded. "Would some greasy pork chops fried in lard settle that stomach? I know how about some oysters...raw, can you feel them sliding down your throat?"

"Oh God no," Bobby said, turning greener. "Frank when I get back you better not be anywhere around here. If I catch you, I'm going to spit in your ass and wear you like a boot!"

"Oh be nice. Come here, let Momma take care of you," Lora said as she grabbed Bobby's arm and started pulling him towards the house.

"That's right, go with Momma," Frank teased.

After a somewhat successful test flight, they celebrated. Frank made it safely through the night as Bobby eventually let him off the hook; he was in no shape to rough anyone up. Garrett broke out the good stuff for them to enjoy, all except Rob. He was still embarrassed; it was hard for him to face the guys knowing that he had been duped by Alex Wright's plan. He started becoming a recluse, even though they all had been duped. But they survived, and he needed something to pull him out of his funk.

38

"You have to come out here and hear this," Bobby said to Lora.

Due to his stomach not feeling right, Bobby had chosen wisely not to participate too long in the festivities. He, and only a few others, actually found their beds that night. Pulling Lora on to the front porch, he wanted her to hear the imitation thunderstorm that was rolling across the desert valley.

"Oh, this is priceless," she whispered.

With the exception of Rob and Shou, the rest of the men were fast asleep on the porch. The symphony of snores echoing off the desert hills livened up that old valley. Garrett, tucked into his ragged old recliner, conducted that little symphony. One by one, each would snore at a different time.

"I should record this, this is a great blackmail opportunity," Bobby said as he pulled his cell phone out of his pocket. "And…I think I will."

Lora retreated to the kitchen to retrieve a pot and a wooden spoon. As she returned she motioned for Bobby to go ring the bell. He counted down with his fingers, three, two and one, and they both started making a god-awful racket that scared the other men back to life.

"Good morning sunshine!" Bobby yelled. "How're your heads?"

"Now who wants a greasy pork chop?" Lora asked.

Standing back and laughing as the others looked startled and befuddled, they watched as Frank smacked the roof of his mouth like a cow chewing its cud.

"Are you looking for that cat, Frank?" Bobby asked.

"What cat?"

"The one that shit in your mouth." Bobby gave the bell another few rings, only to be pelted with empty beer cans.

Atsa pulled in front of the house, arriving for his daily watch. Sitting in the jeep he looked over the carnage on the front porch.

"Luckily there were no more visitors last night, I see."

"Nope Atsa, only visitor here was the Grim Reaper. Said he wouldn't take this one, he's pickled," Bobby said pointing at his Uncle, who was still asleep and unfazed by the commotion.

Atsa raised his rifle and fired it into the air. The old man sprang to life for a few seconds to look around; seeing no signs of trouble he closed his eyes and drifted back off to sleep.

"I'm going to get started on breakfast. You boys really need to go clean up before you come in here and sit at my table," Lora said. "Don't come in here smelling like a brewery."

"Yes ma'am," John huffed. "As soon as I can feel my legs, I'll do just that."

Breakfast was quiet. There was no talk of flying, diamonds or great escapes. Does anyone really know why one night of celebration leads to a morning of misery?

Garrett finally joined them, stumbling through the door and plopping down in his usual seat at the head of the table. Fumbling to grab at the silverware in front of him, he started to load his plate full from what was left over, which was a lot, as the rest seemed to be eating light this morning. Much to Lora's surprise, the old man motioned for her to retrieve his bottle, but she did so at his request. With a quick draw off the end and a scowl upon his face, he slammed the bottle back down on the table. The others shuddered from the sound of the thud, as if a little man were pounding a hammer inside each of their heads.

"Do you have to be so loud?" John asked.

The old man leaned back in his chair. Pushing himself back with both arms against the table, he stared down his nose, looking underneath his spectacles, and answered, "Damn rookies! Can't hold your liquor!"

"We held it just fine," John responded in a raspy voice.

"Okay then, why do your eyes look like two pissholes in the snow this morning?" Garrett teased.

John didn't even bother to respond; he just folded his arms on the table and buried his head. He was in no mood to trade insults with the old man this morning.

Breakfast was finished and the kids were off to play. The men all went in different directions. It didn't seem like there was going to be any work accomplished today. Shou insisted that Hideyoshi at least search for the items that he needed before he let him heal any further. Bobby resorted to setting up a plan all by himself, without acknowledgment or approval from the rest of the group.

Bobby took a stroll up into the hills to meet with Atsa. After the week's events he wasn't so keen on letting things lie. If he had his way, Alex Wright and his posse would have been dealt with differently. He was certain they weren't going to give up.

"Good morning Atsa, care if I sit with you?"

"Not at all, it would be nice to have some company." Atsa offered the rock to his left, which Bobby took obligingly.

"Let me ask you a question, because I'm not so sure about it. Do you think those guys will come back again?" Bobby asked. "Do you think they'll try to come back and take everything, and try to kill us?"

"Yes I do. We were lucky it turned out like it did."

"So what do you think we should do?"

Atsa pondered the question for a few seconds before breaking his silence.

"We need to man a perimeter, we need more security and we need more guns."

"That's easier said than done. Besides you and Shou, the rest of us aren't fighters. I don't think Frank has ever fired a weapon and Rob has no business with a gun after finding out about Heather."

"Would you like me to arrange something?" Atsa asked.

"What do you have in mind?"

In all honesty the plan Atsa hashed out was a pretty good one. Who knew the hills and area better than his people? Members of his tribe who were also ex-military and didn't want to work in one of casinos or take some mediocre job, they were looking for decent work. In Atsa's mind, if there was an acceptable wage negotiated he could convince them to cover the ranch. Bobby agreed without negotiating or even consulting the others.

"It's a deal. We should do it immediately."

With Bobby taking over for Atsa on the hill, he was off to find help. He didn't even think about people tracking Hideyoshi's moves. How was he going to pay for this new security team?

The rest of the team would awake mid-afternoon from their naps. They all gathered back on the porch where they found Bobby sitting, grinning as if he was the cat who ate the canary.

"What are you so happy about?" Frank asked.

"Let me show you boys," Bobby answered proudly.

Reaching down by his chair, he pulled up a garbage sack. Standing up with bag in hand, he took off towards the barn. Looking around as if he was measuring distances, he started placing empty cans on the ground. Stepping back ten feet, he studied his work. He looked up at each hill surrounding the ranch, confirming a clear angle. The others had no idea what he was doing; some thought he was losing his mind. They continued watching as he returned to the porch.

"Gentlemen, what happens if Alex Wright returns?" Bobby asked, his chest puffed out.

"I don't know, I guess we need to be better prepared," John answered.

"Damn right we do. Let me show you what happens if he returns!"

Bobby casually pranced towards the bell, grasping the clapper. "Are you ready?"

"Ready for what?" Rob asked.

As soon as Bobby rang the bell, gunfire erupted immediately. Cans flew everywhere as the men all dove for cover. Shot after shot, the cans were torn to shreds as Bobby stood there cackling at its magnificence.

"What the hell was that?" John screamed.

"That, my friend, is our new security team. Come here and take a look at this," Bobby said. Waving his hand, he encouraged the rest to follow him. He walked out to where the cans used to be. "Don't be scared, come on."

The others, timid and confused, eventually followed.

Looking up to the hills around them, Bobby suggested they do the same. Men started appearing from behind rocks, showing their hiding places, each with a rifle on his hip and standing proud.

"Who the hell are these guys?" Frank asked.

They all took notice as Atsa appeared from behind the barn, walking towards them.

"Atsa?" Garrett asked.

"This is your new security force. These are my people."

"I hired them this morning," Bobby said.

"You did what?" John said, turning to Bobby with an astonished look on his face.

"Yep, hired them this morning. Anyone else wants to stop by, we have a little surprise for them," Bobby said as he smiled over at Atsa.

"How you going to pay them Bobby?"

"Have Hideyoshi make them a card."

"And what, get them tracked back to their homes? Put their families in danger?" John asked angrily.

"We could get a cash advance off one card I guess, maybe pay them that way…or…I, I, I, really didn't think about that John," Bobby stuttered.

"Bobby, there's got to be twenty guys up there. Nobody gives that big of a cash advance," John said firmly, standing with his hands on his hips, looking the big man in the eye. "I understand what you were thinking and trying to do, but you didn't think this fully through."

"I'm sorry John, I was just trying to help," Bobby pleaded.

"I don't know how we're going to pay these guys Atsa," John said.

"Should I tell them to go home?" Atsa asked.

In John's mind he was trying to figure out a way to make it work; he didn't want to say yes. They had been lucky so far, and some more people looking after them would be a good idea.

But not paying men with guns and mouths to feed could be a disaster.

"John-san, if I may interrupt," Shou said, stepping up to him. "I have an idea. I may be able to pay them."

"How's that?"

"In my business, in order to protect our assets, we started fake companies to hide money. I would need to move one of those accounts here, it will take some time, but they will be paid if they are willing to wait."

"Atsa, what do you think?" John asked.

"I will go ask them John. Give me a few minutes to discuss it with them. How long would it take?"

"Two weeks' time," Shou answered.

Standing by waiting for Atsa to return, they watched as he made his way around the valley. Bobby was still apologizing, but John wanted no part of it. Part of him realized there was nothing to be sorry for, he had good intentions, but he should have consulted the group.

"Okay John, they will wait and work. But they want more money."

"How much more?"

"Four hundred a week," Atsa answered.

"Shou?" John needed confirmation.

"That will be fine John-san."

"Okay Atsa, they have a deal," John said, shaking hands with him. "First things first, order them to shoot Bobby."

They watched as Bobby's face turned white.

"I'm kidding, of course. Let's all go get cleaned up. Then we can go around and meet everybody."

"Then can we have them shoot Bobby?" Frank said.

39

Hideyoshi hooked back up with the company that he used to purchase the original heat shield for the car. They all hoped that with such a large order, they wouldn't contact the authorities. Shou had him make another purchase from a tech company that manufactured what was called Buckypaper, an experimental thin sheet of carbon nanotubes. It was one-tenth the weight of steel but five hundred times stronger.

With heat shields they could go faster, and if they were capable of making space flight, they would be protected reentering the earth's atmosphere. They knew if they actually made it to space, radiation would be a risk. With a one-inch titanium alloy shell, they needed to make up another two inches of protection to shield them from all radiation. Shou's theory was to use a one-inch plastic filler against the shell with a covering of the Buckypaper, and then apply another layer, creating a little over three inches of protection. It snugged up the cockpit, which was a tight fit to start with. They guys would have to make it work.

"What are you guys doing?" John asked.

"Insulating and installing thermal heaters to the water lines," Bobby answered.

"Won't the heat make the water evaporate?"

"We won't get it that hot John-san." Shou laughed. "The higher you go, the colder it will be. In parts of space, it could be very cold."

"Around negative four hundred and fifty five degrees," Bobby pointed out.

"That would suck," John said.

"At seventy thousand feet John-san, it should be around negative sixty-nine degrees. If your water lines freeze up, you will drop like a stone, crashing before they unthaw."

"Continue on and sorry I asked. Please, don't let me get in your way," John said, grinning.

"I knew he'd see it our way. Hand me the Elmer's glue," Bobby said to Shou.

"Elmer's?" John blurted.

"Just joking John, just joking."

It was getting close to the next test flight. Issues from the first test flight were almost resolved, except nobody knew how to hide. They were going to show up on radar again eventually. And what if another country saw them? They didn't want to cause an international incident or possibly start a war. It was still risky.

Lora assisted in suiting John and Bobby up. This time they were wearing G-suits. The plan was to try and keep Bobby from blacking out. It also allowed them to wear a full helmet. And of course Bobby's had to be modified to fit, again.

"Okay boys, see if your visors work. This will allow you to block any sunrays that might hurt your eyes. Of course the cockpit windows are shielded. But hey, it's better to be safe than sorry."

"Mine works fine," John said.

"Mine too, but it's getting harder to breath in this suit," Bobby said.

"Turn on the oxygen Jethro."

Leaning over Frank's shoulder, Garrett said, "You'd think that jack wagon would remember that from the first time."

"You'd think."

Whispering in Little John's ear, Frank encouraged him to speak on the mic.

"You're go for off-take Daddy! I mean take-off!"

"Roger that Control," John said, giggling.

Frank handing the headset to Thomas, and he sent them on their way.

"In three...two...one...kick it!"

John flipped the switches as the new-looking aircraft came to life. If the aircraft didn't look like an unidentified flying object before, it did now. The new heat shield was a unique design, polygon-shaped with a bright green stripe around the edges of each panel. The panels were roughly six inches wide by six inches tall. If anything, with the green accents, black skin and now the blue flames, she was pretty.

John lifted the aircraft off the pad to the amazement of their new security team, who had never seen her before. They were a proud people, and now they were even prouder to see what they were protecting.

"What's our course Control?"

"Head south, take her back to the Gulf. Stay around five hundred or so feet and for God's sake, try and keep her off radar this time."

"Roger that, and will do."

John banked to his right and gave Lucy a little throttle. Picking up altitude, he did his best to stay closer to the hills than before.

"Okay, we are at four hundred knots. How do I get this to read miles per hour again Control?"

"Look at your panel, bottom right, second button from the bottom. So you're at four hundred sixty miles an hour. Little fast for canyon flying don't you think?"

"Hard to tell, other than Jethro back there praying, I couldn't tell."

"Might want to slow her down."

"She's handling like a dream, I think we'll be okay Control."

"Then proceed on."

Thomas inserted a disc in Hideyoshi's laptop. He urged Frank to key the mic.

"Hey, is that what I think it is?" Bobby asked.

"And I blame you for it Bobby," John laughed as he responded.

"'Down around the corner, half a mile from here,'" Bobby started singing.

"Bobby!"

"Yes Big Daddy," he answered sarcastically.

"Let's let the Doobie Brothers sing this one."

Wasn't nothing wrong with a little accompanying music for their journey, other than it made John go a little faster and bank a little harder. Who would object? Other than Bobby, who didn't care for it at all.

John passed over into Mexico and set course towards the center of the Gulf. Once they were over water, John got a little braver and stepped on it.

"Control to Lucy, come in."

"Go ahead Control."

"We may be experiencing a malfunction. Our readings indicate you're only ten feet off the surface and you aren't moving."

"Negative Control, you are not experiencing a malfunction."

"Could you clarify what's happening Lucy?"

"We're watching dolphins Control." John burst out laughing.

"Dolphins?" Frank asked before realizing. He turned back to face everyone else in the trailer. "They're watching dolphins. Now that's fucking cool!

When they reached their destination, John noticed the dolphins swimming and took her down for a closer look.

"Okay Lucy, if you're done sightseeing, you want to take her up, and see what's she got?"

"Just tell me what you want Control."

"Air-traffic will be around thirty to forty-five thousand feet. Climb to sixty-five thousand feet, and you should be clear at that altitude."

"Roger that."

"And this time please watch your controls. They will let you know if something is in your airspace."

John pulled back on the left joystick, raising the altitude. When he hit one thousand feet, he mashed the right pedal and brought the nose up, sending Lucy into a steep climb. It only took a matter of seconds to achieve his targeted altitude.

"All right Control, we are here, we need to get out of here too. We're sitting over Miami, Florida!"

"Copy that Lucy, let's take our time with this one. No need to do it like last time."

"Do you want Mach three?"

"Lucy, the question is, do you want Mach three?"

Turning to Bobby, John asked, "What you think Bobby?"

He wasn't going to say no, but he wasn't happy about it either. He was still trying to settle his stomach from the climb.

"I guess so…fuck it…let's do it," he answered, about as unexcited as anyone could get. He sounded pitiful.

"Do it now Lucy, you're on radar for sure."

John took off east, not adhering to the request to build up to it. He gave her hell and quickly broke the sound barrier. He wanted the record; he wanted to go faster than a Blackbird. He watched closely as the speed quickly ticked off numbers on his monitor.

"Bobby, you doing okay back there?"

"Yeah, I'm getting bored. When you going to fly this thing?" Bobby said, putting on a front. He didn't want to admit he was scared shitless.

"You got it!"

John again pressed the pedal down as far as it would go. They were now zipping across the sky at unbelievable speeds.

"Control to Lucy."

"Go ahead Control."

"Keep your altitude, you're losing it."

John had been watching speed and speed only. Hitting something at this speed would be a disaster. He was able to make the adjustments unfazed. He would need to get better at his avionics or there would be a disaster.

"Mach two!"

"Go get it Lucy!" Frank shouted through the microphone.

The others watched on the screen as the blip on the radar, which was Lucy, was crossing Africa and entering the air above the Indian Ocean. Everyone cheered for John to go faster.

"Mach three!" John screamed.

"Get that point three and slow this fucking thing down!" Bobby screamed back.

Water and real estate were passing by so quickly underneath them, Bobby tried to focus on something towards the horizon. But things were moving so quickly.

"Point three!"

John wouldn't let up.

"Point four!"

"Point five!"

"Holy shit John!" Bobby screamed.

"Point eight!"

"Mach four!" John happily shouted before letting off the throttle.

Cheers rang out in the small trailer as they celebrated with John. They had just become the fastest aircraft in the world. The sad part was they thought they were the only ones who knew about it. They were wrong.

"Lucy, Lucy, Lucy…come in!"

"Go ahead Control," John said, his chest still heaving from the excitement.

"You've been up for a while now, congrats on Mach four, but now everyone knows you're up there. You better turn around and head back."

"I'm on it."

"Let's do it on the way back Bobby."

"You have to be kidding me?"

"I'll slow down when we hit the gulf. Just for you!" John smirked.

Bobby didn't share John's enthusiasm. At first he was excited to go to space, but now he wasn't so sure. The aircraft rattling freaked him out, and the speed terrified him. The Blackbird was said to have traveled the distance from New York to Los Angeles in about sixty-seven minutes. Lucy was faster, but how much faster? John had let off at Mach four. If they were going to try for space, Lucy would be going a lot faster, and Bobby would have to *nut up,* if he was going to complete the dream he and John both wanted to share.

40

After dinner, they decided to gather outside around the fire pit. It was a clear night with a beautiful full moon. The stars were impressive as they sparkled against the dark of night. The gathering was to discuss the success of the recent mission and what the current possibilities might be.

"Lady and gentlemen," Frank started off. "We hit Mach four today, congratulations to everyone."

"Thank you, thank you, no autographs please," Bobby jested.

"Autographs for puking," John said.

"Don't you pick on my baby," Lora said, coming to his defense. She attempted to wrap her tiny arms around the giant as the others continued teasing him.

"Anyway, Shou and I've been going over the numbers. It should be known that you only used forty percent of your available throttle."

"So what are you saying Frank?" John asked.

"I'm getting to that point John. Just hear me out?"

"Roger that, jackass," Bobby said, winking at Frank.

"Listen, unlike a conventional aircraft that uses air intakes, Lucy doesn't do that. She's a flying rocket. There is no air to suck in, heat up and exhaust. She just creates exhaust."

"Am I the only one lost? Or does everybody get this?" Rob said.

"The Blackbird could hit speeds of over Mach three. We did Mach four. Lucy is the fastest manned aircraft to have accomplished this. We know about it, well, so does of the rest of the world now. They just don't know it's us, they think it might be alien or some sort of weird missile test."

"Get to the point Frank," John demanded.

"I'm trying, but you assholes keep interrupting me." Frank took a more firm position, his hands flying about as he spoke. "Lockheed has supposedly revealed that they have an unmanned vehicle, called a scramjet spy plane, that can reach Mach six. Just a little over forty-five thousand miles per hour. That's hypersonic if you didn't know."

"So what were we doing today, flying gin and tonic?" Bobby spouted off again.

"No, you were supersonic, you big dick!"

"Bobby behave," Lora said, smacking his leg. "Go on Frank, he's just being silly."

"Shou and I both believe that you guys can hit Mach seven in a manned aircraft. We believe this technology, being the first of its kind, is the missing key to a manned craft achieving these speeds."

"Let me say this, the recalibration gave me the right amount of throttle so that I didn't break our necks or kill us both," John said, leaning on the edge of his chair. "You want to give me more throttle? Knowing that force will cause both of us to black out? So that we can crash and die? Is that what I'm hearing?"

"It would only be to your rear turbines John-san," Shou spoke up.

"And how would I slow Lucy down? Remember, there are no front turbines now."

"John-san, you would be flying at seventy-two thousand feet. You would pitch the nose up to ninety degrees and fire your bottom thrusters."

"What if I freak out and stomp the pedal again? Wouldn't I be heading to space?"

"I don't like the idea of this John," Bobby stated firmly.

"Me either Bobby. Hang on here a minute guys. At those speeds, where would that put us? I mean, we've already been to Africa and back!"

"At that altitude and that speed, if you could sustain it, you would circle the earth in three to four hours," Frank said nervously.

"Look at it this way," Shou said. "The space shuttle travels at over seventeen thousand miles per hour just to leave earth. This would be a perfect test. However, they waste most of their fuel to do so. If we give you one hundred percent of your capabilities you will be much faster. I would recommend that you attempt this feat."

"Bobby, what do you think?" John asked.

"I think I'm scared shitless! That's a lot to manage inside the cockpit. I mean, this is ridiculous, we've had two test flights and you guys want to go breaking more world records!"

"John-san, if you would give me the honor. I'd like to be the pilot to test Mach five. If I return safely, would you consider going for Mach seven?"

"Who's going to be your co-pilot Shou?" John asked.

"Well, I hate to fly, but I guess it's my turn," Rob said stepping up beside Shou.

"You guys are fucking nuts," Bobby said.

"Well honey, if Rob or anyone else didn't step up, I was going to," Lora said. "But expectant mothers shouldn't be test flying."

As the men continued arguing amongst themselves, they didn't even realize what Lora just said. She turned towards Garrett with an astonished look upon her face. He was in on the news, which somehow in the heat of the moment went unnoticed.

Clearing his throat, raising from his chair and standing by the fire, Garrett cleared his throat again, trying to get the feuding bunch to pay attention.

"Stop it you bunch of ninnies!" Garrett screamed. "Didn't any of you meatheads hear what that little woman just said?"

John was the first to speak, "Yeah, she's expecting a baby." Turning back towards Frank, he continued to argue before catching himself. "How do you expect me to kill anyone here? Really how do...wait...baby?"

Bobby dropped to his knees in front of Lora, tears welling up in his eyes. He reached out and took her hands.

"We...you...we're having a baby?" he asked tenderly.

"Yes you big dope, you're going to be a daddy!" Lora said, hugging the now-gentle giant.

"But how?" he muttered.

"I may have married a man by accident, but at least I know how to make a baby. Do we need to have that birds and bees talk Bobby?" Rob said.

Lora, laughing at Rob's joke, motioned for him to join and then the others. They stood by the fire in a group hug. She was even able to persuade Garrett to join.

"When did you find out, baby?" Bobby asked. He wasn't letting go of her. Her feet dangled high above the ground. "Oh my god, we've tried for like twenty years, this is wonderful."

"Put me down and I'll tell you," she gasped. Bobby's grip was a little tight around her tiny frame. But in the big guy's defense, he was excited.

"The other morning I wasn't feeling well. I took Garrett a cup of coffee out on the porch and sat with him. He noticed I wasn't feeling well, said I looked like I had the morning sickness."

"She didn't look well at all, while you boys were out there tinkering around with that toy. We took a little ride into town to get one of those pee sticks."

"Pregnancy test," Lora corrected him.

"Whatever. She peed on that thing right there in the store."

"I was in the bathroom, oh my god," she said, slightly embarrassed.

"I'll never forget the look on her face when she finally got back to the truck. It was like she had seen a ghost." The old man started laughing.

"So Garrett took me to the nearest doctor, and sure enough, you're going to be a daddy!"

They weren't flying Lucy, there were no G-forces, but Bobby was out again. He collapsed right there next to Lora's chair, sawing logs.

"He's out again!" John hollered.

Garrett came to the rescue. He stood over Bobby and emptied the contents of his beer can on the ginormous new daddy.

As he came to, wiping the beer from his face, he looked up to see Garrett standing over him and Lora looking down at him.

Smiling back up at Lora he said, "I'm going to be a daddy. I love you baby."

"I love you too," she said, smiling back warmly.

"Love her later you big blue ox, you still owe me for the doctor's visit. And no, I don't accept bad checks."

"Be nice Garrett," Lora said playfully to the ornery old man.

"Come on boys, let's go to the house to get more beer, and let these two lovebirds be alone!"

41

Frank and Hideyoshi worked countless hours reprogramming the computer systems. Shou checked the craft time after time for any damage done from previous flights; he was obsessively thorough.

Even though he would break any record ever placed, part of him knew it wouldn't last long, as the plan was to have John break his.

They both surfaced from the trailer where they suited up. There was no time to wait for suits that fit. Shou would take John's and Rob would try to take Bobby's. Shou walked out, his suit a little baggy. But Rob, he walked out looking like he was wearing a green tarp held together with a few extra belts. His suit legs were tucked and bunched into his boots; he looked like he was working for the Royal Canadian Mounted Police.

To the sounds of flirty whistling and perverted catcalls, they made their way past the barn to Lucy.

"Are we sure Rob's suit's going to hold air?" John asked.

"Yes John-san, we took precautions."

"What precautions?"

"We used duct tape John-san."

"Oh boy. Good luck gentlemen, see you when you return."

John watched as the men fought to enter Lucy, Rob fighting with the excess material on his suit as it hung up on the hatch. He had to wait a few seconds before he could even close it.

"Are you guys on yet?" Frank asked.

"Go ahead," Shou said coming across the radio.

"Call signs?"

Bobby spoke up from behind Frank. "I vote for Pee Wee and Rainbow!"

"Not funny, Shrek!" Rob shouted, much to the amusement of John and Bobby.

Given a few minutes of silence, they waited for a response.

"Control, we are Bandit and the Snowman," Shou said. He was wearing a pair of mirrored sunglasses underneath his helmet.

"Holy shit, I bet Jerry Reed is rolling over in his grave right about now," Frank said.

"Why Frank, cause Rob got the shaft?" John chortled as the others burst out laughing hysterically.

"Hey Big Daddy!" Rob said. "Technically she didn't have a shaft, just so you know. But boy, would she get pissed if she wasn't on top."

They could hear Rob giggling over the radio, which made them laugh even harder.

"Snowman, it's good to see you can finally laugh about it. Big Daddy out!"

"Enough of the silly shit. Bandit you're good to go on your own mark."

John wasn't paying attention. Little John was standing by the door listening.

"Daddy?"

"Hey buddy, what's up?"

"On top of what?" Little John innocently asked.

John rushed from his chair to capture the little intruder as the others sat hiding their faces.

"I'll be right back, guys. You should be inside helping Lora," he said, scooping the little guy up. Carrying him back to the house, he had to stop. It was the first time he had seen Lucy fly.

"Pretty cool huh?"

"It sure is. Come on, let's get you back to the house."

Shou was a natural at the controls. He took a few laps around the valley before turning south. John walked backwards as he accompanied Little John, amazed by the sight and sound the craft made.

"Control to Lucy."

"Go ahead Control."

"You're over the hill and out of sight, you're a dot," Frank said at the view he was tracking on satellite.

The plan was to go past the gulf and down to the equator. They traveled down the coast of South America over the Atlantic before he gained altitude. Unlike John, he took his time getting there, trying not to freak Rob out too much until the actual testing started.

"Frank-san, we are not only ones tracking on satellite. Listen," Hideyoshi said as he handed Frank his headset.

"Damn!"

"What, Frank?" John asked.

"Air Force, Navy and any others who have a military satellite are tracking him. This could be fucking disaster."

"Control to Lucy, you've gone live!"

"Control do we have visitors?"

"Not yet, so if you're going to do it, you better do it now!"

A man's voice came across the radio that sent Frank running.

This the United States Air Force. This is a secure channel. You do not have the permissions to access this channel. Unauthorized user, please identify yourself.

"Fuck!" Frank screamed as he pulled the main on the breaker box. Everything shut down, even the lights.

"What the hell Frank, what are you doing?" John asked.

"It's over, they found us piggy backing on their system. If they were tracking us they know exactly where we are. This is bad." Frank started pacing. "This is so fucking bad. This is life in prison bad."

"We have two men still up there, Frank," John said.

"I know, but what can I do? I'm hoping they didn't get to finish tracking our location, that's why I killed the power!"

John could feel the sunlight warming his back as Frank opened the door. He didn't move. They hadn't planned for this, and he didn't know what to do.

"Is there any other way to contact them?"

"What John?" Bobby asked. He could barely hear him.

John joined them outside and asked again, "Any way we can contact Shou and Rob?"

"There is no way John-san," Hideyoshi answered. "I will need to destroy all our systems. It would take days to replace, and then I would need to find a way to hack back in. Possibly into another satellite system."

"Okay Bobby, you get Atsa and alert the men. If anyone shows up, no shots are to be fired. Frank and Hideyoshi, grab Yuuki and you guys find a way to get us some money. If we get out of this, we'll need to get back online or it's over. Garrett, we will need a place on your ranch to hide all this stuff, see what you can find. Nobody says anything to the kids or Lora, is that understood?"

They all agreed.

John climbed to the highest peak. Watching with a pair of binoculars, he waited for Lucy to return. But she didn't.

Day turned to night as John stood watch in the hills. He turned away anyone who came to check on him. Being the leader, he felt responsible. He kept a southerly view, praying for his friends' return. He didn't know if he should give up hope as the sun eventually rose.

Atsa called to John. He pointed out a white sedan pulling down the long dusty drive to his west.

"Shit!" John said.

Quickly he ran down the hill, trying to beat the car to the house.

Garrett, Bobby and Frank were sitting on the porch pretending to play cards. John snuck behind the trailers, coming up behind the house out of view of the visitors. Slowly he crept up the side of the house so that he could hear.

Two uniformed men exited the car. It was the Air Force. *Damn, they know it's us*, John thought as he peeked around the corner.

The others paid them no attention as they walked up to the front porch, one man coming on to the steps.

"Good morning gentlemen. Can I ask you a few questions?"

Garrett peeked over his glasses at the man standing on his porch. "Don't they teach you boys manners in the military? I didn't invite you up here."

"Oh, my apologies sir," he said, retreating back down the steps. "Could I possibly ask you a few questions?"

"There's a sign up there by the road, no soliciting. So if you're looking for donations, you came to the wrong place," Garrett huffed.

"No sir, not looking for donations. My name is…"

Garrett cut him off mid-sentence. "Boys, I don't want whatever it is you're selling!"

"No sir, not selling anything either. As I was saying, I'm Major Harold Jennings, and this is Captain Paul Taylor. We would like to know if you saw anything strange, anything you can't identify in the sky the last few weeks. Have you seen anything like that?"

Garrett laid down his cards, looking even more irritated.

"Out here, we see all kinds of lights. For the most part, we just think it's you guys. You know, you military types, up there playing with your expensive toys that you build off my hard-earned tax dollars."

"Sir, have you seen anything with blue lights? We have reports from the area that there may have been some unusual blue lights in the sky?"

"Ain't seen them, good day," Garrett answered sharply.

"Have you heard anything unusual sir?"

"Boys, I ain't heard or seen anything you are lookin for! Now if you don't mind, I need to get back to my card game. These two yahoos got me down thirty cents, and I aim to get my money back!"

"Thank you for your time, we'll leave you to your card game."

Garrett watched out of the corner of his eye as they drove off. John came out from hiding as the car disappeared out of sight.

"Son of a bitch, that was close," Bobby said.

"I didn't hear a word of what they said, all I could think about was orange jumpsuits and gray bars," Frank declared.

"Well, they don't know it was us, yet. And our boys still aren't home," John said.

"They'll find their way back, I know it. I feel it in my bones," Garrett said, trying to comfort

John. "You need to go get some sleep. If they show up, we'll come wake you."

"I won't be able to sleep."

"Sitting in them hills won't bring them back any faster. You go on and get some sleep. If we need you, we know where to find you."

As John headed in the house to check on the kids before finding his bed, Lora traded looks with him. She knew. John didn't have to say the words, and at this point he couldn't. That could be him and Bobby out there right now.

42

A week's time passed, and there was still no sign of Shou and Rob. The first couple of days every news channel ran stories of unidentified flying objects over numerous countries. Everyone thought it was a hoax, but the team knew better. The stories ended, and there was still no sign of Lucy.

Out of the twenty-four hours in a day, John would spend twenty-two sitting on that hill waiting. Waiting was the worst thing he could do; he was haunted by thoughts of losing his friends.

It was the eighth night, just before midnight. John had dozed off leaning up against a rock. He had no sooner drifted off when he was brought back to life. It sounded like a thunderstorm rolling in. It was loud and was getting closer.

Coming from the southwest, Lucy was rolling hard across the hills. Shou was giving her all she could handle. Not only did the sound wake John, it woke everyone on the ranch.

Standing on his perch, John watched as Shou masterly slowed the vehicle in front of the house, swinging her to face the barn. He flew Lucy inside, the first time this had been attempted.

John tried to run down the hill, but he wound up falling and rolling most of the way. Too excited to feel pain, he picked himself up and sprinted towards the garage.

Shou and Rob exited Lucy just before the others made it to them. Both men, scraggly and a little worse for wear, were met with a hero's welcome. Ignoring the hugs and hellos, they slammed the barn doors shut to hide Lucy.

What turned out to be an adventure of lifetime was also the scare of a lifetime. Rob had to dismantle the communication system in Lucy as they flew. But they finished the mission, achieving the desired goal of Mach five and then some. The surprise was they reached Mach six point seven before Shou attempted to slow down; he stated that she had more to give.

However, they needed to run for their lives as every military in southeast Asia came knocking on their backdoors. They were chased from continent to continent, looking for a place to set her down and hide. They were able to finally set down on a small island in the South Pacific. They found an abandoned atoll southeast of French Polynesia on which to hide.

Covering Lucy with palm leaves and brush, they hid. The United States Navy was on a search and discovery mission looking for them. They eventually gave up, and when the search flights became few to none, they made a run for it.

"How did you guys survive?" Frank asked.

"Shou fished and I picked what fruit I could find. Coconuts were plentiful so we did okay," Rob answered.

"What about water?" John asked.

"We drank what was left in Lucy," Shou said. "When it was time to leave, we took turns filling the tank with salt water. We used coconut shells to transport the water back from the beach."

"Do you know how heavy those things are?" Rob said. "And the heat there, oh my God it was so humid. Every trip carrying water, I must have sweated out a gallon, just myself."

"We didn't think we'd ever see you guys again," Bobby said. "Damn good to see you boys!"

"Hell, we didn't think we'd make it back either, we were chased by, oh let's see, the United States, Russia, China, Australia, Japan, and don't forget the fucking Indian Air Force. I didn't even know they had an Air Force. None of them gave up easy. The Chinese and Russians actually fired on us!"

"Damn Rob," Bobby said.

"Yeah, if Shou hadn't pulled off some crazy maneuvers, we would have been toast!"

"Good job, Shou," John said as he embraced the man.

"It was my honor John-san. They were not going to capture Lucy. I would have given my life to protect her."

"I'm thankful it didn't come to that. We need to figure all this out. I got to say, I'm so proud of both of you, so it pains me to say this. But you both stink, you really need to go take a shower," John said, releasing his grip on Shou.

"That is understandable John-san."

"Shower and some real food, I can't wait," Rob said.

"I'll go grill these guys a couple of steaks," Bobby offered.

"Why don't you let Lora do that? We've had your cooking. They deserve a good meal, not to be poisoned," Frank kidded.

It was still a tense situation. They failed to mention that during their escape they flew directly over a Navy aircraft carrier. It only caused them to get tracked again; the military wasn't quite sure just exactly where they were, but they were close.

Sitting by the fire the others watched as the two men scarfed down their meal. They hadn't had one in days, and it showed.

"So I can't believe it, you hit Mach six," John said, pleased.

Talking with a mouthful of food, Rob tried to respond. "And she had more in the tank." Morsels of food flew from his mouth. "If it wasn't getting dark, we were going to go for it!"

"John-san, I know how to slow her down without tilting the nose up."

"Yeah, how'd you do it?"

"We didn't. On the island we had plenty of time to think." Shou took another bite of food. "We push back the cockpit and re-install two turbines. Reinforce a panel like we planned for protecting the bottom one. In space they should not get damaged when engaged."

"That's going to be a lot of work," Bobby pointed out.

"We have time Bobby-san. We also discovered that the oxygen system is insufficient. It will need to be replaced."

"Why would we do that?" John said. "It was working fine for us, and we hit altitudes of sixty-five thousand."

"John, we went higher. At one point, we hit seventy-six thousand. Shou noticed the change when our water bottles were crushed. He immediately took us down to re-establish cabin pressurization. And to boot, I got sick. Our suits weren't sufficient to prevent decompression sickness."

"So what's this mean, Shou?" John asked.

"You will eventually black out and die. You will be trapped in space until your orbit decays. If you're able to return to earth you will crash, burn up, or even possibly miss earth, skipping back out into space and becoming lost forever."

"That would really suck," Bobby said.

"There's an old plane graveyard somewhere around here," Garrett spoke up. "I heard they salvage most of those planes of equipment before the government gets to them."

"How in the hell will that help us if they're stripped?" Frank asked.

"It won't you jack wagon, let me finish!" Garrett stared at Frank, waiting for a response. Frank quietly signaled for Garrett to continue.

"Go to some of these surplus stores and you might find what you're looking for. They might not have it on the shelf, but they might have it hidden in the back. You have to ask the right questions, so they don't think you're working for the government."

"Okay, say they have what we're looking for, that doesn't fix the suit issues. Tell me if I'm wrong Shou, we need actual space suits. Ones that aren't relics. How do you all think we are going to come up with those?" John asked.

"Hideyoshi, would you like to answer this one?" Rob asked.

The team turned to face Hideyoshi.

"The company who provided the heat shield is Russian. They have an experimental suit, which has not been tested yet in actual space. It's lightweight and would provide the operating pressure you need if your onboard system fails."

"I'm lost," Frank said. "If we improve the system, why would we need the suits? The suits you already have should be adequate then."

"Frank-san, if the systems fails, the suits fail. They will die," Shou said.

"I don't like this at all," John said. "We've been flirting with death since we started this whole thing."

"Why don't we just stop here?" Bobby said, perplexed. "Why don't we just stop the whole space thing? We can sell this as alternative energy and leave it at that. We could sell it as nothing more than a more efficient way to produce and sell electricity. Nothing's worth any of us dying."

"Could you live with that?" John asked.

"Yes I could. I mean, I wanted to go to space just like the rest of you, but now I have a child on the way. I'd hate the fact we never made it, but I could learn to live with it."

"Dad?" Thomas said. He had been hiding in the shadows the whole time, listening.

"Thomas, what are you doing out of bed?" John asked.

"Listening," the boy answered. "I want to say something."

"You should really be in bed, son."

"Please Dad, let me say something? I really want to say something to all of you."

"Well, go ahead. Come over here and say what you got to say."

Thomas tentatively walked towards the others, nervously rubbing his hands together as he approached them.

"I know I'm just a kid and what I have to say doesn't matter much at all. But Dad." Thomas turned to face his father. "You're teaching us to never give up, follow our dreams. My dream is the same as yours; someday I want to go up there to. Everything that has happened to us brought us here together. And I love it here with all of you, there isn't anywhere else in the world I'd want to be. I know you Dad, and if you don't do this, you'll be miserable. And Bobby, if your kid is like us, then your kid would be proud to know that you're an astronaut that didn't give up. I'm proud of my dad, and I want to be like him. He's an astronaut, and I know he won't give up."

Silence fell around the fire pit as the wisdom of the innocent child took center stage.

Looking up at the stars surrounding the heavens, Thomas pointed up.

"I wasn't asleep in the car when you and Bobby were talking about going to space. I heard every word. Both of you said that this was your dream, so if you let me have a say in this, my vote is for space. Whatever you decide, I'm still proud of you."

"I love you son," John said, standing and picking the boy up to embrace him.

"I love you too Dad."

Walking around the circle, Thomas hugged everyone, trying to increase his plea for space, wanting to improve his chances of turning the vote.

"Go on, get back up to the house and get to bed," John ordered. "When we finish here, I'll come up to check on you and your brother."

They all watched as the wise young man ran towards the house. It wasn't until John heard the screen door shut that he turned to address the circle once more.

"Well, I guess all of you know what my vote is. I'm going."

Around the circle they went, answering. Even Bobby threw his hat back into the race, with Lora encouraging him. Not a single person said no, everyone agreeing with the dreams of a child.

"That's it then," John said. "We're going. We have a lot of work to do. Get new suits, modify Lucy, install a bigger water tank and upgrade our oxygen system."

"We'll get you the money you need John," Frank said, nodding to Hideyoshi.

"That's great. I think what we need most of all though is…is prayers."

43

The team worked day and night, engineering what they thought was impossible. The retractable panel for the front turbines would be tricky; Frank had to write safeties into the programming in case the pedal was pressed accidently. It would have the same control, but would only engage if the panel were detected open.

Other life support systems had to be installed, such as food, medical and waste disposal. If a guy has to go the bathroom, a guy has to go.

The idea for the oxygen system was to find one from a jet airliner and modify it to support space flight. Bobby and Shou installed two huge oxygen tanks, one on each side of the water tank. They teetered on the idea of installing one that would take oxygen from water, but didn't have the time frame to locate one. They went with the obvious.

"You boys about ready?" Garrett asked as he sat on the front porch waiting.

"We're coming," Bobby yelled from inside the house.

"Come the hell on, while I'm still young!"

John walked out through the screen door. Looking down at the old man he tilted his head, smirked and kept walking.

"You haven't been young since the forties," John mumbled.

"I heard that bucket head. I might be old, but at least this old man can leave on time."

Garrett was taking the boys surplus shopping as he'd promised. Only twenty stores fit that bill in the Tucson area, and Garrett aimed to hit every one of them.

Store after store they visited, each with the same story. No airplanes parts sold here. They agreed to let Garrett do all the talking. Who'd think a man his age worked for the government? It got to the point that maybe he just rubbed most people the wrong way.

The eighteenth store, which also turned out to be the closest to the ranch, carried just what they need. They were uncertain it would, due to the excessive UFO propaganda hanging in the store's windows, but sure enough, they had the system, and at a fair price. The guys were back in business and on their way with their new but ancient system.

Giving into Garrett's request to stop for a drink, they pulled up to a little hole in the wall just outside of town. It was a long day and why the hell not; a little drink could be just what the doctor ordered.

Walking into the dirty, dimly lit establishment, they knew right away they chose the wrong bar. The bar was filled with men in uniform. A poor decision had put them smack dab in the Air Force's lap. This was one of their hangouts. And the guys stuck out like a sore thumb.

Bobby hesitated and tried to retreat; thinking quickly, John stopped him and pushed him towards the back of the bar. They each took a seat away from the action.

"Let's just have one. Try not to look suspicious," John whispered to Bobby.

Garrett sat closest to the door, which was not a good idea. He was instantly recognized.

"Excuse me sir," Major Jennings said. "Do you remember me?"

"Mmmhmm," Garrett moaned, sarcastically acknowledging the major.

"If you gentlemen would allow me, could I buy you a round of drinks and possibly ask you a few questions?"

"This ain't one of those funny bars is it?" Garrett turned his chair. He squared off with Jennings, facing him directly.

"No sir." The major laughed. "I was just being neighborly."

"My answers aren't for sale, and I can buy my own beer," Garrett said as he threw a twenty on the bar. Sticking up three fingers, he placed his order with the unattractive woman tending bar. Smiling lovingly at the old man, she placed three lukewarm beers on the bar in front of them. "Keep the change, honey."

"Sir, I'd just like to ask you a few questions."

Again Garrett squared off against the major, who took the liberty of sitting in the chair beside him.

"Boy, you'd better listen to me good." Garrett wagged his finger in the man's face. "I served this country too, and you'd be wise to learn some respect for those who came before you. Just cause you wear that uniform, don't give you the right to harass an old man."

"No sir, I wasn't trying to harass you. I would really just like to ask you a few simple questions is all," Jennings pleaded.

"You don't get it! I don't want to be bothered by you. Now if that don't click in that simple brain of yours, tough shit! And if I was twenty years younger, I'd mop the floor with that sissy flyboy uniform of yours!"

Garrett now had the attention of every flyboy in the room, which was very unsettling to John and Bobby, as there turned out to be around thirty of them. Last time they counted.

The major stood, a conceited smile across his lips, and threw another twenty on the bar.

"Sweetheart, their next round's on me," he said to the bartender. "You gentlemen have a good day."

Sighing with relief, John watched from the corner of his eye as the major walked down the bar and took a seat. He positioned himself in clear view of John and the others.

"You believe the nerve of that pantywaist?" Garrett huffed.

"Just finish your beer, and let's get the hell out of here," John said. "Keep it cool and don't look at any of them."

"Darlin, take that twenty and put it in your tip jar," Garrett offered. She was quick to comply.

Garrett leaned over and whispered in Bobby's ear.

"Did you see the teeth on that broad? Looks like she sucked off a stick of butter."

"Shhhh…Uncle Garrett," Bobby whispered back.

"Looks like she got hit in the face with a phone book, the yellow pages, and they stuck!" Garrett wheezed and coughed as he started to laugh.

John was in disbelief as Bobby began to laugh as well. He needed to get them out of there, now.

"Down your beers, let's fucking go!" John murmured angrily.

After taking their final gulp of the watered-down suds, they headed for the door. Casually trying to get out the door and get on their way, it was Garrett who stopped for the last word.

Leaning on the bar facing the major, Garrett asked him a question. "You know how you bury one of you flyboys?"

"How's that, old timer?"

"Give him an enema and bury what's left in a shoe box. See you around, flyboy," Garrett said as Bobby was pulling on his sleeve to leave.

"I don't get it," the major said to his peers.

The bartender spoke up at the moment the door closed behind Garrett.

"He just said you're full of shit."

With his ego bruised, Major Jennings took off out the door to address the old man, who luckily was just pulling out of the parking lot with the others. Bad timing for the boys. The major heard the old truck roar off down the street. That sound didn't come from a normal engine; it sounded like a miniature jet engine under the hood. Now he was really suspicious.

44

"We got major issues John," Frank said, panicking.

John didn't even get to sit, exhausted from the trip and having to deal with Garrett and the flyboy.

"What now?" he asked wearily.

"That company discontinued their flight suit division. Nobody was buying or interested, so they shut it down."

"So we don't have flight suits. Now what do you suggest?"

"They still have models that weren't picked up, but they won't let go of them."

"So find somebody else."

"There is nobody else John. Everyone else has a contract with NASA or some other space agency."

"Buy from them, it's that easy," John said, finally plopping down to rest his tired feet.

"They aren't permitted to sell to anyone else, they're under government contracts. Even attempting to buy will get us more unwanted attention."

"So what are you telling me Frankie? It's fucking over?"

"Not necessarily. We found the design engineer. He is an American, hired by a Russian company, and now he's unemployed."

"And this means what to me?"

"He's back in the States and living in California." Frank smiled.

"Why are you smiling Frank? Did he bring the suits home with him?"

"No, those are still in Russia."

"So what's to smile about? Am I missing something here?"

"John-san," Hideyoshi said. "He also has a strong presence on the internet, through his video channel. He's mocking two suits up as we speak."

"So what do you suggest? Drive to California, pick him up? 'Hey we need your suits, come check out the space ship we built in Bobby's Uncle's barn?'"

"Exactly," Frank said.

"You two have lost your minds." John laughed. "He worked for a Russian company who made these suits, don't you think the government is watching him? Especially if he's broadcasting it all over the fucking Internet!"

"John-san, if you want suits, ones that will even fit Bobby, we need to act now."

"John, I know it's a risk. But everything we've done to this point has been risky, am I right?"

"Where in California?" John asked.

"Burbank," Frank answered.

"How far is that from here?"

"Seven and a half hours, give or take."

"I'll give you twenty-four hours. Yuuki stays here and finishes the launch programming."

"Can we take Shou?"

"Absolutely not. He and Rob are still installing the retractable panel and front turbines."

"Bobby then?"

"Are you kidding? Why don't both of you nut up and go ask Lora for yourselves. I'll pop some corn and watch her whip both your asses."

"We're doing this alone Hideyoshi," Frank said.

"And I'm okay with that Frank-san."

"I thought you boys would be," John snickered. "You better get going and don't forget you need to hurry back here and help finish all this computer stuff."

"We're on it. See you in a few John."

Brody Harper was your typical California boy, with blue eyes and blond hair flowing down to his shoulders. He may have looked like the average surfer you found strolling on the beach, but this surfer was highly educated. To hear him speak, one couldn't tell he held several degrees from several top colleges; he sounded like a character in an eighties coming-of-age movie. One look under the hood of that old Chevy pickup and he was in, if they would let him drive it back. Seeing what that old truck could do was like a young boy getting to feel his first boob. He was in heaven.

Now if bad timing wasn't one thing that always hurt the team, it was about to happen again. If anyone looked out of place in the desert, it was Brody.

Atsa called everyone out on the porch. That familiar white sedan was pulling down the drive one more time. Garrett grabbed his shotgun. He was upset these guys didn't get the message the first time or the second time.

"Those stubborn sons a bitches, they've gone and pushed my jackass button!"

Garrett met the white sedan as it pulled up. Bobby was trying to block Garrett from getting to the car.

"Mr. White, good afternoon," the major said as he shut the car door.

"How you know my name?"

"We know more than you think we do Mr. White."

"You got a search warrant?" Garrett screamed.

Everyone stopped, pausing as the old truck came tearing up the drive toward them.

"There's what I wanted to look at," Jennings said.

"Hang on Major," John spoke up. "That's private property, you have no right to look at anything."

"And just who are you?" Jennings asked.

"I'm the guy who's going to sue you for harassment and illegal search and seizure."

"What seizure, we haven't seized anything?"

"Well you're trespassing, and if this big gorilla would get the hell out of the way, I'd pump about five rounds of buckshot up your flyboy ass!" Garrett yelled, still wrestling with Bobby.

"Don't threaten me old man, I'll take everything you got!"

"According to the fourth amendment you would be in violation and as for the second amendment, he does have the right to bear arms," Brody calmly said, walking up to confront the major. "And according to the 'Castle Doctrine,' he's allowed to defend his abode from unwelcome intruders like yourself, that have not been invited on said property. The use of deadly force would be considered justifiable homicide."

In awe, the major stood back and looked at Brody. His eyes got wider, and a look of disgust washed over his face.

"And who the hell are you, some sort of hippie lawyer?" Jennings asked.

"No sir, I'm Brody Harper, probably the most intelligent man you'll ever meet. Now will you vacate this property, or do we have to contact the local authorities and have you arrested for trespassing? The decision is yours to make."

They watched as the major complied. Getting back in his car, he aggressively flew back down the drive in disgust.

"That was amazing, how the hell do you know all that?" Bobby asked.

"I read, and fortunately he doesn't. If you had shot that man, you'd be heading to prison," Brody answered.

"Excuse me?" John said.

"Merely just entering the property is not enough to shoot the man. He would have had to do something that made you feel you were in danger for your life. Anyway, he's gone. Hello, I'm Brody Harper, it's nice to meet you all."

"Well, I'll be a monkey's uncle." Garrett started laughing, pointing at Bobby.

45

"You gentlemen will be up there for twenty-four hours, you will need to go to the bathroom. So in order to provide a good seal, you'll need to shave the area where the device attaches or you'll have urine floating all over the aircraft," Brody instructed, handing John and Bobby each a long tube attached to a triangular cup.

"What the hell is this?" Bobby asked.

"Attach the tube to the vacuum, turn on the switch to start the vacuum and insert your," Brody paused, coughing. "Your thing into here. The urine will be sucked into the waste system, where it will be contained. Wipe out the cup, and place the towel into the toilet to be discarded. Once the toilet is clear of debris, shut off the vacuum and store the hose."

"You want me to poop in a vacuum?" Bobby said, puzzled.

"You want me shave off my...?" John asked.

"Just where it needs to seal...and yes...you poop in a vacuum."

Frank stood up, taking center stage in the kitchen.

"Since this location is compromised, with the help of Atsa," Frank gave him a nod of acknowledgment, which he gratefully returned, "we have a new location to launch from. We...us...in the truck, will head east on Highway

10, almost to the New Mexico border, down by the Chiricahua Mountains. We'll pull my trailer behind the truck and run control from the there. You two," Frank pointed at Bobby and John, "will fly Lucy to our location. We'll top off her water and start the launch sequence from there."

"We will be there as well. My men will cover from the mountains. If the Air Force comes you will know," Atsa said.

"What about us?" Lora asked.

"You, Garrett, Brody and the kids of course, will be able to watch remotely from here. We thought it wise that if things go south, you're nowhere close," Frank said, reaching over to rub Little John's head. "You'll be able to listen and of course talk back. Brody will run the station here for you."

"The international space station flies two hundred and thirty miles above the earth's surface. We are targeting to take you to three hundred miles. She orbits the earth every ninety-two minutes at around seventeen thousand miles an hour," Hideyoshi said.

"Once you're in stable orbit, you'll be directly behind her. We'll have you start our program that will have you up to three times her speed. That's right, you'll orbit the earth every thirty minutes. So in twenty-four hours you will have orbited the earth forty-eight times," Frank stated.

"That's cool," Thomas said, grinning at his father.

"Now for the bad news," Frank said. "Once we get up there, we are live! Everyone will know that we exist; it won't be a secret anymore. The reason for the speed is so that the space station doesn't actually get a good picture of you. But they'll know that they aren't alone."

"What about space debris?" John asked.

"Good question," Brody said. "We'll be monitoring through their satellites. We detect any debris, and we'll make an adjustment down here that will allow you to avoid it. Chances are at that height, you should be okay."

"We did that once and got busted," Bobby pointed out.

"That's understandable. However, this time we'll accommodate communication satellites for our communications. You know, there may be a satellite television outage, for say…twenty-four hours," Frank said. "And they'll be too busy looking for you to realize we're piggy backing this time, so NASA and those folks probably won't know we're there. But the television companies, they're going to be pissed."

"Bobby-san, we've already hacked in. We've ran some tests and they haven't found us yet," Hideyoshi said.

"We need to leave here at three-thirty in the morning. So everybody should turn in early and be ready to go. You guys got some shaving to do, and we still have some tests to run. So if anybody has any questions, now is the time."

"Just how fast will we be going, say, when we leave the atmosphere?" Bobby asked.

"Sure you want to know that Bobby?" Frank asked.

"No and yes, but tell me anyway."

"When you hit the stratosphere, you'll be at eighteen thousand miles per hour."

"So what you're saying is, I will have peed myself, puked, also shit myself and passed out...again...somewhere in the stratosphere?"

"Knowing you big man, it's highly likely," Frank answered.

Little John started to giggle.

"Cool. I thought this was going to be hard, why break the trend. I mean really, only eighteen thousand, let's do twenty. I mean, if I have to man-scape we should at least do something the hard way?" Bobby said, smacking John on the back. "I know...you can shave me and I'll shave you."

"Only if we can cuddle after," John answered.

"You wouldn't like it. I snore."

"All right, all right you clowns, let's get to bed. See you all in the morning," Lora said.

The morning would bring a big new day. Not only would they introduce Lucy to the world, they would make history with the unlikeliest crew ever assembled. If Wilber and Orville Wright could see them now.

46

Lora ran down the stairs tee-heeing like a little schoolgirl who just found out about the first boy who had ever liked her. Her eyes were beaming with pleasure. What she shared next kind of perplexed everyone sitting at the kitchen table.

"When Bobby gets down here, ask him about his turtle."

"His what?" Frank said confused.

"His turtle…shhhh…here he comes."

They all watched as Bobby turned the corner into the kitchen. He was walking bowlegged. And as if he had something biting at him as he walked, his hips would twitch and his right leg would jump.

"Howdy partner. What happened, did you go for a late night horsey ride?" John said in the best southern accent he could muster.

Bobby unhurriedly sank into the seat next to John, everyone still watching as he squirmed to get comfortable.

"Did you wear your chaps and nothing else, got a little road rash going on down there?" John kept at it.

"It's not that," Bobby answered, sounding perturbed.

Lora was standing by the counter, hysterical. She turned her back and hid her face so that Bobby could not see her laughing.

"What's this about a turtle?" Frank asked.

"Lora!" Bobby said, shocked. He knew the cat was out of the bag, or was is it the turtle?

"Sorry honey...love you...got to go!" Lora said, still giggling. She quickly skipped out of the kitchen to avoid capture.

"Oh, this is embarrassing."

"What's embarrassing?" John asked.

Shaking his head, he tried to think of a way to explain what was just exactly going on without adding more fuel to the fire.

"I got carried away with the razor. There, I said it."

"So you shaved...a turtle?" Rob asked.

"No...damn...I can't believe I'm going to say this." Bobby's face turned redder. "I shaved everything, and I mean everything."

"Oh, I see," John said.

The others tried to avoid eye contact with Bobby, hiding their amusement.

"So you just didn't trim the hedges, you um...um...um...well, you bush-hogged that bitch!" Frank said, unable to contain himself any longer. The others all broke out in an uproar at Bobby's expense.

"It's not funny," Bobby said, scowling. "It's really not funny!"

Lora chimed in from the living room. "Oh yes it is!"

Some fell out of their chairs, others were bent over, but Garrett didn't see the humor just yet. He didn't fully understand what was going on.

"So what the hell does this have to do with a turtle?" The old man sat staring at Bobby, still pondering the situation.

Leaning back in his chair, Bobby pulled out the elastic waistband on his shorts and looked down.

"He looks like a sad little turtle peeking out of his shell."

"Oh, I see what you're saying now." Garrett leaned over, trying to peek.

Bobby let go of the waistband as his shorts snapped shut, avoiding further embarrassment.

"Hey!"

"Seen one, you've seen them all. What are you worried about? So what you're telling me is your tortoise lost to the hair."

"Oh my god, I can't breathe," John said, holding his stomach. "Stop it!"

To Bobby it seemed like forever before they all calmed down. Of all of the days for this to happen, why on launch day? But at least the mood was light, even though it was at his expense.

Breakfast was short and sweet. Today was a big day for them all. They loaded up the truck, attached the trailer and watched as Frank and the others headed out for the launch pad.

"Guess we better get suited up," John said.

"Gentlemen, follow me," Brody said.

Those remaining at the ranch waited in the living room as Brody suited up our two pilots. Little John was bouncing off the walls with excitement. Thomas was trying to contain his enthusiasm, but he had to let it go when his father walked out of the bedroom and made for the stairs.

"Oh that's fuc….sorry, that's freaking awesome," Thomas said.

Brody had designed a lightweight, fully functional dual-purpose suit. It could be worn for launches and actual space walks. It wasn't much larger than the high altitude suits they were already accustomed to wearing. The boys would have preferred another color, but this one would have to do. The suits were bright red with a black seam down each side.

"Well, we stand out if anything," John said.

"I like them Daddy," Little John stated before jumping off the arm of the couch into John's arms.

"How'd I know you'd say that?"

"I like them too, and my Bobby looks very handsome in it," Lora said, pulling Bobby over for a kiss.

"Brody, can you make me one?" Thomas asked.

"Slow your jets son, let's see how these work out first. And it's going to be awhile before you go flying," John said, pulling Thomas in to join him and his brother.

With goodbyes out of the way, Garrett and Brody escorted them to Lucy. Brody assisted in strapping them in, making sure that when they launched, they were secure.

This was the first time John flew Lucy out of the barn. Of course Shou had put in her in there with ease, but John hadn't attempted the feat yet. He took his time, much to Garrett's disapproval; years of dust and dirt made visibility poor. Garrett tried to guide them, but for his own safety he was forced back. It took some time, but John finally cleared the old barn.

"You ready to do this Bobby?"

"No, but I have a feeling you aren't going to stop and let me out."

"You would be correct sir."

John took a few laps around the valley before stopping in front of the house to give one last wave goodbye. Hopefully this wouldn't be the last time. He didn't want to admit it, but the thought was on his mind.

"All right John, head east. Frank said keep her about two hundred feet off the ground. So take your time."

"Roger that, wave goodbye and let's go."

Both men waved out the cockpit window, gave a thumbs up and headed to the launch site. Even taking it slow they still beat Frank there by thirty minutes.

Staying strapped in they sat patiently as Rob refueled Lucy. Frank came on board to go over the flight one more time.

"Gentlemen, this is a big day. Are you ready to do this?"

"I think so," Bobby answered.

"Don't worry Bobby, you'll do just fine. We're good Frank, let's do this."

"Gentlemen, godspeed," Frank said. He gave each man a squeeze on the shoulder, and he exited the craft.

John sat a few minutes with his eyes closed, praying. Bobby stared at a picture of Lora he had glued to the back of John's seat. They didn't speak during this time. One might think they were nervous or scared, but they were just remembering the journey that led them to this moment.

"Control to Lucy, do you copy?" The radio broke through the silence.

"We have you Control, you are loud and clear," John answered.

"Control to Home Base, do you copy?"

"This is Home, we also copy," Brody answered.

"Okay guys, put on your helmets and start your life support systems."

Each man pulled the helmet on to his head; with a quick little twist to the right, they were secure. Bobby flipped the two switches, turning on life support.

"Control, we are ready to commence."

"Hang on boys." Garrett came across the radio, taking the headset from Brody. "We got one thing left to do, before you go."

"This is Control, go ahead Home."

"I normally don't this, so bear with me, but it seems fitting for the moment," Garrett said. "Dear heavenly father, I ask that you look after these two fine men. Bring them home safe to us, we love them. And if it's not too much to ask, can you have them stop and get me a bottle of whiskey on the way back?"

"Very fitting." John laughed.

"Bet you won't read that in the history books," Bobby said. "They may leave out that little touching part."

"Roger that Home…okay Lucy…take her up to one thousand feet and we'll begin launch sequence."

"Roger that, here we go!"

47

The greatest day of their lives was finally upon them, except it was about to be ruined. Alex Wright had found his way out of the desert, and he was headed right for them. Somebody was going to lose their life today. He was embarrassed and angry, and he wanted revenge.

"Control to Lucy."

"Go ahead Control."

"Go ahead and switch over to launch control, sit back and relax and enjoy the ride."

John flipped the switch they had installed on the front of his dash. It gave the computer complete control of Lucy.

"She's all yours Control."

"We'll start in ten. We'll need both of you to grab the straps on your upper seatbelt and hang on tight."

"We are a go Control," John said, trying to hide his nervousness.

Frank started the countdown.

"Ten...nine...eight...seven...six...lift the nose!"

Shou flipped the first switch on his panel. Lucy's nose raised up to a sixty-degree angle as the thrusters held her steady at one thousand feet.

"Five...four...three...two...one, mark!"

Shou flipped the remaining switch on his control panel, bringing the engines fully to life.

Lucy's rear engines howled across the desert valley. It was the first time they had full power. The long blue flames shot out two hundred or so feet behind her and sent her screaming upwards into the sky.

"Control, we're out of here!" John yelled into the microphone.

"Roger that Lucy, it might get a little bumpy."

"A little bumpy?" Bobby said. He was bouncing from side to side as much as his harness would allow. He could feel his helmet bouncing off the headrest.

"Prepare for rollover and nine Gs!"

The others ran out of the trailer to watch the sight. It was magnificent as Lucy lit up the desert morning sky.

"Come look, come look!" Little John screamed, urging the others to come outside. Even from the ranch they could see Lucy, which meant so could the rest of the world.

"Lucy, from down here you're a beautiful sight!" Frank said.

"Roger that!"

Lucy rolled over and was now leaving the earth's atmosphere. John could hear the engines cut in and out, trying to maintain one constant speed. The strain from the thrust wasn't as strong as zero gravity set in.

"Control to Lucy, go ahead and turn on cabin air system, you can pressurize the cabin."

"Roger that Control," John responded.

Bobby switched systems.

"We are good Control."

"Roger that Lucy, you can remove your helmets now, but don't unstrap. We'll be taking you up to three hundred miles above the earth's surface. You'll need to put the helmets back on when we get there. Just enjoy the view until then."

"What's our estimated time to achieve?" John asked.

"Twenty minutes Lucy. Right now you're traveling at eighteen thousand miles an hour."

"I wish you guys could see what I'm seeing, it's unbelievable," Bobby said.

"Wow, look at that," John said.

"It's the Aurora Borealis, pictures don't do it justice. Green waves dancing across the top of the atmosphere, it's amazing," Bobby said, his eyes as a wide as three-year-old on Christmas morning.

"Home to Lucy." Lora's voice came across the headset.

"Yes baby, I mean Home," Bobby answered.

"Take pictures. Your child might want to see what his father saw someday."

"Will do honey. Sorry, got caught up in the moment."

"Bobby?"

"Yes John." Bobby snapped photos, one right after the other.

"You might be interested in this," John said, pointing out the other window. "Look out here, look up."

"My God…there are millions of them, billions!"

"How's that for a view?"

"It's amazing. I wish we could get out of these seats and get closer to the window. I've never seen this many stars in my life. And John, look over there."

A satellite was floating by, as if it was suspended in air.

"Lucy to Control," John said.

"Go ahead Lucy."

"Did you guys see that satellite? That was a little close."

"Yes we did Lucy, believe it or not that satellite was three miles away. Nothing is in your flight path, if so we will make corrections. Sit back and relax, keep on enjoying the view."

"Roger that."

"Home to Control, we are experiencing some communication issues. Everyone is breaking up," Brody said.

"Home, you may need to reboot," Frank suggested.

"Will do Control, be right back."

Alex Wright pulled the cables from the wall as Brody shut down the computer. With his pistol, he hit Brody in the side of the head, knocking him unconscious. With all of Atsa's men at the launch site, they had left the ranch unguarded. It allowed Alex Wright to walk right up to the front door and take everyone hostage without even a struggle.

"*Where the fuck are they?*" Alex screamed at the terrified hostages.

"Unless you can grow wings out your ass and hold your breath for a real long time, you ain't going to find them, you jackass," Garrett answered.

Alex fired the pistol at Garrett's head, only missing by a couple of inches. The bullet lodged in the wall behind where he was sitting.

"Next one that insults me dies, do you understand that?"

"They aren't here," Lora pleaded.

"Then where the fuck are they?"

Alex walked over and snatched Thomas off the couch. He placed the pistol to his head.

"Does one of these little brats have to die before one of you answers?"

"Let the boy alone, I'll tell you where they're at," Garrett said.

"Speak old man!"

"About two hours or so east of here."

"Doing what?"

"Don't tell him any more Garrett," Lora begged.

"Bitch! Open your mouth again and I'll put a bullet in it!"

"They're flying that contraption they built," Garrett said.

"Get him up," Alex said, pointing at Brody. "You're taking me there, I'm getting what's mine. Try and stop me, and I'll kill this little brat!"

Alex Wright made them get in his car. He made Garrett drive while Lora attended to Brody. Alex rode in the backseat, keeping his hold on Thomas with the pistol still placed to his head. Little John rode next to them, holding onto his brother for dear life.

48

"All right Lucy, need you boys to put your helmets back on."

"We copy Control."

"And Lucy, we might as well tell you now, the world knows you're up there. The media is going nuts. When you get up to speed and fly by the space station, wave and try to smile pretty. I'm sure they are going to be trying to snap a picture of you."

"Will do Control. Helmets secure, we are on our own life support."

"Roger that. Now you are going to feel some G-forces. Nothing like during takeoff, but they will be there."

"How long until we are up to speed?"

"With that kind of power, in space? Shouldn't take long."

"We're ready, on your mark Control."

"In three…two…one…mark, and away you go."

Shou flipped the switch, and now Lucy was roaring through space, high earth orbit. She wasn't as bumpy as during takeoff, but the guys knew she was moving. The G-forces only last a few seconds in the beginning as they set her at high-speed orbit.

"Hey the engines shut off, the engines shut off!" Bobby yelled.

"You don't need to keep them on to maintain speed Lucy. Once she hits the desired speed she'll maintain it. You will hear one kick on every now and then, if she needs to make a course adjustment," Frank responded.

"Should have covered that in the prelaunch meeting, then I wouldn't have shit myself Control."

"We would have big man, but you were so excited to go shave your turtle."

"Not funny," Bobby said.

"Okay boys, you can unstrap. Take off your helmets and feel free to float around. Secure your things or you'll be bumping into them, and you don't have a lot of space to float around in. Release the latches on your seats and you can fold those down."

"Copy that control, and trust me when I say this, we have a lot of space up here," John said.

"Copy that Lucy, you've got five minutes and you'll fly by the space station."

As they prepared for their first live appearance, John took point in the cockpit, searching for the first sign of the space station.

"There it is and it's coming quick, come here Bobby."

Floating up to John, they both took a window. The space station was massive compared to Lucy. Even in space at seventy miles away, the space station was an impressive sight.

"What are they saying Control?" John asked.

"They are trying to figure out what country you're from, or if you're alien."

"Greetings earthlings," Bobby said, waving out the cockpit window.

"And she's gone." John laughed.

"Not for long, you'll see the space station again in thirty minutes," Frank said.

"Only twenty more hours to go, we should have thought this out a little more. What do you want to do Bobby?"

"No kidding, twenty hours? Let's grab something to eat and figure it out."

Amusing themselves with food and water in space, they missed the space station's second flyby. They would stop every hour to document readings, but other than that, they just enjoyed the ride.

Atsa was stationed a mere mile from the launch site. He was watching for unexpected visitors. The entire morning he saw no cars, until one finally came pulling up. With rifle in hand he motioned for the car to stop.

Seeing Garrett at the wheel, he was relieved, at least for a few seconds.

"What are you guys doing out here?"

Garrett nodded for Atsa to look behind him, in the back seat.

"Holy shit!"

"Don't fucking do it, don't try to be the hero. One wrong move and I'll blow this kid's brains all over his brother. Now put your weapon down," Alex ordered.

"No problem Mister, just don't hurt the kid," Atsa bargained.

"Now take that radio, tell anyone with a gun to come down, disarm. And if anyone tells John Kemp I'm here, I'll kill his kid."

Atsa complied and alerted everyone; they were all in disbelief that Alex Wright would even attempt to return. They followed Atsa to the launch site, where his men all gathered, unarmed and waiting.

Frank stayed in the trailer as the others poured outside. Shou took his place in front of the entire group. Given the chance, he planned on killing Alex. Alex ordered everyone out of the car and told them to join the group, with the exception of Thomas.

Alex exited the car, holding on firmly to Thomas. Looking over his accomplishment he picked out one man. "You, come here!"

Rob hesitantly walked towards them.

"What...what do you want?" Rob asked.

"Gather up all those guns and put them in here," Alex said as he unlocked the trunk on his car.

Disgusted, Rob did as he was told. Once he loaded the trunk, Alex shut it and shot the lock, damaging it.

"Now there's only one gun left. Don't try me either, I will kill this kid."

"Let the child go," Shou said bravely.

"You walk over here and get him."

Shou proceeded to walk towards Alex to retrieve Thomas, but Alex didn't let him make it; halfway there he raised his pistol and fired. Shou was hit in the right shoulder just above his lung. The bullet went clean through and kept going, hitting Rob in the left thigh. The others scattered, diving into the dirt, trying to avoid the shot.

"Would you look at that boy," Alex said to Thomas. "Two for one. Damn I'm good."

"You're an asshole is what you are," Thomas replied.

"You got a little spunk, don't you boy? I like that, but if you ever call me an asshole again. I will shoot you."

"Leave him alone!" Lora screamed.

"Bitch, I've warned you once, don't make me do it again. Now where is John Kemp?"

Lora was the only one to answer. "In space, they flew to space."

Puzzled he looked at Lora. "You're not lying are you? Now that's fucking amazing. That power source can send a man to space. Too bad for all of you that I'm taking it."

"You won't get away with it," Garrett said.

"Yes I will, and you'll help me."

Alex made the men undress. With their clothes he tied them all up, leaving them face down in the Arizona desert. Lora he tied up, sitting her in the trailer with Frank, Thomas and himself.

Alex sat, listening intently as Frank ran flight operations, amused that John and Bobby, three hundred miles above the earth, had no idea he had their families. And they had his soon-to-be space ship.

49

"Here they come again Bobby," John said, referring to the international space station.

"We are in space, let's moon them! It seems fitting," Bobby suggested.

"Seriously?"

"Yes, I'm serious!"

"Well, why the hell not? It is seventy miles. They won't know exactly whose asses they're looking at, if they can even see them."

The sad part was, they could see, unbeknownst to them as they prepared to flash.

Like prankster teenagers, two adult men dropped trou and pulled off a moon-by instead of a flyby.

"Lucy to Control."

"Go ahead Lucy." Frank sounded disheartened.

"Whoa, somebody's not having a good time down there. But we are up here. Control, just how much trouble do we get in for mooning the international space station?" Bobby said, laughing.

Alex motioned for Frank to give him the headset.

"Hello boys. The trouble is, you lose your space ship. Now go ahead and bring it on down, before you get into more trouble."

"Control are we compromised again?" John said, panic setting in.

"No, you're not compromised John—boy! This is your old pal Alex Wright. Now bring my space ship down and I won't have to shoot any more of your friends."

What Alex didn't know was that he was compromised. When Hideyoshi went outside to join the others, Frank jumped on his computer and quit running a few programs, those programs that were blocking people from finding them. It was risky, but Frank didn't have much of a choice. He prayed somebody out there was listening.

"No problem. Put Frank back on the line," John said.

"Go ahead John, guess no more need for call signs huh?"

"Is everybody all right Frank?"

"No. Shou and Rob have been shot, they're still alive, Shou barely."

"Wright you rotten son of a bitch, when I get down there I'm ripping your head off!" Bobby screamed.

"Probably not a good idea Mr. White, I've got your pretty little wife too. Threaten me again, and I might just have some special fun with her," Alex said after ripping the headset off of Frank.

Alex waited for a reply, but Bobby was fuming and didn't want to antagonize Wright, so he remained silent. Alex threw the headset back down in front of Frank.

"Get us down Frank," John said.

"Suit back up, get your helmets on and get buckled in. We'll have to get you to slow down, get you into position so we can bring you down."

"We're on it."

Putting the gun to the back of Frank's head, Alex nudged him.

"Get them down now!" Alex ordered.

"I can't, they're going too fast, at that speed they'll burn up on re-entry. Wrong angle and they'll skip off and fly out into space. We do this wrong and they'll die," Frank pleaded.

"I won't tell you again, get them down…fucking…now!"

Alex pushed the weapon harder against Frank's skull, pushing his head down towards the desk.

The glass window in front of Frank shattered. Scared, Frank's eyes slammed shut quickly. Frank thought he heard a gunshot, but he wasn't sure. Alex Wright fell to his knees; slumping forward, his head came to rest on Frank's back. The trailer door blasted open, coming off at the hinges as men entered screaming for everyone to get down.

Cringing, Frank opened his eyes. Major Harold Jennings was standing at the door. Frank was able to take a deep breath of relief until he realized there was a dead man leaning on him. He jumped to his feet, nauseated as Alex Wright fell to the ground.

"Get those kids out of here, get the woman too," the major said. "And get those men out there off the ground!"

"You're here to arrest us, aren't you?" Frank said.

"Maybe, what laws did you break?" Jennings asked.

"Possibly a few, maybe a lot."

"I don't actually know what you have up there, but from what we've seen, if you're willing to work with us. I'm sure we'll cut you a deal. The president himself has been glued to the situation all morning. You've garnered a lot of attention all over the world."

"It won't be my call to make. I'll need to get them down first."

"Mr. Kemp and Mr. White, yes, bring them home," Jennings said.

Frank's computer was damaged from the blast. As he tried to reboot it up, it lay dormant.

"We have a big problem here Major, we've lost all communication with them. I can't bring them home. This fucking thing is dead."

"Yes you can, get your team together. We'll take you to the base. We have much better equipment, trust me on that."

Sirens blaring and lights flashing, they rushed towards Tucson.

"Damn it, we lost everything," John said. "Communications are down!"

"It's been like thirty minutes John, how the hell do we get down from here? They have my wife!"

"I know, they've got my kids too, or have you forgotten?"

"Sorry, I haven't forgotten, didn't mean it that way. Let's just get down; we need to get to them. We need to save them."

"I'm going to have to switch from auto to manual and slow this thing down, hang on."

"Sure you want to do this?"

"We don't have much of choice now, do we?"

John raised the retractable panel; exposing the front turbines, he flipped the switch to activate them.

"Here we go," John said.

Stepping on the pedal carefully, he waited for the turbines to engage, but nothing happened. He pressed down further, and still nothing. He smashed it to the floorboard; they weren't slowing down. The front turbines were dead in the water.

"We have a problem."

"Check the others, bump the throttle a bit, see if the rear ones engage," Bobby said.

Sure enough they fired. Bobby knew right then that the front ones weren't insulated enough, and the water lines had frozen.

Suddenly another voice came across the radio. Communications were back up.

"This the United States Air Force to John Kemp, do you copy?"

"Fuck Bobby, even they know we're up here!"

"Talk to them, we don't have much of a choice. We need help, we have to get down from here."

"Go ahead, this is John Kemp."

"Stand by Mr. Kemp, we have someone who wants to speak with you."

"What the hell?" John said to Bobby.

"Hey John, it's Frank, did you miss me?"

"Frankie!" both men cheered.

"You boys ready to come home? We had some technical difficulties down here and had to phone a friend, but I'll explain that to you later, after we get you down."

"Good to have you back, but we got a problem up here Frank. The water lines are frozen, and we can't slow Lucy down. Front turbines are shot."

"I've got good news, and I've got bad news. Good news is everybody down here is safe, bad news is I don't know how to slow Lucy down just yet."

"Think of something Frank," Bobby said.

"Hang on, be right back," Frank said handing the headset to Major Jennings.

"Frank…Frank…Frank!" John said.

"Mr. Kemp, this is Major Jennings. How you guys doing up there?"

"Well a madman has my kids and Bobby's wife hostage, and we're stuck in space. I'd say we're having a stellar day."

"As your friend said, everyone down here is safe. And Mr. Wright has been dealt with. Trust me when I say he has been totally and inarguably incapacitated."

"Sucks for him, might suck for us too if you can't get us down Major," John said.

"We'll do our best Mr. Kemp."

"Tell Lora I love her," Bobby said.

"She heard you and she loves you too, now can we get you home?"

"Please," Bobby begged.

Major Jennings started directing traffic, letting John's team take control of the terminals.

"Airman, give that man your terminal. That's an order!"

The airman complied, standing to let Hideyoshi sit down.

"Let me log you in," the airman said.

"No need, I already have your password," Hideyoshi said, smiling. "And you should pay your credit card bills on time, your credit really sucks."

"I'll work...on...that, and thank you, I guess." The puzzled airman surrendered.

"Okay Mr. Kemp, do you have side thrusters working?" Jennings asked.

"Let me check," John said. Bumping the stick he felt Lucy turn. "Yes, I've got them."

"Good. You're going to want to turn her one hundred and eighty degrees. Flying backwards, we'll have you use your rear thrusters to try and slow her down."

"Major, will that work?" John asked.

"I have no idea. I've never flown in space, and you don't have many options, now do you?"

"Guess not. Hang on, I'm going to turn her."

John slowly pushed on the joystick. Lucy began to turn.

"Almost there John-san," Hideyoshi said. "Current rotation one hundred thirty degrees."

"You're doing a good job John," Frank said.

"Good," Hideyoshi said. "Let off now!"

"All right Kemp, don't give it too much throttle. But try to slow her down," Jennings said. "We've got your speed down here at fifty-one thousand, you need to be about sixteen to seventeen to safely re-enter."

"Here we go!"

As John pressed on the throttle, Lucy began to shake, and Bobby began to pray. The more he gave her the more she shook; he wasn't used to having so much throttle. This worried him; he wasn't sure how that would respond in earth's atmosphere.

"Seventeen thousand John-san, you're good."

"Turn her back and start descending," Jennings ordered.

"Turning back now," John said.

"Awful demanding down there, ain't they John?" Bobby said.

"No shit. This thing ain't as easy to fly up here as it is down there."

As Lucy started to descend John lost the angle of approach. He came dangerously close to missing.

"You're coming in too high John, you need to bring her down," Frank instructed.

"*That's hard to do Frankie, she's fighting me!*"

"*Just a little more John, almost there. You have to get her down or you'll skip off!*"

"*I'm trying!*" John screamed back. "*Any minor adjustment and she's all over the place, it's a lot of power to try to contain!*"

"*Reentry in fifteen seconds, come on John, we'll lose communications soon!*"

"*I'm trying!*"

John was fighting for all he was worth; Lucy had already picked up resistance upon reentry. He needed to make a choice, so he throttled down and risked the chance of burning up on reentry instead of skipping off. In his mind, he thought at least they could find the bodies. Skipping off back out into space, nobody would ever find them.

"We've lost them, we can only wait now," Jennings said.

Silence fell over the control room at the Air Force base as they waited.

It seemed like an eternity not knowing.

"And we are through ladies and gentlemen, please stow your tray tables and put your seatbacks in the upright position, Lucy is coming home!" Bobby shouted over the radio, to cheers breaking out across the control room.

They entered somewhere over the Indian Ocean, falling like a rock. John was too busy to talk; he was still fighting the controls, trying to get Lucy to respond.

"Frank we aren't out of the doghouse yet, she won't slow down!"

"John, you have to pull the nose up! Pull up on your left joystick slowly until she starts slowing!" Frank instructed.

"Damn he's in a steep dive," Jennings said to Frank.

"Left joystick is dead Frank, any other ideas?"

Frank was confused now; they should have full flight capabilities after reentry. He started flipping through his drawings of Lucy, looking for a quick answer.

Rob hobbled up behind him on his wounded leg, jerking the headset from Frank.

"John, did Bobby open the bottom panels after reentry?"

Bobby started searching over his panel, looking for the switch as Lucy started to spiral. His vision was getting blurry, and he felt like he might pass out again.

"Bobby!" John screamed.

Bobby was finding it hard to even lift his hand at this point; reaching out to find the switches he kept missing. Finally he was able to grab the panel. Securing his fingers behind it, he found the switch.

"It says they're open!"

"Flip it again Bobby, they may be jammed," Rob ordered.

With only his thumb, his fingers still secured behind the panel, Bobby flipped the switch down and then back up.

"Try it now John!" Bobby shrieked.

John pulled back on the joystick, feeling the turbines wake up and join the party.

"We've got them!" John yelled over the radio.

"You better hurry Mr. Kemp, you're losing altitude quickly!" Jennings said.

John was able to stop the roll and bring the nose up. Pulling back as hard as he could he gave the bottom engines all the power they had. She was finally slowing.

Still fighting to not pass out, Bobby watched through half-closed eyes as the water below them was fast approaching.

"Come on John," he tried to desperately whisper. A whisper was all he could squeeze out as the G-forces pulled on his body.

John almost had it. Lucy splashed down about twenty miles off the coast of Africa. As she hit the water, the splash rose at least a hundred feet in the air.

"We lost them," Jennings said.

"No!" Lora screamed and started crying, as heads in the control room sunk in sadness. Not a word was spoken until Jennings stood up.

"Airmen, send out a message. See if the Navy has a ship in that area." Jennings started pointing around the room. "Captain Taylor, target her last location and get us a flight to Africa. Mr. Yarborough, Mr. Henry, gather your people, we'll be leaving within the hour!"

All watched as the major gave out orders.

"Don't sit there staring at me! Let's go people! We're losing time!"

Frank whispered one last message into his headset. "I'm sorry guys, I'm so sorry."

"What are you sorry for Frankie?" John came across the intercom.

"We were just taking a little bath is all," Bobby said.

"Guys! Oh my god you made it!" Frank was elated.

Cheers of joy erupted in the control room, anyone and everyone started jumping, hugging and dancing. Hats went flying across the room, papers tossed in the air. Even high-ranking officers were seen giving a few high fives.

"Believe it or not, I'd say we went down about hundred feet in the drink. Lucy had the power to bring us back out," John said. "Now we're going to bring her home."

"Mr. Kemp, please set a course for the Air Base," Jennings instructed.

"Negative Major, not today. If you're going to arrest me, you can come get me. I'm taking her home," John said, and then he reached down and flipped his communications off.

"Where the hell is he going?" Rob asked. "Back to Ohio?"

"Major Jennings," Captain Taylor said. "We are still tracking him, he's headed this way."

"He's going home," Garrett said. "Lucy belongs at home."

"Captain, get everyone in the choppers. We're going to Mr. White's ranch."

One would think after everything that happened, John would take it easy coming back. Well, everyone would be wrong. John knuckled up, much to Bobby's distaste, and targeted beating Shou's speed record. He got Mach seven and then he hit eight just for good measure. And yes, Bobby eventually passed out.

Arriving back at the ranch, they noticed all the people. It looked like the Air Force was having a family barbeque. Everybody was standing around, waiting for them to appear. There were seven choppers, fifteen trucks, twelve cars and more uniforms with guns standing around than they could have imagined.

"Looks like they aren't rolling out the red carpet Bobby," John kidded.

"It's been one hell of journey."

"Yes it has. And I wouldn't want to take it with anyone else but you."

"Do you think they'll let us be cellmates?"

"I think we're getting ready to find out."

John set Lucy down on the old launch pad behind the barn. Popping the hatch they both fell out of Lucy, landing on their backs in the dirt. To much surprise, they were met with cheers. The team, including Lora and the kids, came running towards them.

As they celebrated and hugged their loved ones, Major Jennings stepped in.

He extended his hand to John. "That was one hell of a flight you pulled off Kemp."

Boggled, John accepted the major's handshake.

"Thank you Major, thanks for the help getting us home."

"It was my honor," Jennings said, extending his hand to Bobby. "Mr. White?"

Bobby obliged. "Thanks Major."

"Gentlemen, and lady, we might want to move. You have another visitor coming. It might get a bit windy here," Jennings said.

"Who's...what?" John asked, as the major ushered them off the landing pad.

"Look John," Rob said, pointing at the hill.

They all watched as Marine One crested the hill, coming straight for them, two Apache helicopters at her side. Those in uniform around them snapped to attention.

Marine One landed gracefully behind Lucy. She looked tiny in comparison to that monster of an aircraft. But the fact was, she was prettier. Once her blades quit rotating, the door opened on her side and out stepped the president.

"Major, the president came here to arrest us?" Frank asked.

"Not exactly," Jennings laughed.

They watched as the president stood and looked over Lucy. He began to walk around her, even running his hand down her side as he went.

"Mr. President, these are the men who built and flew the aircraft," Jennings said.

"That's a nice little bird you have there," the president said.

"Thank you sir," John said. "Sorry about all the trouble we've caused."

"What trouble?" He was being coy. "This didn't happen, you understand what I'm saying?"

"I believe I do, Mr. President," John said, relieved.

"We'll keep this our little secret, under one condition."

"And that condition is what, Mr. President?" John asked.

"When you get the bugs worked out, I'd like to fly that little bird."

"I think we can arrange that," John said, laughing. "Anything else?"

"And you attempt to work within the law. Speaking of which, your friend with the questionable past. He'll be fine; he came out of surgery and is resting. The others will need to fix their mistakes, which I know nothing about…cough…cough, if they want to stay a guest in our country." The president paused and looked over at Hideyoshi, who nodded in agreement. "And will somebody get that man, medical attention," he said, referring to Rob.

"Yes sir," the major said. He escorted Rob to a waiting vehicle.

"Excuse me, Mr. President," Bobby said.

"Yes."

"After every mission, we have a beer. Care to join us?" Bobby said, his sly little grin coming out.

The president didn't think long, "Yes, yes I would like that. It's hotter than hell out here. How do you all stand this damn heat?"

"That's what the beer is for. After a few you won't notice the heat, or anything else for that matter," Garrett said. "Follow me. And try to keep up."

To be continued:

Highway to the Stars: The Beginning/Book one of the series

www.ingramcontent.com/pod-product-compliance
Lightning Source LLC
Chambersburg PA
CBHW071159250626
47159CB00001B/140